COMPLICATION

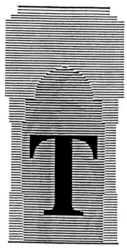

THE
FRIENDS
of the
Beverly Hills
Public Library

COMPLICATION

ISAAC ADAMSON

SOFT NT

Library of Congress Cataloging-in-Publication Data is available.

ISBN: 978-1-59376-432-6

Cover design by Elke Barter
Interior design by Elyse Strongin, Neuwirth and Associates, Inc.
Printed in the United States of America

Soft Skull Press
An imprint of COUNTERPOINT
1919 Fifth Street
Berkeley, CA 94710

www.softskull.com
www.counterpointpress.com
Distributed by Publishers Group West

10 9 8 7 6 5 4 3 2 1

Complication (noun)

1. A condition or event that is complex or confused.

2. An intricate and often puzzling relationship of parts.

3. (*Medicine/Pathology*)—A secondary or negative reaction during the course of an illness.

4. (*Horology*)—Beginning in the sixteenth century, any feature of a timepiece beyond the standard display of hours, minutes, and seconds. Used to refer to both the mechanism itself and the timepiece housing it. Examples include calendars, phases of the moon, signs of the Zodiac, and automatons engaged in various acts erotic, whimsical, or religious in nature.

5. A big can of worms.

PART

ONE

CHAPTER 1

■

The Saturday morning before my life went out the window, I opened the front door to find two policemen holding their hats in their hands and examining them like unfamiliar, vaguely distasteful things. Both men were balding, beads of perspiration glistening on their heads. Both had mustaches so stereotypically Chicago cop I wondered if these mustaches were meant to be ironic, even if Chicago cops aren't famous for their sense of irony. "I hate to be the one," the less-bald policeman told me, "but I'm afraid I have to inform you that Lee Holloway is no longer with us."

Obviously there had been a mistake.

Lee Holloway was me.

But then Lee Holloway was also my father. We shared our first name. Mr. Holloway, the policeman told me, had experienced a major cardiac event while mowing his lawn a few hours ago.

"Heart attack," he clarified.

"The EMTs did everything they could," said the other.

"We're sorry for your loss," the first finished.

The police told me the name of the hospital where the body was being kept and offered to give me a ride. I said no thanks, they nodded, replaced their hats, and strolled off toward their squad car. As they got in, I tried to imagine and simultaneously not imagine the last moments of my father's life, wondering whether he realized what was happening, wondering what thoughts might have been going through his head. Instead my mind kept returning to the image of an abandoned lawnmower running in the middle of his big backyard in the south suburbs, the battered old thing spewing plumes of blue smoke into a cloudless sky until it ran out of gas with a shudder.

I made phone calls and handled the funeral arrangements with a numbed efficiency that now strikes me as slightly deranged. When I called into Grimley & Dunballer Recovery Solutions on Monday and said I wouldn't be in, my boss must have been in a good mood because she didn't quote me the company bereavement policy. Instead she told me she was terribly sorry and to take as much time as I needed. We both knew this meant not a minute longer than dictated by the company bereavement policy, but I'd learned to appreciate those occasions when she revealed her human side by, say, making a facial expression or ingesting food. Grimley & Dunballer was the second-largest debt collection agency in the Midwest, and I'd been there for five years working as a client services liaison. If my job sounds dull, that's because it was.

The funeral was held on a Tuesday. My dad's sister Sally flew in from Tampa for the services and acted as ringleader like she always did at family functions. Two women my dad had dated at different times, a couple neighbors, and few of his real estate coworkers also attended. During the wake, one of these colleagues recounted at length the hilarious e-mails my father used to send, mostly jokes unfit for repeating at a wake. A guy named Gus kept going on about how my dad was booked to show a place in Bridgeport the day he died.

"He would have made that damn sale," Gus told me.

"I'm sure you're right," I replied.

"A people person, your dad. Could talk to anyone."

I nodded, unsure what to say.

"He died with his boots on," Gus said, clutching my shoulder, narrowing his gaze. "Never forget that. Your dad died with his boots on."

Why this should be important to me I didn't know. I'm sure Gus was trying to be kind, which is what kept me from pointing out that my dad had in fact been wearing green and white striped flip-flops when he'd died. Later someone remarked that I was doing a good job holding myself together, but stoicism had nothing to do with it. I was numbed out, not so much dealing with my grief as refusing to acknowledge its existence, unwilling to process on any but the most surface level what had happened. For the rest of the wake, I stood around eating sandwiches and shaking hands with decent people I barely knew and keeping myself from punching the wall, and then it was all over.

It wasn't until much later that I thought it was a little strange that no one, not even my Aunt Sally, mentioned my younger brother Paul. No one talked about my mother either, who'd taken off to join a New Age commune of sorts in Albuquerque when I was thirteen, never to be heard from again, although her absence from the conversation was decidedly less strange as most of the people present never knew her. Aunt Sally was convinced that my dad would've lived longer with a strong female presence in his life, and she was probably right. He smoked and drank and ate like it was the 1950s and had predictably developed a heart condition as a result. A second wife might've nagged him into shape, but he had no interest in a second wife. And so it was as if it had always been just the Three Holloway Men. Or, as I often thought of it, the two of them and me.

Both were beer-and-a-shot kinda guys, diehard Southsiders who enjoyed tinkering with their motorcycles and bitching about the White Sox and listening to Steve Dahl on the radio. After returning from college, I'd moved to Wicker Park, a northside neighborhood not far in terms of geographical distance but in other ways a whole different planet. As adults, my dad and I hadn't been what you would call close. Not that there was any animosity between us. We still talked on the phone fairly often and I made a point of dropping by during the holidays. We just didn't have much in common. I was supposed to be the smart one in the family, but I had not gone on to land an especially smart job or lead an especially smart life, and in some vague way I felt like I'd disappointed him.

By Wednesday evening I'd already done most of the heavy lifting in getting his affairs in order. An estate lawyer and longtime family friend agreed to act as executor, and the real-estate company Dad worked for would be putting the house on the market. I boxed his clothes save for a couple of suits. Whether he needed it or not, my father bought a new suit each year, and the two I saved looked like they hadn't ever been worn. I dropped the rest of the clothes off at the Salvation Army but decided to keep his watch. A Tag Heuer—the same kind, he would tell people with a pride only half ironic, worn by Steve McQueen.

In the basement I found a box full of photo albums and loose pictures. I dug around for a good photo of Dad and me together to take home but couldn't find any. There were lots of pictures of him with Paul, though. Ones I hadn't seen in years, ones my Dad obviously wanted to keep but didn't want hanging on the walls, as if Paul's absence was too much to confront on a daily basis. I kept all the photos, even though I knew they'd just remain in the same box until the day someone found it in my own basement and wondered what the hell to do with them. All the furniture that I could carry on my own, along with his books, pots and pans, dinnerware, tools, golf clubs, and aptly-named stationary bike, I moved to the garage. I put a notice on Craigslist—SUNDRY HOUSEHOLD TREASURES FREE TO GOOD HOMES— and left the garage door opened. Nearly all the possessions my father had amassed over six decades were gone within the span of an afternoon. The one object nobody took was the crappy lawn-mower he'd been pushing when his heart called it quits.

Looking back, I realize I was in a fugue state of sorts, narrowing my brain to one small task at a time to keep it from being over-whelmed by the wide enormity of grief I knew was waiting. It was just like when my mother had left us, that feeling of having the ground beneath your feet suddenly open like a trap door and leave you in freefall. By Thursday night, the bedroom, kitchen, living room, and basement were taken care of, and the only thing left to do was clean out his home office. A large, unframed poster of a climber silhouetted against the setting sun and dangling from the edge of a steep rock cliff was tacked above the desk where his laptop sat. IT IS NOT THE MOUNTAIN WE CONQUER, it announced in giant type, BUT OURSELVES. I ripped the poster down and threw it on top of the growing mountain inside the gar-bage bag and then started in on the file cabinet, tossing anything that didn't need to be passed on to the estate lawyer. My father was organized when it came to paperwork. Tax forms, credit card bills, auto and home insurance policies, bank statements—each had its own manila folder with all its contents meticulously arranged by date. It was like he'd been expecting an IRS audit for the last twenty years. It didn't occur to me that maybe he'd instead been anticipating the scenario I was now enacting.

His desk was mostly empty. Left drawer: a pack of unopened sticky notes, pens and pencils, a stapler, a desktop calendar with no appointments noted. Right drawer: envelopes, larger envelopes, two reams of printer paper. The top drawer held nothing but a single white envelope with his name and address penned in a tight script. No return address was provided. I removed the letter from the envelope and read.

Dear Mr. Lee Holloway,

> *My name is Vera. I live in Prague and I was close with your son. Please know Paul spoke very kindly of you.*
>
> *I am writing to you for reasons that I believe your son's death is not what was reported. I think he did not drown in the flood. I cannot tell you more at this time because it would not be sensible for all manners of reason. But I am urgent to meet you, so that I can share with you an important part of Paul's life I'm sure is unknown to you but which I am certain will be of great interest.*
>
> *Please come to a café called the Black Rabbit on Ostrovní Street in the Nové Město district of Prague 2. I will be there every day between 6 and 8 pm for three months from the date of this letter.*
>
> *My hope is I will meet you soon.*
>
> *Sincerely Yours,*
> *Vera*

No other correspondence from Vera or anyone else was in the desk. I checked the file cabinet again. Nothing there, either. His Rolodex (he had a state-of-the-art laptop but still used a Rolodex) didn't reveal an address for anyone named Vera or anybody else in the Czech Republic. I sat down at my father's desk and reread the letter. One hundred and fifty-eight words counting the signature. A greeting, ten economical sentences, a closing. No last name. No return address, e-mail address, or telephone number. The letter was postmarked two months and twenty-eight days ago.

Which meant only two days left.

I started up the laptop and opened his e-mail program. A search for "Vera" yielded nothing but a couple messages containing words like *veracity* or *veranda*. I scrolled through the e-mails roughly corresponding with the date of the letter but found nothing. It was while picking through his latest messages I discovered confirmation of his purchase of an open return ticket from Chicago O'Hare to the Ruzyně Airport in Prague, Czech Republic. Using the same online travel service, he'd booked reservations at a place called the Hotel Dalibor.

His flight was leaving in four hours.

Before I realized what I was doing, I was thirty thousand feet in the air somewhere over the Atlantic. There had been no time to go back to my house and pack before racing to the airport, and I was saved by the fact that I'd kept my passport at my dad's place. I never used the thing, and during a period of my life a few years earlier, I'd been moving from apartment to apartment so often that I was afraid I'd lose it. While cleaning out his house I'd been wearing a ratty T-shirt, cargo shorts, and Adidas flats, an ensemble that didn't seem appropriate for intercontinental air travel, though I realized no one really gives a damn anymore. With no other clothes at hand, I ended up wearing one of his suits, a black Italian number two sizes too big. In my wallet I carried his credit cards. In his jacket pocket, I carried his e-ticket stub, his hotel reservation, my passport. Getting through airport security posed no problem as the name on the e-ticket matched the credit card and the name on the credit card matched the name on my passport. I stretched out my legs and marveled that my father had bought a seat in first-class. This from the same man who routinely called the phone company to argue over surcharges.

I knew almost nothing about the last days of Paul's life—last years, even—and I assume my father didn't either. What we knew, what we'd always known about the trajectory of his life, was that Paul would either win the lottery or get struck by lightning. There was never any middle path for him. Back five years ago when he disappeared, I'd been shocked, but not surprised. Crucial difference being that having knowledge about light sockets won't preclude you from being shocked should you stick your finger in one, but unless you're an idiot, this shock should in no way surprise you.

Since the arrival of Vera's letter, my father had no doubt spent a lot of time studying Vera's terse correspondence, prodding its stonewalling sentences in hopes the words would suddenly give way and reveal whatever truth their author used them to conceal. But the letter never told him anything new, either about his son or the woman who claimed to have known him.

Your son's death is not as reported.

Was this Vera person saying my brother wasn't really dead? Or only that he'd died in a manner inconsistent with what was reported? And did she mean "reported" as in covered by the press, or was she just referring to official "reports," like the inquest or whatever it was they had in the Czech Republic?

My father must have had similar questions. Weeks after receiving the letter, just two nights before he'd died, he'd booked the flight I was now on. He'd bought the ticket on a Friday for a plane that didn't leave until the following Thursday. Maybe he'd wanted to finish something at work, had a house showing or closing he couldn't miss. Maybe tickets were simply cheaper on this date. But it seemed strange to me that he would finally resolve to satisfy the curiosity Vera's letter provoked and then purposely delay the same satisfaction. Had he wanted a chance to back out, room to change his mind?

I didn't have that luxury. After reading the letter, the choice was either immediately get to Prague or let the unknown Vera slip away and leave me forever wondering what it was she knew about Paul's disappearance. I reread the letter one final time then ate a meal of salmon and overcooked potatoes. After dinner I tried to watch an in-flight movie starring Sandra Bullock but twenty minutes in realized I'd seen it before. At some point I fell asleep, and when I awoke, I was beginning my final descent into Prague.

CHAPTER 2

■

My plane touched down only fifteen minutes late, and not having any luggage, I was able to get out of the airport and find a taxi without much delay. Before leaving the airport, I rented a SIM card from a kiosk that gave me a temporary local cell phone number. I didn't anticipate using it much, but like most human beings from the richer countries of the early twenty-first century, I felt naked and lost if I was unable to access all information in existence at every conceivable moment, felt practically stripped of my identity. As it was already 6:30 PM, I told the driver to take me directly to the Black Rabbit. No time for the hotel.

Outside the airport lay weedy fields and encroaching darkness. On the four-lane highway, fields disappeared and traffic increased; blocky tenements layered in graffiti towered in the middle distance, foregrounded by newly built corporate offices springing up alongside the road. We entered a tunnel and emerged in a Prague more as I would have imagined it had I ever bothered imagining it at all. Blackened structures from bygone centuries piled dark into the low horizon, and noisy trams rattled along the far riverbank while people ambled by on the narrow sidewalks. On the hill above us, St. Vitus Cathedral rose spotlit and jagged against the night while a steep slope cluttered with tiled roofs tumbled to the riverbank beneath. Across the water, countless spires jutted upwards into the murky eastern skyline like tent poles supporting a sagging canvas.

The cab crossed a stone bridge, and I watched white lights strung from the deck of a tour boat dance slowly in the distance, a ghostly constellation floating downstream, the people onboard rendered faceless by low banks of fog that clung to the water's dark surface. Here then was the Vltava, the river that claimed my brother. The current looked sluggish, stillborn. Too weak to drown a rat.

My cab driver pointed out the window at an imposing stone building as we came to a halt, said it was the National Theater. Atop its roof a winged goddess piloted a chariot pulled by three horses frozen in mid-gallop and about to heave themselves over the edge of the building and into the latticework of tramlines above the street. A block down was Ostrovní Street. No cars allowed. Too small, the cabbie said, too many people. He told me to head for Divadelní Street, then turn right.

The moment I stepped outside the cab and set foot in the city itself, I finally started to ask all those questions I should've asked before I left. Was I in Prague to fulfill a journey my father had been denied? Here to answer questions about Paul I hadn't thought about in years, if I'd thought about them at all? I couldn't say. A friend of mine, upon hearing his mother had died, got into his car and drove straight across the country, from Maine to California, never eating, stopping only for gas. Why California, he couldn't be sure. He would've kept going, he said, but for the ocean. Maybe this was my version of that. But as I stood there it struck me that flying halfway around the world based on a letter from a stranger was more like something Paul would've done.

I headed down Ostrovní Street. The cabbie wasn't kidding—no broader than twelve feet at its widest point, the tilting and cobblestoned lane was hemmed in by low buildings crowded one into the next. Above a door on a building halfway down the block hung a wooden sign depicting an emaciated rabbit raised on its hindquarters. The rabbit's ears were drooping, mouth agape, milk white eyes sagging like melted dinner plates. A diseased, demented Bugs Bunny.

The Black Rabbit said the sign in English.

The door opened onto a hallway leading to a curved stairwell cut from red stone and descending into a catacomb cellar enclosed by vaulted ceilings. Small white candles flickered atop sleek black tables, and well-dressed patrons chatted quietly over wine or beer. Too well dressed to be tourists, I figured. Czech professionals, Euro yuppies. No one paid me any attention whatsoever except a woman sitting alone in the far corner.

Thin and shapeless inside a loose black sweater, she was in her mid-thirties, her straight black hair swept forward with just a little window carved out for a face with jutting cheekbones and hard blue eyes almost gray. She was less pretty than striking. More striking was that she made no effort to hide the fact that she was openly staring at me as I approached.

"You must be Vera," I said.

Her mouth parted, but no words came.

"My name is Lee," I said. "Lee Holloway."

Closer, she looked less thin than simply frail, her skin ashen, mouth inelastic and sad. When I'd received the letter, I wondered if Paul and this Vera person had been romantically involved, but seeing her now, there was no question. She was exactly his type, only more so. Thinner, darker. From the looks of it, more troubled.

I'd bet anything she had some weird tattoo hidden somewhere, some Goth leftover from a youth that was further away than she maybe wanted to admit.

"Paul was my brother," I prompted.

She blinked. "He never mentioned he had a brother."

This didn't surprise me. Paul liked to act like he had no family at all. A lone wolf.

"I'm sorry," Vera said. "This is strange for me. You look just like him."

People said this often enough that I'd stopped pointing out that my brother was at least three inches taller and forty pounds heavier. When last I'd seen him, he'd sported a bald head and a goatee. His nose bent to the left where it had been broken by a girl in a punk rock bar on North Avenue when he was twenty-four. He had a tattoo on his left forearm of Elmer Fudd, which he didn't like to explain but had to do with the way he laughed—a stuttering, gravelly monotone that surfaced and disappeared often for no apparent reason.

She motioned me to sit. A thin silver bracelet orbited her wrist, and a bottle of Matoni sparkling water sat half empty next to a glass on the table. She extended her hand and I moved to take it before realizing she wasn't offering a handshake but had merely paused in an upsweeping motion aimed at getting the waiter's attention.

"Your father sent you?" she asked.

"Not exactly. My father is, well, he's dead."

She placed a hand over her mouth.

"Heart attack," I said. "Mowing the lawn."

"*Ježíš Maria*. That's terrible."

"A lot of people die mowing the lawn. More than you might think. Not that you probably have any thoughts about lawn mower fatalities. Happened just Saturday."

Some part of me wondered why the other was talking about lawnmowers.

"That's awful. I'm so sorry."

My throat suddenly felt constricted, my face hot. Bad time to get choked up, but when is a good time? "Thanks," I managed. "He was a good guy. A people person."

Christ, I thought, next I'd be telling her he'd died with his boots on. I wondered whether my dad might have met Vera when he had flown out when Paul's personal effects were recovered. He'd returned without saying a word about his trip. Nothing about what he'd eaten, where he'd stayed, how much paperwork he had to fill out, whether he'd been treated with kindness or indifference. He came back carrying only the same suitcase he'd left with, and if he'd had Paul's possessions shipped back, I never saw them. *Are you going to be okay?* That was all he'd said in the car as we rode back from O'Hare. Worrying about how I was taking the news was I guess his way of trying to keep his own emotions at bay, to hold himself together. Not knowing what else to do, I'd reached out to squeeze his shoulder. He started crying and stopped in the same breath, like the sound a dog makes when you step on its tail. But thinking back to Vera's letter, I knew they hadn't met before. It was clearly a letter written to a stranger.

We sat in silence while she rummaged through a handbag and produced an unopened pack of cigarettes. "Do you smoke?" she asked. I'd hardly noticed up to now that she had an accent, slight though it was.

I shook my head.

"I also don't smoke." She tore the cellophane wrapper and tapped the pack against the inside of her wrist. "I stopped long ago. But I told myself if your father came, I would make an exception. For you, I will also make an exception. Finally a waiter. Do you like beer? Czech beer is very good. Your brother, he very much liked Czech beer. Perhaps I should order an extra one. Who knows if he will be coming back."

For a moment of freefall, I thought she was going to tell me Paul was still alive. That he'd run into some kind of trouble, been forced to fake his own death five years ago. That he'd been hiding, lying low, waiting for things to blow over. She'd written the letter because she needed help. Together we could bring him back into the world. I started feeling guilty for believing all this time that he'd been gone.

But Vera wasn't talking about Paul coming back. She was talking about the waiter, who in the next moment arrived and took Vera's order with an air of weary reluctance. Across the room, a bedraggled-looking fiftyish man with long, unwashed salt-and-pepper hair spilling out of a wool stocking cap shared a joke with the bartender. His eyes had a bleary intensity as he repeatedly glanced over at our table. But then Vera probably provoked repeat glances wherever she went. She lit her cigarette, and the flame illuminated a small U-shaped scar riding across the ridge of her cheekbone beneath her left eye.

"When I wrote the letter," she began as the waiter walked away, "I never believed anyone would come. Many times I tore it up. Always I wrote another. When finally I sent it, I felt difficult to come here day after day. But I came anyway. I've nearly lost count of the days. And now here you are. Why are you here?"

"Because of your letter."

"But you must also have reasons."

"He was my brother. I want to know what happened."

"And if I tell you, what then?"

I shrugged. "Then I go home."

She fell silent, regarding me behind a curtain of cigarette smoke. "Maybe you have a certain way you wish to remember your brother. What I say could change your idea of him. Please understand I have told no one. What I say is only for you. No one else can know." Vera snubbed out her cigarette and edged closer, fingers unnaturally long and white as she placed her hands flat upon the table's surface. "Your brother," she uttered in a low voice, "stole a watch."

I waited for her to go on.

She didn't.

"A watch," I prompted. "Like what, a Rolex? A Tag Heuer?"

"Not an ordinary watch. The Rudolf Complication."

"Is that Swiss?"

Vera leaned back, placing a hand to her throat and blinking in rapid succession. "You don't understand. The Rudolf Complication is not a watch for knowing what is the time. Not something you wear. It's art. An important work of art. Of history. When Paul disappeared, he was planning to take this watch from a gallery near the river. Or had already taken it. I don't know for 100 percent."

"I'm not following you."

"On the other side of the river, between Malá Strana and Kampa Island, is a canal called Čertovka. Means in English 'the Devil's Stream.' Near the—"

"Why do they call it that?"

She shrugged. "Something about an old woman who lived near there in olden times and everyone thought she was a devil. The villagers painted little devils all over her house as a warning for, I don't know, to other villagers I guess. There's a big wooden wheel in the canal. A famous water wheel. You have probably seen it on postcards."

"Paul didn't really do postcards," I said.

But I remembered that he had sent at least one. Nearly a year after he'd left Chicago, six months or so before he died. It was from some place called the Prague Torture Museum and featured a medieval engraving of a man spread eagled and strung upside down by his ankles, hands bound behind his back. Two men on either side of him held the handles of a large saw they were using to divide their prisoner in half at the crotch.

On the back, Paul had written:

Brotherman Lee,

   Hope you're hanging in there (har har!) Would write more, but I've been tied up (ack ack!) Merry XXXmas. Gotta split! (yuk yuk!)

Yours in Masculine Brotherhood,
Paul

"Near this waterwheel is an art gallery called the Galleria Čertovka," Vera continued. "I worked there. I helped Paul plan to steal the watch. Your brother and the Rudolf Complication, they disappeared together. For five days Paul was missing. Then some of his clothing was found in Karlín, in Prague 8, after the flood. An expired work permit in his name and blood stains that matched his blood type. Karlín is far from the gallery. Far from where Paul lived, far from anywhere Paul has a reason to go. The watch was never found. There was another person, a third man helping to steal the watch. It was his idea. His plan. This is why I wrote the letter. Your brother, he did not die of the flood. I believe Paul was killed. That this third person, he murdered Paul."

I experienced the same slow-mo knee-jerk as when I learned Paul was dead five years ago. Shock, but not surprise. Across the room, two women with matching hoop earrings kissed each other on the cheek. The older guy at the bar in the stocking cap was looking our way, but he turned his head the moment he realized

I'd noticed. Or maybe the timing was coincidence. It was a conversation to make you paranoid.

"He was killed," I said. "You're sure about this?"

Vera nodded.

"Did you tell the police?"

She twisted her lips and looked sharply away.

"The police. Did you speak to them?"

"Not about Paul. Of course, they asked questions to all workers of the gallery. Interpol also investigated. But they wanted to know only of the watch. The Rudolf Complication. Nobody asked about Paul."

"This third man you mentioned—"

"I don't know him," she interjected. "Only Paul knew this man. This was for my protection. If this man was caught, he could not tell the police of me. If I was caught, I could not tell the police of this man. Only Paul was in the middle. Paul was not protected."

Except, I reasoned, if Paul was caught, he could have told the police about both of them. Of course, that conclusion depended on him being alive. Which meant at least two people had reason to see that he wasn't, one of whom was sitting across the table from me.

"How did my brother know this other guy?" I asked.

"I couldn't say," Vera said.

"He must've told you something about him."

"He said the man had slick hair."

"Slick like stylish, or slick like oily?"

"Just slick."

"Did slick have a name?"

"Martinko Klingáč."

"That should make things easy enough."

She shook her head. "It's not a real name. Martinko Klingáč

is from a story for children. Slovak fairytale just like, oh, what is it? Rumpelstiltskin. Martinko Klingáč means the same as Rumpelstiltskin."

Before she could continue, the waiter arrived and unloaded two tall beers filled precisely to the .5 liter mark on the glass. Vera insisted on paying right away—or maybe that's just how they did it here. The waiter made change from a coin purse, then wandered off to pick imaginary lint from his shirt as Vera snubbed out her cigarette and pushed the ashtray to the edge of the table.

"I must go," she said.

"Our drinks just got here. I just got here."

"I can't stay. I'm sorry."

"So when can we meet again?"

She pushed back her chair and stood. She was taller than I'd imagined. At least as tall as my brother. "It is not possible," she said.

"I flew ten hours for this?"

"I've told all what I can say. Please understand."

"This isn't even my suit," I sputtered. "These aren't my goddamn shoes. Do you know what it's like trying to walk around in someone else's shoes?" I knew I wasn't making any sense and forced my mouth to stop before I embarrassed myself. Her eyes dropped and she pulled on a thin black leather coat, hands climbing white and spidery as she did up the buttons.

She was really leaving, just like that.

"Why tell me anything at all?"

"Someone should know."

"The police. They're the ones should know."

"They have no interest."

"Why now? After five years."

She slung her purse over her shoulder.

"The word for beer is *pivo*," she said. "If you want more, just tell to the waiter *pivo*. When you wish to leave, have the barman call for you a taxicab to your hotel. One from the street will cost you twice as much. Where are you staying?"

"I'm going to the police."

"That's not a good idea."

"We meet again tomorrow or I go to the police."

She muttered something, her voice drained, inflectionless. Czech seemed a language well suited to muttering. Then she looked at me and said, "In Wenceslas Square there is a statue of a man on a horse. We can meet there at six thirty in the evening. But you must not go to the police. You must not tell anyone what I have told you. I have my reasons for this."

"Fine. Tomorrow. Man on a horse."

"And you will tell no one."

"I won't tell anyone."

"Say that you promise."

"I promise. Cross my heart. Whatever you do here."

She regarded me for a moment longer before reaching some silent conclusion and then turned and walked across the room and was up the stairs and gone. The fiftyish man across the bar, the one with the stocking cap, watched her walk off then smiled and gave me a knowing little nod. Like he and I were in on some secret. I looked away and caught my own twin reflections in the two glasses of beer on the table. Two warped faces wondering what to do next.

INSIDE THE MIRROR MAZE

Report on the investigation into the Zrcadlové Bludiště Incident 12 December, 1997

The following report has been compiled by the Office for the Documentation and Investigation of the Crimes of Communism (ÚDV) at the behest of Detective Zdenek Soros of the Prague Metropolitan Police. Materials herein have been transcribed from audio recordings discovered at the declassified State Security Services (StB) archives. Names of third parties deemed non-essential to the investigation have been withheld in compliance with the 1992 Act on Protection of Personal Data.

These transcriptions and the accompanying documents do not in our estimation constitute a comprehensive record of the 1984 investigation of Eliška Reznícková and the Zrcadlové Bludiště[1] Incident. Recovered audio recordings appear to be incomplete and certain documents explicitly cited or alluded to within said recordings are missing. It's unknown whether files related to this case were intentionally compromised during the days leading up to or in the immediate aftermath of the revolutionary November Events of 1989, either by members of the Czechoslovak Communist Party (KSČ), the Ministry of the Interior, State Security Services (StB), or other parties, or whether

---

1 In keeping with the original StB documents, *Zrcadlové Bludiště* refers to the mirrored labyrinth housed atop Petřín Hill in the Malá Strana district of Prague.

documents have gone missing through some clerical or other institutional error. We do not know the number of related materials that may be missing or destroyed, nor the nature of those potential materials. While its our hope that further documents related to this case may be unearthed as we continue cataloguing and digitizing materials stored in the StB archives, it's impossible to speculate on the likelihood of such an occurrence.

The concluding summary of events subsequent to the StB's involvement in the Incident at Zrcadlové Bludiště is based on our own independent, present-day investigation. Recommendations for any future related investigations and/or legal actions also appear at the end of this report.

———————————

Office for the Documentation and Investigation of the Crimes
    of Communism (ÚDV)

170 34 Poštovní úřad

Praha 7

Poštovní schránka 21/ÚDV

AUDIO RECORDING #3113a

Date: September 24, 1984 [Time unspecified]

Subject: Eliška Reznícková

Case: #1331—Incident at Zrcadlové Bludiště

Interview session #2

Location: Bartolomějská 10, Prague, Praha 1

Investigator: Agent #3553[2]

———————————

2 *The Office for the Documentation and Investigation of the Crimes of Communism (ÚDV) is unable to determine the identity of Agent #3553 at present. For further information, see ÚDV document 12B#141.*

REZNÍCKOVÁ: I don't play the accordion.

[Unintelligible—duration 4 seconds]

AGENT #3553: We must begin again. Please state your name.

REZNÍCKOVÁ: My name is Eliška Reznícková.

AGENT #3553: Your age.

REZNÍCKOVÁ: I'm twenty-seven years old.

AGENT #3553: Occupation.

REZNÍCKOVÁ: You know my occupation.

AGENT #3553: Please state it once more.

REZNÍCKOVÁ: I work at the Black Rabbit. It's a tavern.

AGENT #3553: Located where?

REZNÍCKOVÁ: On Ostrovní Street, in Nové Město. Prague 2.

AGENT #3553: Describe the duties you perform.

REZNÍCKOVÁ: I pour beer. I take money and put it in a cash register. I wash and stack glasses. When the customers leave, I lock the front door. If my boss ████████ is coming in the next day, I sweep up. Those are my duties. I don't play the accordion, either at work or at home. I don't know anybody who plays the accordion.

AGENT #3553: Are you married?

REZNÍCKOVÁ: You asked me that before. The answer is still no.

AGENT #3553: Children?

REZNÍCKOVÁ: Never.

AGENT #3553: Boyfriend?

REZNÍCKOVÁ: I'm too old for boys.

AGENT #3553: Are you a lesbian?

REZNÍCKOVÁ: What does this have to do with accordions? I don't understand. I don't understand any of this.

AGENT: We're not interested in accordions. We're chiefly concerned with—

REZNÍCKOVÁ: Yes, I know, the *case*. Some accordion case. And again, I've never seen it.

AGENT #3553: How can you be certain you've never come across the particular accordion case in question when we haven't even shown it to you? Unless you're telling us you've never laid eyes on any accordion case whatsoever. Only then can we absolutely rule out the possibility of your having come across the specific accordion case in evidence.

AGENT #3553: Is this to be your official statement? That you've never in your entire life crossed paths with a single accordion case fitting any description whatsoever? Speaking plainly, Comrade Rezníckova, we find that difficult to accept.

REZNÍCKOVÁ: Then show me already! Bring it in here. Then I can officially say I've never seen it.

AGENT #3553: To do so at present would be reckless. We believe your vision severely impaired. Please read that poster aloud, if you would.

REZNÍCKOVÁ: This is absurd.

AGENT #3553: You are capable of reading, we assume? Meaning your inability to recite the words appearing on the notice posted some three meters to our immediate left does not indicate a literacy deficiency. You agree the text is perfectly legible and the light is wholly sufficient for the purposes of—

REZNÍCKOVÁ: With my glasses, yes, of course I can read. Glasses I would be wearing were it not for your comrades deliberately stepping on them when I was arrested this morning. Or yesterday morning. Whenever it was. Tomorrow is already yesterday.

AGENT #3553: Meaning what exactly?

REZNÍCKOVÁ: The poster. It says, "Tomorrow Is Already Yesterday." There's a worker with his sleeves rolled up and sledgehammer slung over his shoulder and the poster says, "Tomorrow Is Already Yesterday." I have no idea what it means.

AGENT #3553: Very well. We should note, however, that you had to narrow your eyes nearly to the point of closing them and lean precariously in your chair in the direction of the poster in order to decipher what should be an easily readable message celebrating the achievements of the heroic workers of the Czechoslovak Socialist Republic. Without your glasses, isn't it fair to say you're practically blind, Comrade Rezníčková?

REZNÍČKOVÁ: Fair, yes. I can barely see your face without squinting. But I don't want to make you any clearer. You're just a blur of thinning hair and graying flesh wrapped in stiff layers of green. Dark green military cap, green wool overcoat, pea green tie. The Green Blur, I'll call you. You smell of Stag soap and smoke *Rudá hvězda*, Red Star, proletarian cigarette of the people. Off duty you probably smoke American cigarettes bought with Tuzex vouchers. You're in every apparent way a standard issue policeman. And yet, I think to myself, isn't my situation plainly a matter for the StB, *Státní bezpečnost*, the secret police?

AGENT #3553: Why would you think this?

REZNÍČKOVÁ: Could the Green Blur then be a covert StB operative disguised as a regular overt VB cop? Or are so many secret police already posing as professors and priests, engineers and factory foremen, that a street cop is the only disguise left? Couldn't even be considered a wolf in sheep's clothing. Maybe there are no sheep left. Only wolves and dogs.

AGENT #3553: We've searched your apartment and have discovered a number of items—we shall be discussing those in due time—but you should be happy to learn that we found a second pair of glasses you keep by your nightstand.

REZNÍCKOVÁ: My reading glasses.

AGENT #3553: We'll get them to you once they're examined. At that point, perhaps we can consider allowing you to identify the accordion case.

REZNÍCKOVÁ: You're examining my reading glasses?

AGENT #3553: We examine all evidence that may be relevant.

REZNÍCKOVÁ: How are my glasses relevant?

AGENT #3553: We're not at liberty to discuss your glasses.

REZNÍCKOVÁ: [Unintelligible]. But can you tell me whether playing or owning an accordion is now a crime? If that is really what this is all about. Or maybe you're saying the instrument itself is suspected of some transgression?

AGENT #3553: We find your fixation on this accordion curious.

REZNÍCKOVÁ: I find it curious you've asked me about it some six hundred times.

AGENT #3553: We've merely been discussing the case.

REZNÍCKOVÁ: And apparently my case involves an accordion.

AGENT #3553: Your case involves an accordion case. Which you well know. The accordion as musical instrument has nothing to do with the charges against you.

REZNÍCKOVÁ: Ah. So there are charges?

AGENT #3553: We're not at liberty to discuss any charges. Let's talk about your whereabouts on Sunday morning. You left your apartment at approximately 8 am.

REZNÍCKOVÁ: Permit me one question. Don't you, comrade, have a murderer to catch?

[Silence—duration 3 seconds]

REZNÍCKOVÁ: From one citizen to another, wouldn't it be more in the people's interest to let me be and instead go after this monster we all know is on the loose?

[Silence—duration 4 seconds]

REZNÍCKOVÁ: You know what I'm talking about. The young girl's body found Saturday morning near the Strahov stadium. It was all my customers could talk about. They say it's him, you know. The Right Hand of God.

AGENT #3553: The Right Hand of God is a superstition, as I'm sure you well know. On the morning of Sunday, September 23—

REZNÍCKOVÁ: As long as you refuse to acknowledge the killer's existence, you aren't accountable for stopping his crimes, is that it? Has some official at some ministry or other declared serial killers a cancer restricted to decadent Western societies? The embodiment of capitalism's brutal excesses?

AGENT #3553: We refuse to engage in such demoralizing speculation, but it's worth pointing out that you won't find a single verifiable account of the so-called Right Hand of God's exploits anywhere.

REZNÍCKOVÁ: Of course not. The killer and his crimes have been systematically erased from history. That's what they say.

AGENT #3553: Who is "they"?

REZNÍCKOVÁ: You want me to name names? "They" is everybody. "They" is probably your own mother. Haven't you ever heard the children's rhyme? You people are always listening and yet you never hear anything.

AGENT #3553: If next you plan on asking us about the mysterious black vans that drive through the streets snatching up children to harvest their organs, we can assure you that this story, too, is a fabrication.

REZNÍCKOVÁ: *"When moon is high in August sky, and wind howls through the trees / They say at night a killer walks the gloomy crooked streets . . . "*

AGENT #3553: On Sunday, September 23, you left your apartment.

REZNÍCKOVÁ: You've really not heard it? The song based on that poem by Rentner?

AGENT #3553: You boarded at the redline train at Kosmonautů.

REZNÍČKOVÁ: *"Condemned to wander till time's end, bowed neck hung with clock / His wretched fate to ever hear, the dread tick-tock, tick-tock . . . "*

AGENT #3553: You boarded at the redline train at Kosmonautů station[3] and rode to Muzeum.

REZNÍČKOVÁ: You can ignore it if you choose, but people still talk. In whispers over dinner tables after the children have gone to bed. Between those endless suffering contests the old women hold while waiting in line outside the butcher shop. In slurred barroom tales I overhear at the Black Rabbit. The missing garbage man's corpse found last year in Bubeneč. A year before, the dead girl in the Vyšehrad cemetery. A thirteen-year-old boy named ▮▮▮▮▮▮▮ in a warehouse of rubber tires in Smíchov two years before that.

AGENT #3553: You transferred to the green line and then exited at Malostranská. You caught a tram on Klarov Street to the base of Petřín Hill. Correct?

REZNÍČKOVÁ: For as long as anyone can remember, people have been disappearing. Each autumn, like clockwork. Some found strangled, some bludgeoned, others drowned or with their throats slit. Some are women, some men; occasionally they are children. All are found with their right hand missing. Never the left. Always the right.

AGENT #3553: You transferred to the green line and then exited at Malostranská.

---

3 *Renamed after the November Events of 1989 to Háje Station.*

REZNÍCKOVÁ: As a girl, my mother lived across the street from an antique dealer and his mongoloid son on ██████████ Street in Josefov. The ██████████ family. Just before . . .

[unintelligible—duration 7 seconds]

REZNÍCKOVÁ: . . . in the corner, his face swarming with flies.

AGENT #3553: You caught a tram on Klarov Street to the base of Petřín Hill.

REZNÍCKOVÁ: All stories follow the basic pattern. Grisly stories that stray into the realm of fairytales. The missing right hand is often just the start.

AGENT #3553: You were seen carrying an accordion case.

REZNÍCKOVÁ: And now a little girl. Her body found in Břevnov. Or was it the gymnasium in Smíchov? Stories vary. The girl bled white, or with her eyeballs pushed inside her skull, or with every tooth removed at the root. Asphyxiated, mouth stuffed with locks of her own black, red, blonde hair. In another version—

AGENT #3553: The girl was six years old.

[Silence—duration 2 seconds]

AGENT #3553: Her name was ██████████. She had her skull fractured in four different places from blows delivered by a blunt instrument, and the body was in fact found at none of those locations.

[Silence—duration 9 seconds]

REZNÍCKOVÁ: You would know better than me.

AGENT #3553: Perhaps not.

[TAPE ENDS]

CHAPTER 3

■

Around 8 AM I woke disoriented and enclosed by pale yellow walls empty save for a grim painting featuring two bearded men playing chess in a smoke-filled tavern. You could tell which one was losing by the way he clutched his meerschaum pipe hard between his teeth, his face rigid with concentration, while his younger opponent was casually wiping his glasses on his coat sleeve. All other figures in the painting were subsumed in the shadows, their conversations, I imagined, muted by the blanket of hovering smoke.

My hotel was one of few in Karlín, a neighborhood just north of the city center, the hotel itself only blocks from where my brother's blood-stained shirt and expired work permit were found in the courtyard of a building on Křižíkova Street. A five-story Neo-Renaissance building with a salmon pink façade going gray from its proximity to a highway overpass one hundred yards from my third-story window, the hotel looked out over a small grassy lot, a McDonald's, a tram stop. On the other side of the street, the world's saddest looking shoe store stood next to a seedy establishment with mirrored windows and a neon sign reading "non-stop herna bar."

Heading home from the Black Rabbit last night, I'd been accosted on the street by a little girl no older than eight who trailed me from the subway station. Following close at my heels, she kept repeating some phrase over and over and trying to hand me a used, pocket-sized tourist guidebook called *Prague Unbound*. It looked to be in good condition, its cover even improbably embossed with faded gold lettering and bound in black leather, but I didn't plan on doing any sightseeing. The little girl was devilishly persistent, though. When I finally gave up and handed her a couple crowns, she loosed a grin that gave me shudders. The poor kid had diseased blackened gums and not a single tooth in her mouth.

Prague Unbound had yellowing pages and that singular musty old book smell as I cracked it open and set about finding out what herna bars were. Turned out they were low stakes gambling establishments and not, as I would have guessed, high-energy protein snacks. Oddly enough, the photograph in the book was of the very same herna bar across my hotel and was taken from nearly the same perspective I had looking out the window. In the distance beyond lurked the massive Žižkov TV Tower, rising on a hilltop like a malformed rocket awaiting takeoff. The guidebook said it was the tallest structure in the city, built by the Soviets allegedly to jam Western radio and television broadcasts. After the Russians left, a local artist had decorated it with sculptures of faceless black babies crawling ant-like up its surface.

Prague Unbound also mentioned that the area was the site of a bloody battle between the Holy Cross Army and the Hussites in 1420 which saw hundreds of the retreating Crusaders drown in the Vltava as they made a panicked attempt to flee, the book noting, "in layers of mud and silt the river records bone-by-bone the measure of human folly." The book didn't have much to say about anything else in my vicinity, except for mentioning a nearby museum that housed a huge 3D model of the city handmade entirely from paper and built by a lone man in the eighteenth century over the course of eleven years before he died broken and penniless. "Prague has a genius for inspiring grand ambitions in its most ardent suitors," the guidebook warned in sidebar, "and a history of rewarding such devoted efforts with complete and utter ruination. As perhaps its most famous writer put it, this little mother has claws."

My ambitions for the morning were anything but grand. I had nothing to do all day until my meeting with Vera and no interest in pretending to be a tourist. Maybe I resisted experiencing Prague because in some irrational, abstract sense, I blamed the little mother with claws for Paul's death. Even when he was alive, I'd never gotten used to the idea of him being in Europe. Paul was no liberal arts grad putting off penning the Great American Screenplay, no wild oats sowing trust-fund bohemian with a café-ready copy of *The Unbearable Lightness of Being*, no high-risk entrepreneur looking to score in the Wild, Wild East. You'd never mistake him for a member of the intelligence or diplomatic communities, neither intelligence nor diplomacy being among his noted qualities. Paul was *smart in his own way*, I had been fond of saying. You might think it was like saying a fat girl had a pretty face, but that's not exactly what I meant. Paul certainly knew things I didn't. He understood the intricacies of wagering at off-track betting parlors, could find a good twenty-four-hour diner in any part of the city, knew how to talk shop to bookies and low-level drug dealers and policemen. He knew how much a transmission rebuild should cost before you're getting ripped off, the medical risks associated with ultraviolet tattoo inks, the difference between regular and goofy foot, and which pawn shops were open on Christmas Eve.

I don't know how his kind of smarts served him in Central Europe, but it hardly mattered. Paul had gone to Prague for love, to hear him tell it, though he would've sooner worn a Cubs jersey at Comiskey than used the word love earnestly when speaking of a woman in the company of men. While hanging out with some buddies at a bar on Cermak, he'd run into a girl named Sarka, a Czech who worked as an au pair for a couple in the Gold Coast during the day and tended bar at night. They started hanging out together. Then she had some kind of visa trouble and had to go back to the Czech Republic, re-apply for a work permit. They'd only been seeing each other for three or four months by this time, but she'd invited him to come stay with her in Prague and wait out the slow churn of bureaucracy. When my brother told me about it, I figured that would be the last I'd hear of Sarka. A week later he called me and said he was leaving.

I'd asked if he knew anything at all about the Czech Republic. Its history, its language, food, culture, climate. Could he even name a famous Czech person? Could I? he'd countered. Franz Kafka, I said. Miloš Forman, Martina Navratilova, Václav Havel, Nadia Comaneci (that one was a trap—I knew she was Romanian). Also the model who married that guy from the Cars. Paul laughed, said I'd just made up those names. And even if I hadn't, how famous could these people be if he'd never heard of them? Then he rattled a bunch of Czech names I didn't recognize. All were hockey players or porn stars. And Paulina Porizkova, he said, was the name of the woman once married to that lucky bastard from the Cars.

Nadia Comaneci, he added, was Bulgarian.

I took a shower. Clean tub, good water pressure. Housekeeping knocked, housekeeping entered, I kept showering. Once they'd gone I toweled off and got dressed. My suit reeked of cigarettes from the Black Rabbit, but I had nothing else to wear. As I was putting on my father's shoes, I noticed a large manila envelope sitting atop the writing desk in the corner. My name (or Dad's name) was written upon it in block letters. I walked over and ripped it open. Inside was a small booklet.

Rudolf's Curiosities

Art and Oddities from the Collection of
Hapsburg Emperor Rudolf II
15 July – 15 September 2002
GALLERIA ČERTOVKA
20 U Lužického Semináře, Malá Strana, Praha 1

Even with the date and *Čertovka* and *Malá Strana* printed on the front, only when I started flipping through the pages and landed on a description of the watch itself did I understand what I was looking at.

EXHIBIT 23: THE RUDOLF COMPLICATION

The Rudolf Complication timepiece was originally designed for Holy Roman Emperor Rudolf II during the waning years of the sixteenth century.

Rudolf II (1552–1612) was an enigmatic ruler, a highly cultivated yet deeply superstitious man given to bouts of melancholy and paranoia. He maintained a vast collection of art and esoterica from all over the world inside Prague's Hradčany Castle, which acted as the seat of the Holy Roman Empire during his reign. Rudolf also provided refuge for Europe's greatest intellectuals and eccentrics, ranging in reputation from scientists and mathematicians Tycho Brahe and Johannes Kepler, to heretical visionary philosopher Giordano Bruno, to rogue alchemist Michael Sendivogius, to scheming astrologer Geronimo Scotta.

Englishmen Edward Kelley (a.k.a. Edward Talbot, a.k.a. Edward Engelender) was one of the more brazen charlatans to win the confidence of the Hapsburg ruler. Alleged necromancer, partner of esteemed Elizabethan scholar John Dee, and for a time Rudolf's favorite alchemist, Kelley eventually went afoul of the Emperor for his inability to produce the promised Philosophers' Stone and was imprisoned in Křivoklát Castle, west of Prague. During a subsequent escape attempt, he fell from a high tower and broke his leg.

Upon being pardoned, it is believed Kelley designed the watch in an attempt to salvage his relationship with Rudolf II. Said to be made of magical metals inscribed with cabbalistic symbols that Kelley reputedly learned from famed contemporary Rabbi Löew, the watch contained a hidden compartment that displayed the hours running backward, making time metaphorically stand still for its wearer and granting him literal immortality. For a fearful Emperor enamored of the mystical and the mechanical, there could be no greater curiosity.

Rudolf is said to have paid a large sum for its commission. The details surrounding the completion and delivery of the Rudolf Complication are lost to history, but the Emperor must have felt he'd once again been duped, for he had Kelley imprisoned a second time, this time in Hněvín Castle. In 1597, following a second failed escape attempt that earned him a second broken leg, Kelley committed suicide. He was buried in a pauper's grave in the outskirts of Most village in northern Bohemia.

Rudolf II himself died fifteen years later, and his treasures were lost to waves of conquerors that swept through Prague following the disastrous Battle of White Mountain. Missing for centuries, Rudolf's prized watch has only recently been returned to the people of the Czech Republic. This exhibition marks its first public display.

Ghosted under the text were twin illustrations of the watch, one with the case closed, one opened. Closed, a stylized heraldic engraving of a lion stood out from the watch's gold cover. Inside, black roman numerals circled the yellowed ivory face, and there was a single tapered hand to indicate the hour, no minute hand, nothing for ticking off seconds. A portrait of Emperor Rudolf wearing the piece was featured in the brochure. Jowly, bulbous nosed, heavy-lidded, and long of chin—considering the artist surely flattered the royal subject, Rudolf must've looked like the Richard Nixon of his day. The watch was shaped like a tambourine and not much smaller than one, less like a watch you'd wear on your wrist than one of those clocks East Coast hip-hop clowns draped around their necks in the eighties.

How much was it worth?

Thousands? Hundreds of thousands? Millions?

Paul did think big. Had to give him that.

Never clearly, rarely deeply, but often big.

Smart in his own way.

Beneath Rudolf's glum stare, on the corner of the page, someone had penned a message in black ink still so fresh it glistened under the morning light streaming in through the hotel window.

Astronomical Clock, Old Town Square, 9 am.

Vera had evidently bribed one of the maids or another hotel employee to bring this to my room. She'd bumped up our meeting and changed the location, a shrewd maneuver as there would now be no time for me to get wired with a listening device or arrange for an undercover cop to tail me to our meeting, a notion that had occurred to me and been instantly rejected as ridiculous even as I tossed and turned with jetlag at 4 AM.

I looked up the Astronomical Clock in *Prague Unbound*. It was a big tourist attraction, one of the most famous clocks in Europe. "Legends abound regarding this celebrated horloge," said the guidebook. "Tales of conspiracy and mayhem and eye-gouging. Pay them no more heed than you would a drunken Turk." I read the sentence twice, but it came out the same both times. Guess the cultural sensitivity movement hadn't reached Czech tourist literature yet.

I wondered if Vera was being ironic in selecting a famous old clock as our new meeting place as I tore the cover page from the booklet in case I needed the address later, folded it inside *Prague Unbound,* and slipped the guidebook in my jacket pocket. The two figures hunched over their chess game in the painting were still pondering their next moves as I headed out.

INSIDE THE MIRROR MAZE—
PART II

AUDIO RECORDING #3113b

Date: September 26, 1984 [Time unspecified]

Subject: Eliška Reznícková

Case: #1331—Incident at Zrcadlové Bludiště

Interview session #5

Location: Unknown

Investigator: Agent #3553

AGENT #3553: You then took the funicular up the hill?

REZNÍCKOVÁ: It was broken.

AGENT #3553: So you walked up the hill? Comrade Reznícková?
Please pay attention. You took the tram to the base of Petřín.
You went up the hill. You were carrying the accordion case.

REZNÍCKOVÁ: I never said that.

AGENT #3553: We have witnesses. Where were you going?

REZNÍCKOVÁ: Ask your witnesses.

AGENT #3553: Where did you go after exiting the funicular?
You said you rode it up Petřín Hill, correct?

REZNÍCKOVÁ: I said the funicular was broken.

AGENT #3553: Who were you planning to meet atop Petřín? What were you planning to do? Where were you going?

REZNÍCKOVÁ: Matthew twenty-five thirty-one.

AGENT #3553: Good, an address. Where is this Matthew Street, exactly?

REZNÍCKOVÁ: It's not a street. It's from the Bible. Matthew 25:31. "When the Son of Man shall come in his glory and all the holy angels with him, then he shall sit upon the throne of his glory. And before him shall be gathered all nations: and he shall separate them one from another, as a shepherd divideth sheep from the goats. And he shall set the sheep on his right hand, and the goats on the left."

AGENT #3553: Why the left?

REZNÍCKOVÁ: You'd have to ask Matthew.

AGENT #3553: A political allegory?

REZNÍCKOVÁ: I'm not that clever.

AGENT #3553: Do you consider yourself a religious person?

REZNÍCKOVÁ: I avoid considering myself when possible.

AGENT #3553: How is it you know the Bible so well? This passage clearly has special meaning for you. Why?

REZNÍČKOVÁ: It doesn't. I'm tired. I need sleep. I can't be of any use to you when I don't know what I'm saying.

AGENT #3553: Allow us to read you something.

[Papers being shuffled—duration 4 seconds]

AGENT #3553: "... and Prague below a sleeping city where time passed like so many snakes through a bramble, each era leaving behind its molten skin cast in stone. But this Sunday morning as he stands on the Letná Plain, no time passes and the city looks not so much sleeping as abandoned. The Butcher once read that the Americans had invented a new weapon which could obliterate entire populations in a flash but leave buildings and bridges and highways completely intact. The neutron bomb, they called it. The Butcher envisions a Prague devoid of people and life, the city a silent, sprawling monument to the end of itself. But then a bird twitters, a little goat girl skips into view on the other side of the empty plain, and the city is resurrected."

REZNÍČKOVÁ: Please stop.

AGENT #3553: "Snow slips from a rooftop in the distance and lands with a muffled thump in a drift below and The Butcher blinks and blinks and tries to retrieve the thought he was thinking but finds his thoughts are gone and will not be summoned. The little girl in the brown dress appears at the far end of the empty Letná Plain, and when she walks by him he snatches her up and hoists her upside down by her naked rear ankle hooves and drives her goat head into the concrete. She cries and brays and her arms flail and then she doesn't cry and

*her arms stop moving and her goat blood spills over everything.
He stretches her right arm limp upon the pavement and withdraws his knife and rolls his eyes to the blue heavens. The blade
comes down and her five-fingered hoof is no longer part of her
body. The Butcher slips the appendage in his pocket. His fingers
intertwine with hers in a secret embrace as he walks down the
hill, the old city vibrating and shimmering before him.*

[Silence—duration 5 seconds]

AGENT #3553: Do you recognize this passage?

[Silence—duration 2 seconds]

AGENT #3553: This is your writing, correct? You didn't tell us
you were a writer.

REZNÍCKOVÁ: Your evidence I am may be evidence I'm not. But
yes, it's mine. It's a project I'm working on. For my own amuse-
ment. It has nothing to do with anything.

AGENT #3553: It's demoralizing.

REZNÍCKOVÁ: I can assure you no one has been demoralized but
myself.

AGENT #3553: Still, there are a number of elements we find
interesting. Particularly your evident obsession with this Right
Hand of God figure.

REZNÍCKOVÁ: It's hardly an obsession. Just an interest. Really
it's you people who should be interested. Don't you think?

AGENT #3553: Let's talk about your protagonist. You mention in passing that his proper name is Martin Vlasák, but he self-identifies according to his vocation, referring to himself as "The Butcher." We find this interesting, as your own surname, Reznícková, is a feminization of one Czech word for "butcher." Furthermore, the entire piece is in the first person, written in the form of diary entries, and set in the present.

REZNÍCKOVÁ: If you're insinuating that I'm playing some kind of literary shell game—

AGENT #3553: When did you author the passage I just read to you? Before or after you went up Petřín?

REZNÍCKOVÁ: Before. Long before, months ago.

AGENT #3553: Your neighbors in the Kosmonautů complex reported excessive toilet flushing the night before you were arrested.

REZNÍCKOVÁ: Really? And just what is considered excessive? Is there a limit recommended by the Ministry of Toilets?

AGENT #3553: We know you were trying to dispose of your writing. Why didn't you flush this document, too? Did you really think we wouldn't find it? Let's read another passage, where your hero goes to a tavern called the White Rabbit. Familiar ring to it, no?

REZNÍCKOVÁ: It's nothing to do with the Black Rabbit, before you start down that path. The name refers to a Jefferson Airplane song, which is itself a reference to *Alice in Wonderland*.

AGENT #3553: Let's listen to what you wrote. *"Ten to midnight inside the White Rabbit and smoke crawls thick along the ceiling. The Butcher doesn't need to look at the clock. He knows it's nearly closing time by the number of condensation marks from emptied glasses forming disjointed ringlets on the tabletops, by the way conversations have slurred into blinkered repetitions rife with sloppy hand gestures and emphatic nods that threaten to send their nodders headlong to the floor. President Husák was on TV yesterday, asking the hardworking people of Czechoslovakia not to drink so much. Maybe this is their way of protesting, of living in truth."*

REZNÍCKOVÁ: A fictional character is saying these things.

AGENT #3553: Indifference is an obstacle to progress that even fictional entities must work to overcome.

REZNÍCKOVÁ: Oh my. Well, I'll keep that in mind in the future. Do I get to sleep now?

AGENT #3553: Let me continue. *"Among these men are many thrust from their former lives, exiled from their truer selves. Unproduced playwrights, cameraless filmmakers, tenure-stripped professors, decommissioned architects. They now work as street sweepers, coal shovelers, and drill press operators. They wash windows; they scrub corpses. They pretend to work, and the government pretends to pay them. The Butcher sometimes thinks of his fellow drinkers as old bears in hibernation sleeping through a winter that just won't end. Other times he envisions the White Rabbit as some kind of spiritual bomb shelter where irradiated souls could for a few hours and imagine they'd remained untainted by the psychic fallout occurring all around them, where they could dream of some velvet morning when they would emerge from the darkness triumphant and whole, blinking into a bright, sunlit future. But none of them are whole anymore, and the future doesn't even know they exist."*

REZNÍCKOVÁ: Alright, stop. We both know this conversation isn't really about anything I've written. Can we quit pretending this is about some manuscript you found at my apartment?

AGENT #3553: So you are at last willing to concede that you have some understanding of why we asked for your assistance.

REZNÍCKOVÁ: His name is Vokov[4].

[Silence—duration 3 seconds]

REZNÍCKOVÁ: And yes, I carried an accordion case up Petřín Hill. There, I've said it. And yes, I left it in the child's castle, in the mirror maze. I'm sure you already have Vokov in custody anyway. And what was he expecting me to do? Rot in prison for him? I was carrying the accordion case for a man named Vokov. Inside the case were fifty copies of *The Defenestrator*. An underground newspaper. A *samizdat*. That's all I know, and it has nothing to do with some desk-drawer novel. Please, let me sleep. Two hours and I will tell you everything, I promise.

[Silence—duration 2 seconds]

---

4 As questions pertaining to the identity of the person referred to herein as Vokov are germane to the ÚDV investigation into the case of Zrcadlové Bludiště, it has been determined by the Czech Office for Personal Data Protection that they should appear in the text as relayed by Rezníckavá to the interviewer.

AGENT #3553: There will be plenty of time for rest when we're finished. Tell us about this Vokov. What is his first name?

REZNÍCKOVÁ: I don't know.

AGENT #3553: Where did you meet him?

REZNÍCKOVÁ: At the White Rabbit.

AGENT #3553: Meaning the rock and roll song or the character from the Lewis Carroll novel?

REZNÍCKOVÁ: The Black Rabbit. I meant the Black Rabbit. You're confusing me. Please just let me rest.

AGENT #3553: When did you first meet this man?

REZNÍCKOVÁ: It was on Saturday night. At closing time. Every night it's the same. Customers wince and grumble and rise wobbling on puppet legs. They don heavy coats and pull hats crooked over their heads and stagger up the stairs. When everyone is finally gone, I lock the door and put on "One O'Clock Jump" while I'm sweeping. A scratchy recording of the Count Basie version I found in an old crate in the basement. Did you know Count Basie was once banned by the government? They thought he was a member of the aristocracy. Because of his name. Same is true of Duke Ellington.

AGENT #3553: Is that a joke, Comrade Reznícková?

REZNÍCKOVÁ: You can never be sure, can you? Saturday we
had closed, and I was just about to put the needle to the record
when suddenly a chair squeaked across the floor. At a corner
table barely visible in the shadows, a large man sat slumped in
his chair, arms crossed. I couldn't tell if the man's eyes were
opened or not.

AGENT #3553: Please describe this man.

REZNÍCKOVÁ: A thick beard covered his neck. His ears were
buried beneath locks of wavy hair that fell nearly to his shoulders. Nested at the center was a face like a roughly chiseled
sculpture. Solid brow, great lump of a nose. Cheekbones wide,
flat, uneven. He was perhaps in his mid-forties, though it was
difficult to tell. His shirt was buttoned to the collar and his shoes
were large, comically so. A glass of beer sat untouched on the
table in front of him. I made my way over to the man and was
just about to give his shoulder a gentle shake when he jerked his
head upward. When his eyes opened they were the hard, mottled gray of old statues. I was momentarily unable to speak or
look away. "We're closed," I told him.

AGENT #3553: This man then was not a regular customer?

REZNÍCKOVÁ: I'd never seen him before. It was then I saw the
accordion case resting under the table. Its corners dented, its
surface scuffed and marred. He told me his name was Vokov. I
repeated that we were closed and that he must leave. "Do you
know what's going to happen next?" he asks. "Do you know what
will happen starting now and ending where such things end?"

AGENT #3553: What do you suppose he meant?

REZNÍCKOVÁ: I have no idea. I told him I imagined the future would be much like the present, only longer. This seemed to amuse him. He took a sip of beer, wet lips glistening in his beard. "A man followed me here," he tells me. "I've seen this man before. He thinks I haven't, but I have. He's out there now waiting. And so I know exactly what is going to happen next." I look reflexively in the direction of the street, which is pointless as I'm standing in a subterranean room with no windows. "He's waiting for other men like himself to arrive," the man resumes. "When I leave the Black Rabbit, a car will pull up to the curb. They'll make me get inside this car. They'll take away my accordion case. They'll scrutinize the contents of this case with the rigor of Talmudic scholars. There will be questions, many, many questions. There will be talk of Paragraph 98 of the Criminal Code. Subversion of the Republic. There will be threats, perhaps beatings. These men are patient men. They will wait for answers. They'll take me down the rabbit hole and they'll wait. This is what will happen to me. What will happen to all of us."

AGENT #3553: And how did you respond to this?

REZNÍCKOVÁ: I told him he was drunk. But I could see he wasn't drunk. "What happens is we die in jail," he says. Talking like a radio announcer reading an official report about grain production. "In Ruzyně, in Mirov. Or maybe they don't let us die right away. Time itself can be used as an instrument of torture. Maybe we're sentenced to reeducation labor. We work in the mines. We develop bent frames and aversions to the sun."

AGENT #3553: You knew by this point he was deranged.

REZNÍCKOVÁ: Who is to say? There was something about his voice, wise and unreachable and sad. "Coughs blossom into respiratory illnesses," he says. "Our lungs fill with fluid. Blood colors our sputum, our hair falls out in clumps, our voices subside into watery rattles. We drown of our own bodies. This is what happens. To me, to my friends. Because I've been careless. Because I've made a mistake."

He gives the accordion case a sudden kick. It rings metallic, and the sound brings me part way to my senses. Now is the time to make a run for it. But then if he wanted to attack me, why the big speech? Besides, I am standing closer to the door, and once I get to the street, if police really are there waiting, then I will only have to scream. But then I know none of these things will happen because the question is already escaping my lips even as my teeth clench to hold it back.

"What's inside the case?" I ask him.

AGENT #3553: And he tells you?

REZNÍCKOVÁ: Vokov lifts the accordion case and lays it on the table. Neither of us speak, both studying the dull metal box as if some complicated chess problem is posed upon its surface. He takes from his inner coat pocket a curled sheaf of papers several pages in number and unrolls them atop the case.

"This," he says, "is *The Defenestrator*."

AGENT #3553: A samizdat[5].

---

5 The existence of this underground newspaper remains unverified. Nowhere is it referred to in other materials obtained by the ÚDZ, and a search of the non-profit *Society of Libri Prohibiti*'s exhaustive archive of samizdat and exile literature circulated between 1948-1989 yielded no results.

REZNÍCKOVÁ: I guessed as much, though he didn't say so, and I'd never actually seen one before. It was just a handful of plain, typewritten sheets. He flips through the pages, explaining how all previous issues had been hand typed, page by monotonous page, copy by mind-numbing copy, on cheap onionskin. Quality paper is a tightly controlled commodity, he says, difficult to acquire without drawing attention. Every printing press and photocopier in the country is state owned and as closely monitored as materials at the Semtex plastic explosive factory. But Vokov says his friends have recently gained use of a cyclostyle stencil printer from an old parish school in Podolí.

AGENT #3553: Did he give you the name of this school?

REZNÍCKOVÁ: He did not. "Now we can crank issues out in no time," he said. "Which means we can include news, real news transcribed from the radio broadcasts that sneak through unjammed. BBC, Radio Free Europe, Deutschewelt." But news, he explains, is not their primary focus. *The Defenestrator* publishes short stories, serialized novel excerpts, feuilletons, poems, even an essay written by a famous exiled novelist living in London that had been smuggled across the Austrian border by members of the French Human Rights League. The people behind their publication know the *Parallel Polis* contributors, who know the *Revolver Revue* writers, who help distribute *Edice Petlice*, who have connections with *Vokno's*[6] people. Among their number included half the signers of Charter 77. Or so he told me.

---

6 *Parallel Polis, Revolver Revue,* and *Vokno* were some of the more widely circulated dissident publications as verified by *Society of Libri Prohibiti.* However, it's unclear whether all were active at the time this interview took place.

"Fifty copies are inside the accordion case," he says. "Tomorrow I was to take them to the top of Petřín Hill and deliver them to a man unknown to me. You know the rest."

AGENT #3553: And did you know the rest?

REZNÍCKOVÁ: Each copy would be passed hand-to-hand in secret, I suppose. One trusted friend to another. I've heard there is or was a special pew in St. James Cathedral under which you could find such materials. Though if I know it, so must you. In perhaps six months time, I figured, each copy of *The Defenestrator* would have been read by some fifty or one hundred people. With fifty copies, that meant nearly five thousand individuals.

AGENT #3553: You really think so many would be interested in unsubstantiated [unintelligible] printed on cheap onionskin?

REZNÍCKOVÁ: What I wondered was why Vokov would share all these incriminating details, why he would trust someone he'd never met. But then he's got nothing to lose, I thought. And by telling me of this operation, he is also implicating me. If I choose not to go to the police with what I know, I become an accomplice.

AGENT #3553: Pity you did not immediately act upon this thought. Didn't you resent him using you?

REZNÍCKOVÁ: No. I knew I should. But no, I didn't.

"Fifty copies," he resumes. "Each a prison sentence as soon as I walk out that door. So now, I ask of you a favor." Vokov glances over his shoulder, nods toward the fireplace in the corner. "Burn these," he says. "Each and every copy." Which shocked me.

AGENT #3553: Why should it shock you that he wanted to destroy evidence of his wrongdoing?

REZNÍCKOVÁ: Think of all the work involved. All they'd been through to make this thing. "It's already too late for me," he insists. "One way or another, I'm finished. But the others still have a chance. The choice is simple. Preserve the work or destroy its authors."

AGENT #3553: Remarkable. So he not only presented himself as a martyr willing to sacrifice himself for a greater good, but also placed any blame for what might happen to his co-conspirators onto your shoulders? You must have been struck by the arrogance of such a tactic.

REZNÍCKOVÁ: I don't know how to explain my reaction except to say the man was very convincing. I said I could take them. I could deliver the case to his contact. The man on Petřín Hill.

AGENT #3553: But why? Such actions are irrational.

REZNÍCKOVÁ: I have my reasons.

AGENT #3553: Did it not occur to you that even if Vokov really was being followed, and the police knew or suspected what was in the accordion case, that it would make much more sense for the police to not arrest him right away, but to instead wait and see who he gave the case to, in order that this member of the conspiracy might also be brought to justice?

REZNÍCKOVÁ: I don't think like a policeman. Or like a criminal. I had my reasons and I don't care to dwell on them. Isn't it enough that I'm cooperating?

AGENT #3553: Are you? It's of tremendous importance that you make us understand why you did what you did.

REZNÍCKOVÁ: Alright, fine. I had an idea that maybe one day *The Defenestrator* might consider publishing my work. No one else is going to, let's face it. Not in this lifetime. And if they couldn't publish it themselves, then maybe they could find a place for it outside the country.

AGENT #3553: And you calculated this action would put you in their good graces. Make you a member of the club.

REZNÍCKOVÁ: Something like that.

AGENT #3553: We must tell you that this answer is unsatisfactory on a number of levels. You would do well to drop this whole samizdat charade and tell us what really happened.

REZNÍCKOVÁ: I am telling you.

AGENT #3553: We know what you've done. The enormity of your crimes. These lies you tell us about this imaginary figure Vokov—

REZNÍCKOVÁ: Imaginary? I assure you—

[Loud banging sound consistent with fist hitting table]

AGENT #3553: We will bring you to reality! We will bring you to reality!

[Banging sound repeated 3 times]

AGENT #3553: We will bring you to reality. All we need is time, comrade. And we have all the time we need.

[Session terminated]

CHAPTER 4

∎

The graying edifices near my hotel were graffiti riddled and timeworn, and in places I could still see the watermarks upon the walls five years after the flood, but in Old Town's winding, cobblestoned lanes, the buildings wore fresh coats of paint and sunlight bounced off clean-scrubbed windows. Tourists squeezed down constricted passageways past storefronts bursting with Bohemian crystal, wooden puppets, garnet and amber jewelry. There were Franz Kafka T-shirts, Franz Kafka coffee mugs, Franz Kafka refrigerator magnets. Window after window of Russian nesting dolls, watercolors of the Charles Bridge, replica swords, Golem keychains, hand-carved wooden chess sets, plastic replica handguns, more puppets, more Kafka, more garnet, and more amber. Arched doorways proffered glimpses of courtyard beer gardens and outdoor cafés; ATMs and international currency exchange kiosks were everywhere. Prague was so thoroughly in the business of Prague it made you almost feel sorry for the old Communists. If history was a sport, capitalism would have drawn a penalty for excessive celebration.

I found the Astronomical Clock housed in a large stone tower whose spires echoed the Týn Church opposite, a site where, *Prague Unbound* noted, "to this day a small bell rings in a tower in memory of a local servant girl killed by a wicked noblewoman for spending too much time in prayer." The main clock face stood maybe sixteen feet off the ground, surrounded by a gothic canopy, stone arches, columns. A gold-breasted rooster perched above the clock; wooden statues depicting death, an angel, and some dude in a turban looked on while upon the clock face, discs turned within discs, Roman numerals and Arabic numbers shared space with esoteric mathematical symbols, and three or four hands of differing lengths pointed this direction or that. I had no idea what any of it meant.

I took a place at the perimeter of the crowd and scanned for Vera. Tour guides stood before the gathering, holding aloft brightly colored umbrellas. The guide nearest me was speaking English through a miniature bullhorn. More people were arriving every second.

"Work on the Astronomical Clock began in the year 1410," the guide announced, "but the clock wasn't perfected until the great Master Hanuš arrived at the end of the fifteenth century." Adjacent guides were broadcasting the same narrative in German, Japanese, something that sounded like Russian.

The clock soon became the envy of all Europe, the guide said, and its growing fame alarmed the town authorities. Worried that clockmaker Hanuš might be lured to another city and by large commission be spurred to even greater clock-building feats, the town councilors held a secret meeting. A few nights later, three men wearing black hoods paid a visit to Hanuš. Two of them bound the clockmaker while a third grabbed an iron poker from the fireplace and gouged out his eyes. Master Hanuš never built another clock, in Prague or anywhere else.

The assembled tourists reacted with nervous chuckles, those near the German guide laughing hardest. Maybe it was funnier in German. They'd coined the term *schadenfreude*, after all.

But the story didn't end there. Hanuš learned of the council's betrayal, but he did nothing. Years passed. Now a sickly old man and near death, he approached the councilors and was given permission to visit the clock house one final time, a chance to say goodbye to his life's finest achievement. The Japanese and German tour guides stopped speaking and turned to gaze expectantly at the clock. The English guide glanced over her shoulder, and realizing time was running out, finished in a breathless rush, trumpeting through the bullhorn about how the blind Master Hanuš went inside the clock house and listened to the great gears clicking and meshing and waited for some tell-tale auditory sign, some precise moment of maximum mechanical vulnerability known only to its designer, and then threw himself bodily upon the clock and grabbed at the gears and wheels, ripping and tearing with the last of his strength. By the time the guards wrestled him from the clock, it was too late. The hands of the Astrological Clock had stopped turning. They were to remain idle for two hundred years.

A murmur swept over the crowd as the new hour arrived. Cell phones and cameras were hoisted as a mechanical rooster cockadoodledooed. Flashes went off as Death yanked a rope, the bell tolled above, and a procession of wooden apostles creaked past the opened windows above the clock face. Then the windows clapped shut, Death clanged the bell again, and the show was all over. The tourists erupted in spontaneous applause. Despite their enthusiasm, the clock refused an encore, at least for another hour, and people began shuffling off after their guides toward the next medieval wonder.

Still no sign of Vera. I imagined she was hanging back, watching from a distance. She'd waited five years to send a letter. She could wait a few more minutes to make sure that I really was alone, that I hadn't brought the police or anyone else along with me.

"Cocksuck there, you see him?" someone said.

The voice belonged to a shaggy-headed man wearing a wrinkled green warm-up jacket over a loose knit black sweater decorated with a blocky white snowflake pattern. He was standing to my left in gray slacks that ballooned at the knees and a pair of black basketball shoes like Michael Jordan might've worn twenty years ago. The guy wasn't looking at me as he spoke, his eyes instead fixed on a clean-cut blonde kid wearing shorts and backwards baseball cap strolling leisurely across the square. "Watch this, man," he said, his thick accent coagulating the words into a single, jagged mass. "Pickpocket. Now they dress sometimes like tourists."

Was Vera watching? It wouldn't look good, me talking to some random someone. But I couldn't resist asking, "How can you tell he's a pickpocket?"

"Once I arrest him. Tram 9. And his girlfriend. She's still in jail now. "

It was a lot easier to imagine the speaker getting arrested than doing any arresting. He was maybe five seven, on the thin side except for a second-trimester paunch. With the ruddy face of a drinker, and a mess of salt and pepper hair, it was easy to overlook the bleary intensity of his eyes. I realized suddenly I'd seen him before. It was the man from inside the Black Rabbit. The one who'd been watching me speak with Vera.

"You are waiting for someone?" He snorted and wiped his nose with his sleeve. "You seem maybe nervous. Are you nervous, Mr. Holloway?"

"How do you know my name?"

He tapped a finger against the whitewall of his temple then turned and loped toward the massive Jan Hus sculpture at the center of the square, hunch-shouldered and half-limping through a flock of pigeons rising startled to flight. A beaming young woman stepped up and handed me a flyer for a performance of Vivaldi's *Four Seasons* being held in some church. I scanned once more for Vera. Pigeons beat their wings in gray swirl. Another girl tried to hand me a flier for a puppet show.

By the time I caught up with the man, he'd already crossed the square, moving past Jan Hus and through the serrated shadows beneath the Týn Church onto a sharply veering street marked Dlouhá. "Who are you?" I asked. "Did Vera send you?"

"My name is Soros. Long time I am waiting for you, man. Long time."

He pivoted down another winding lane with the agitation of a man pacing a prison cell. I was trying to note the streets on the red nameplates fastened to the walls, but it was hard to tell where one ended and another began. No alleyways or even gaps, only walls meeting walls, as if in a maze or a dream.

Then I understood there was no need to worry about making my way back to Old Town Square. Vera wouldn't be coming. She wasn't the one who'd arranged to have the Rudolf II exhibit booklet in my room with *9 am Astrological Clock* penned in the margin. No, that would be the man charging ahead of me, pushing through the crowd like someone about to be sick.

"Did you know my brother?" I called after him.

"Brother?" He stopped walking, and I watched his face drop as the realization hit. "You're not Paul Holloway? Well, fuck on me. You're not who I was waiting for. But then always I think he is dead anyway."

"You knew him?"

"Yes. But when I know him already he is gone."

"What does that mean?"

"He is my case for two days. When I am Detective Soros. Before I am just Soros."

"You were a cop?"

"No, milkmaid," he deadpanned. "Babies they drink my hairy tits. Yes, I am police. When Paul Holloway is missing, I am chief investigator. Two days on his case. Third day, everything fucks out bad. Different case I am stucked in my leg. Fifteen years old *pervitin* junkie in Holešovice, he stucks me with dirty fucking screwdriver also he stucks in his sister's *cikanka* asshole or I don't know what. My leg, it's poof! Like balloon. Red black blue. So, hospital. And when I get out, case of Paul Holloway is closed. Missing, they think dead. No body, no investigation. Nobody else looks for this man. No friends, no family here. Nobody we talk to, nobody is suspect. No case, my bosses say. And what are bosses but bosses? But I don't forget about Holloway. Not him, not the others."

"What others?"

"Like your brother."

The crowds were thinning, shop signs going from English to Czech, buildings losing their color, streets going cold in the morning shadows. Every passage looked like an echo of the one before, intersections a disharmony of wrong angles that reminded me of a Just Say No poster I'd seen in junior high featuring webs spun by spiders that were administered LSD. I remembered wondering what genius scientist decided to give spiders acid. I still kind of wondered, but it had been pushed down the list of life's unanswered questions.

"Are you saying there was some kind of cover-up?"

"After the flood, some parts of the city, they are destroyed. We're for many hours working, for many days no sleep. Move families from bad flood places, drag old women out of houses. Put down bags of sand, put up steel fences, go around the streets in

little boats. Smíchov, Malá Strana, Karlín—these places are turn
to lakes. Old buildings, some are destroyed, collapse. Your brother
is reporting missing. Anonymous call. In the area of Karlín, his
clothing, it is found in the courtyard of a fallen apartment house.
So they say maybe drowning, an accident. Missing, presumed
dead. Is there suspicion? I think yes, but bosses think no. The
body taken by the water, say bosses. Accidents don't need men to
investigate. Accidents don't need evidence, paperwork. No suspects, questions, courtrooms. And the police, everyone in Prague,
we are tired like fucking dogs then. Your brother is a victim of the
flood, yes, but the flood doesn't kill him."

"What makes you think not?"

"Because of where was the blood. On his shirt. On his right
sleeve. Also because the time he disappears."

"I don't follow."

"Who are you speaking with last night?"

"I don't know her name," I said.

"You say the name Vera. Already just now."

"I don't know her last name."

A shadow of anger flashed over his features before vanishing
in the next instant. "I say your brother is murdered. You have no
surprise. Why? Because already you know. Because I think the
woman tells you. But who can know Paul Holloway is murdered?
The person who kills him. Maybe a person who helps. Who are
you speaking with last night?"

"None of the above?"

"Dog shit!" He seized my arm and yanked me violently sideways. I struggled to regain my balance and wrest myself from his
grip, but it was no use. He could've punched me in the face or
thrown me up against the wall or lead me in a foxtrot, but instead
he just froze and pointed at a mess on the pavement. "Dog shit,"
he repeated, relinquishing his hold with an uneven grin. "You

don't know the woman's last name? Then I tell you. Her name is Vera Svobodova."

We passed a trio of old men sipping from paper bags on a bench outside a low gothic church, its doors yawning open to reveal an opaque darkness inside. Across the street, drying laundry and faded rugs hung from the balconies, and somewhere inside a television was blaring. Funny, no matter what country you're in, television always sounds like television. Soros resumed speaking while his shoes slapped a disjointed rhythm on the cobblestones.

"In Paul Holloway's shirt are two things. Expired work permit and matchbook from the Black Rabbit. I go there, show picture on the work permit. A barman says yes, I have seen this man. This man he has been there with a woman. Tall woman, black hair. Small tits, pity, otherwise a hot bitch looker, he says. I give this man my mobile number, tell him to call me if again he sees her. Five years happen. I leave the police, but still I have same phone. One day the woman appears again in the bar. Two nights, three nights. The barman, he remembers her. Men, they remember a hot bitch looker, tits or no tits. Again and again she visits the Black Rabbit, every night for two weeks maybe. Always she is alone. The barman calls Soros. I go to the Black Rabbit. For a week. I go and I watch. Every day is there Vera Svobodova. Then one day she is not alone. At her table is a man. Paul Holloway. Only next day I find out he's not Paul Holloway but Paul Hollo-way's brother. Fuck on me. But he knows Paul Holloway is mur-dered. And he doesn't want to be my friend."

His story prompted so many questions my head was spinning. Probably didn't help I hadn't eaten since the airplane. The name-plate mounted on the building said we were on Bartolomějská Street, a pinched lane with the air of a film set after shooting had ended and everyone had gone home. I wondered where the hell Soros could be taking me, but moments later, we were once again in tourist central. Crowds thickened, graffiti vanished, shop signs went from Czech to English, buildings from stony gray to pastels. We were in front of the clock, right where we'd started.

"The person who kills Paul Holloway is still alive," Soros said. "Still here, in this city. This person will kill again. It will happen just like every year. Maybe this is too much for you now. Maybe you need time to understand. But there is no time."

He dug into his pants pocket, came up empty, then reached into an inner pocket of his green warm-up jacket to produce a crumpled business card. "You don't believe me, maybe you will believe Bob Hannah. Tell Bob Hannah the detective sent you. Ask of your brother's right hand. Next time, maybe you will want to be friends."

"His right hand?"

"Ask Bob Hannah."

He hobbled off across the square, a bedraggled figure bobbing and weaving through the crowds until a carriage pulled by a horse with red velvet blinders eclipsed my view and he was gone. Twenty feet away, a policeman in riot gear stood carrying a semi-automatic submachine gun. The German shepherd at his side lowered on its haunches, yawning and unfurling a pink gray tongue as a girl in a sandwich board advertising BE SOMEONE ELSE—PHOTOS IN HISTORIC OUTFITS walked by. I stood unmoving at the edge of Old Town square, studying the card.

> Bob Hannah
> Managing editor
> *The Stone Folio*
> Prague's Leading English Weekly
> Karlovo náměstí 502/40
> 128 00 Praha 2 - Nové Město
> Czech Republic

I slipped the card into my pocket, pulled out *Prague Unbound*, and flipped to the map at the back in order to figure out the quickest route back to the hotel. Just left of the meandering Vltava River, in Old Town Square, northeast of Jan Hus and friends, beneath the Astronomical Clock, was a tiny dot. Beneath the dot, a handwritten scrawl reading, *Here you are again.*

■

CHAPTER 5

My dad's shoes were half a size too large, and I could feel my feet blistering as I slumped down on a bench at the edge of the river. On the other side of the Vltava, a giant metronome sat on a high plateau, unmoving atop a concrete pedestal. Praguers were evidently nuts about all things timekeeping. Clocks in the metro stations, clocks on streetlamps, the Astronomical Clock with its creaky wooden effigies. But then, if my brother had died in a plot to steal a Maltese Falcon, I'd probably be noticing birds everywhere. *Prague Unbound* mentioned that the plinth where the metronome now stood was once the site of the largest sculpture in the world, one depicting Joseph Vissarionovich Dzhugashvili, Liberator of Nations, Gardener of Human Happiness, better known as Josef Stalin. The sculptor responsible for its creation suicided before the statue was unveiled, while the model drank himself to death because his friends turned on him and refused to call him anything but Stalin. The statue stood for only six years. When the Soviet leader's crimes were brought to light, Czechoslovakian authorities were further embarrassed because they couldn't figure out how to dismantle the 17,000-ton eyesore and had to call in West German demolition experts. "Remnants of Stalin's exploded head may still be found in the stygian depths of the Vltava River below," noted the book, "a reminder that men great and small may come and go but the Vltava is forever."

I sat pondering my encounter with the ex-detective. What he'd told me was troubling enough—willful police indifference, a killer of some sort on the loose, something having to do with my brother's right hand—but what he didn't say was equally puzzling. He hadn't mentioned anything about the Rudolf Complication and didn't seem to know much about Vera beyond her name, the fact that she'd once been seen with my brother at the Black Rabbit, and that five years later she'd decided to start frequenting the place again. Could he be ignorant of the fact that my brother was part of a conspiracy to steal the watch? Maybe—but then why would he have arranged the exhibit booklet to be left in my room?

Maybe he was the third man. Martinko Klingáč.

Didn't seem likely. Nothing slick about wild hair, his wrestling-match-inside-a-Salvation-Army-drop-box outfit.

I'd also been thinking about the map in *Prague Unbound*, the one strangely marked with my exact location when I'd opened the book in Old Town Square, and decided this at least presented less of a mystery. It was a used book, after all—obviously its previous owners had drawn the dot and hand written *Here you are* in tiny script when trying to get their bearings. The Astronomical Clock was one of the biggest tourist draws in the city, after all, along with the Charles Bridge, one of two places probably everyone who came to Prague visited. This person, I guess, came twice, and either a frustrated or humorous impulse caused them to add *again*. Whatever the case, the coincidence wasn't that striking, and I had bigger things to worry about.

Somewhere church bells started ringing, and the sight of an old guy in a canoe fishing near one of the tiny islands in the river

got me thinking back to a trip to Wisconsin the three Holloway
men had taken the summer my mom left—a memory I hadn't
dusted off in years. I was thirteen, which would've made Paul
nine or ten. It was a weekend thing where we stayed at a lake-
side cabin owned by one of my dad's friends. Rained the whole
first day, and we were stuck in a cramped cabin with no TV, no
video games. Instead of grilling hamburgers, my dad had tried
cooking them on an old potbellied stove and turned them into
hockey pucks. By Sunday the three of us were sick of each other
and began retreating into the silences of our separate worlds. But
when the rain cleared we made a go of it anyway and headed out
in a rowboat with rented gear. None of us knew what the hell we
were doing, though my Dad talked a good game, having spent the
previous afternoon reading *A River Runs Through It*. He insisted
we not call them fishing "poles" but "rods" and talked about a four
count rhythm and keeping our casts between ten and two o'clock,
never mind that we were using lures rather than flies. No bites
all afternoon, although we nipped at each other plenty, bickering
about lures, the best spots in the lake to fish, whose fault it was we
had forgotten to bring the cooler.

Then out of nowhere Paul had a hit, rod jumping as if touched
by something electric. He started reeling the fish in too fast, and
the thing leapt out of the water trying to spit the hook. Biggest
fish I'd ever seen, a bass, its enormous black spine breaking the
surface of the lake as Paul cranked on the reel, his rod bowing
like a curled, twitching finger. I remember the look of terrified
concentration on his face as the thing thrashed and twisted. We
didn't even know enough to put a net under it, my dad and I just
standing there in our bulky orange life jackets giving him useless
advice, *reel him in, pull, you got the sonofabitch*. Paul somehow
hoisted the fish into the boat without ripping the hook out of
its mouth. The fish flopped around, dull thuds sounding as it

smacked its tail against the floor of the boat. Then Paul dropped his fishing pole and grabbed the bass in both hands and it stopped fighting as he raised it aloft, its only movement the gills opening and closing like a slow bellows, and for one victorious moment, all the tension that had built up the whole weekend vanished.

Then the fish jerked to sudden life. In one spasm it twisted free of Paul's hands. Its midsection hit the edge of the boat as it plummeted, and the next moment was like watching a free throw bouncing on the rim, the ball trying to decide which way to go. The fish just as easily could've landed in the boat. But it went the other way, slipping into the water almost without a sound, disappearing into the depths of the lake. It raced away and took the rented fishing pole with it as Paul stared at his empty hands.

We got stuck in traffic on the way back into Chicago and spent four hours in the car listening to talk radio and staring out different windows, nobody speaking a word. Years later it became one of those stories we'd laugh about, part of family lore. Remember when Paul dropped that fish and it made off with his pole? Paul would smile as my dad told the story, shake his head. Tragedy plus time equals comedy. But I could tell Paul didn't really like remembering it. There wasn't much of that summer any of us wanted to remember.

And here I was remembering it anyway.

I took out the card Soros had given me, the one belonging to journalist Bob Hannah. After a few moments, I gave in and I dialed. If nothing else, it gave me an excuse to see if my localized cell phone SIM card actually worked. A few rings and then a beep sounded. No human on the other end, no voicemail greeting, just a long tone and silence. I left brief message along with my number and hung up.

I looked up the Gallery Čertovka in *Prague Unbound*.

The place was just across the river.

I was up and moving before I could talk myself down.

After wading through tourists for the next ten minutes, I found myself in front of a large waterwheel sitting motionless in the canal, black wood cracked and corroded. Vera's famous postcard waterwheel. Above it sightseers cattled endlessly across the Charles Bridge, only a few veering from the castle route in order to take in what my guidebook called Prague's Little Venice. Little was an understatement, as its only waterway was a walled ditch maybe half a mile long that separated Malá Strana from a small outcropping in the river called Kampa Island. Houses capped with red tiled roofs backed up to the water's edge on either side, sleepy little storybook dwellings painted the colors of Easter eggs. *Prague Unbound* went out of its way to warn that at night, the area was frequented by the ghost of a cuckolded locksmith with a rusty nail driven through his skull, condemned to wander the streets in search of some soul brave enough to remove the spike and release him from his torment.

I didn't run into any ghostly locksmiths, but halfway down the sloping U Lužického Semináře Street on the Malá Strana side of the canal, I found the gallery and went inside. The display room was roughly the size of a racquetball court only with much lower ceilings. A series of photographs was mounted on the walls. There were a couple racks of art books, and a postcard carousel sat near a front desk manned only by a box with a recommended gallery donation sign. I tried picturing Vera behind this desk. The top of her head would nearly have brushed the ceiling.

I dropped some coins into the collection box and wandered the floor, pretending to take in the photographs. The first picture featured a young man standing in front of a tank, his leather coat held defiantly open, as a soldier perched atop the tank's turret half-heartedly aimed a machine gun at his chest. Another showed a gaunt old man dejectedly facing the camera, eyes sunk in heavy

shadows, while behind him people sifted through broken furniture beneath a ruined façade of unglassed windows and walls
mottled with bullet holes.

"Good morning," called a man emerging from a staircase at
the back of the room. He was somewhere in his sixties, had an
oblong face framed by iron gray hair pulled into a ponytail, and
was dressed in a brown sweater, loose corduroys, and Lennon
spectacles. He looked like an old hippie who'd aged into uneasy
respectability through no apparent fault of his own.

"Josef Koudelka," he said, assuming a spot beside me.

"Nice to meet you, Josef."

"Ah, no," he chuckled. "My name is Gustav. Josef Koudelka
is the man whose work you're admiring. Famous Czech photog-
rapher. Our show features his work from 1965–1970, before he
was forced to emigrate." The man's impeccable English was delivered accent free with a genial, avuncular air that reminded me of
one of those professors in the movies, the kind who smokes pipes
and quotes Shakespeare and helps inner city kids rise above their
bleak circumstances through slam poetry or whatever. Even in my
still mostly unwrinkled and expensive suit, curator Gustav had
instantly sized me up as an English-speaking tourist with no clue
what he was looking at.

None of which boded well for my plan.

"This is probably his most famous," Gustav said, directing my
attention to another picture. In the photo, the cameraman's arm
jutted into frame, elbow cocked, wrist turned to show his watch.
A first person POV of someone checking the time, nothing out of
the ordinary until you noticed the watch said noon, and the broad
city avenue spread below was eerily unpeopled.

"August 21, 1968," the man resumed. "Wenceslas Square just
before the Soviets literally entered the picture. They'd taken over
the airport in the middle of the night, shut down the borders,

moved 7,000 tanks and half a million troops into our country. Not so much soldiers as kids really, ruddy cheeked, blue-eyed farm boys with guns and oversized uniforms and no idea where they were or why. We tried disorienting them even more by tearing down all the street signs in the city, rendering their maps unusable. They'd get lost, run out of gas, sit there sweating in the heat and begging for water. Lots of people here spoke Russian then, had to learn it in school, but you'd never have known it if you were a Russian T-55 tank commander. I'll never forget those tanks. Massive, gray, loud as hell. Like antediluvian monsters assembled from scrap metal."

Antediluvian? This was going to be worse than I thought.

"You speak English well," I said.

"I lived in Canada for twenty-three years. Toronto."

"Never been to Canada. Been to Mexico."

"I've heard parts of Mexico are quite pleasant."

"I've only been to Tijuana."

He held a neutral smile in place. In the photo it was still noon, still no one on the street. Looking at the disembodied arm against the motionless backdrop, all I could think about was what Soros had said just before we parted. *Ask what happened to your brother's right hand.*

"Well," Gustav concluded, "enjoy the exhibit. Let me know if you have any questions."

It was now or never. "Actually, I do."

I passed him the card Soros had given me. "My name is Bob Hannah," I said. "I work for *The Stone Folio*. Prague's leading English language weekly. We're working on a story about the flood and I was hoping to ask you a few questions."

"About the flood?"

"Right. The one five years ago."

"You must have very liberal deadlines."

"We're a very liberal paper." When that landed with a thud, I continued, "Actually, our story is more like a five years follow-up piece. A revisitation. Where are they now, human spirit triumphing over adversity, time heals all wounds, water under the bridge. We're considering that, title wise. *Water Under the Bridge.*"

Discs of light reflected off the lenses of his glasses, obscuring his eyes beneath as he inspected the card before tucking it the front pocket of his jacket. "I suppose you'll want to see the window?" he asked.

I had no idea what he meant but nodded anyway. He moved toward the same door he'd emerged from earlier, and I followed. On the way we passed another Koudelka picture, this one not of the Soviet invasion but a creepy shot of a masked figure clad in a black robe and flying through the night sky. The placard said it was taken to promote a play.

"Mluvíte česky?" said the curator over his shoulder.

"I'm sorry?"

"I asked if you spoke Czech. I have reams of printed matter about the Rudolf Complication, but most of it is in Czech. The Complication is really what you're interested in, right? The break-in, the big heist. How much do you know about the exhibit?"

"Only what was in the brochure."

"Some background then." He took off his Lennon specs and wiped them with his jacket sleeve. "The watch, as you know, was the main attraction. The only other object of any real interest was a certain chalice made from a unicorn's horn. Rudolf used it on the advice of his court physician, an Italian who thought it had great healing powers. Of course, being enlightened, modern people, we now know unicorns don't exist, and that their horns hold no magical properties. The chalice was actually fashioned from a narwhal tusk. We had some artwork as well. And a handful of his majesty's bezoars and a few alrauns. You're familiar with them?"

"I've seen some of their early work."

He gave me a cockeyed look and replaced his glasses. "Bezoars are gallstones. Mass accretions in the gastrointestinal system."

"Right. Accretions. Misheard you."

Like I was supposed to know what bezoars were. I was already starting to dislike being Bob Hannah. I curled my lips between my teeth and pocketed my hands. I couldn't let this encounter slip out of my control.

"Alrauns are mandrake roots, *mandragora*, prized for their uncanny resemblance to the human form and a mainstay of witch-craft and alchemy. Rudolf especially cherished those sprouting beneath the gallows. Homunculus roots thought to grow when semen dripped from the corpse of a hanged man and into the soil below, impregnating the earth. The Emperor was known to order the skeletons of executed criminals exhumed so that moss growing upon their skulls might be scraped off and used in var-ious elixirs and alembics."

"Kinda like a medieval wheat grass shot?"

The curator grunted, no sense of humor. I followed him up the stairs, past the second story landing, across the third floor hallway, and through a doorway on the left until we arrived inside an empty room. An opened window looked out over the Čertovka canal, across at the buildings on Kampa Island less than twenty feet away. A breeze carried in the damp smell of the water below as the curator moved toward the window. I thought of how the canal got it's name—the Devil's Stream—and wondered which of the nearby houses the superstitious medieval villagers had painted all those devils on.

"See that line there?" He pointed to a diffuse, chalky white mark about three inches wide that ran horizontally across the length of the building opposite, just above the second story. "That's the watermark. Floodwaters reached nearly four meters in this area. Happens once every hundred years or so. Despite official warnings, people were slow to believe it was really going to be a centenarian."

"A what?"

"Hundred-years flood." The guy grinned, showing off again. "Czechs of my generation have a natural distrust of authority, I suppose. A shame considering once every hundred years or so, the authorities get something right."

Glancing out the window, I saw trees rustle on the other side of the Devil's Stream, throwing fitful shadows over the narrow channel of dull water below. "Transportation was already a mess by the time we got moving, and our only option was to shuttle objects to the upper floors. The Rudolf exhibit, books and postcards, computers, office equipment, rugs, chairs—everything was moved to the room you're now standing in. Five years ago, we had locks on the door, motion detectors, sensors on the windows. Any breach of the system generated a phone call to a private security firm. Cost a fortune. At the time I saw it as a good long-term investment."

He gestured mock grandiose at the naked walls enclosing us, where nothing was left of the security apparatus. "At the risk of sounding sentimental, I will say this for the Communists—they kept a lid on crime. Granted they were all arch criminals. With wolves guarding the hen house, you may not have hens for long, but at least you don't have to worry about foxes."

"Is art theft a big problem here?"

He shrugged. "Walk down Wenceslas Square and ask one hundred people about big problems, and not a single one will mention anything to do with art. But yes, in the early post-Soviet years, democracy and freedom first manifested themselves in a criminal free-for-all. Didn't help that our then-playwright president all but emptied the prisons. Having spent so much time locked up himself, I suppose he could be forgiven. And yes, this transitional lawlessness extended to the art world. Works forgotten for decades under the Soviets suddenly began disappearing from churches, museums, galleries, homes. Seven years after what your foreign journalist brethren dubbed the Velvet Revolution, former members of the secret police staged a heist at the National Museum and walked out with some two-dozen important works. Just a couple years ago, rare pistols from the Napoleonic Battle of Three Emperors at Slavkov were taken in broad daylight. The culprits were caught trying to pawn them off on a local antique dealer just around the corner from the exhibit. Hardly *The Thomas Crown Affair*. Your average art thief, thankfully, proves no smarter than your average car thief."

"Was the Rudolf Complication insured?"

The curator shook his head. "Publicly owned pieces seldom are. Traveling exhibits like *Rudolf's Curiosities* are only covered while in transit from one gallery space to another. Nail-to-nail, in insurer's vernacular. It's a great disappointment for thieves hoping to ransom against an insurance policy, but not much of a deterrent."

"How much do you think the watch was worth?"

The question was slow to reach him as he stared out the window, watching the water move below. "Priceless," he said at length. "But art is only priceless until it's on the market. Van Gogh's *Sunflowers* was priceless before it was auctioned for $39 million. A priceless Picasso then fetched $100 million. Priceless has lost its meaning. Egypt would sell the pyramids if the right offer came along."

"So are we talking Picasso-level priceless, or . . . "

"As a commodity, the Rudolf Complication has disadvantages." He enumerated them on his fingers as he spoke. "One, it's not a painting. Sculptures, textiles, ceramics, jewelry—even the best rarely fetch as much as minor paintings by major artists. Two, the Rudolf Complication wasn't created by a major artist.

Credit for the piece is generally ascribed to one Edward Kelley, court alchemist of Rudolf II. Reputedly also a forger, adulterer, duelist, necromancer, bad credit risk, accomplished liar—but not, despite such an obvious wealth of qualifications, a famous artist. Three, and perhaps most importantly, the Complication has no provenance. No documented trail of ownership. The watch surfaced only a short time before it disappeared, and only then under dubious circumstances. Many believed it to be a forgery."

Now we were getting into Paul territory. I had a hard time imagining him involved in a sophisticated European art heist, but getting himself killed over something worthless, something fraudulent? It was somehow easier for me to swallow. Which probably said as much about me as it did about him.

"Obviously, its questionable legitimacy was not something the Ministry of Culture flaunted in promotional materials," said Gustav. "But the story about how the watch suddenly surfaced after being lost for centuries stretched the bounds of credulity. Those half-dozen people who care about such things were highly skeptical. I don't suppose you're familiar with the name Martin Novotny?"

The curator explained Martin Novotny was the last private owner of the Rudolf Complication—although for only a few hours, if Novotny's story was to be believed. An alcoholic, gambler, occasional burglar, and small-time grifter, he was already familiar to the police. After celebrating what must have been a particularly successful break-in, Novotny passed out drunk on some tram tracks in a neighborhood called Malešice. The police arrived before the tram did and discovered him with the watch around his neck and knew there was no way in hell he was the legitimate owner. He eventually admitted stealing it, though he refused to say from whom. They released him. A week later Novotny came to an unfortunate end when his body was discovered thrown in through a fourth-story window in Strašnice.

"*In* through a fourth-story window?" I asked.

"As opposed to out of, yes," the curator said. "Either very dodgy police work or an unsolved case of reverse defenestration, take your pick. Meanwhile, no individual ever stepped forward to claim the watch. The government declared the Rudolf Complication to be state property. They organized a unique traveling exhibit, one which would first make the rounds of Prague galleries, then galleries throughout the Czech Republic, finally the world, before settling back at the National Museum. But of course, it never got farther than the west bank of the river. Did you bring a camera?"

"Not today."

"Unfortunate," said the curator. "Because we're now standing before The Most Photographed Window in Prague. At least during the two months immediately following the flood. Place yourself, if you will, in my shoes, and imagine it's mere days after the flood. The waters have at last subsided enough that you are finally permitted to return to your beloved gallery. You open that door behind you to find glass strewn across the floor. An iron grappling hook is wedged in the window frame. Attached to it, a nylon rope. Two computers, one security camera, a lockbox with petty cash, books, the alrauns and bezoars, the narwhal chalice—all have been left behind. Thank God, you think. And then you discover the Rudolf Complication is gone. And with it, you understand in an instant, any chance of your gallery co-hosting any further prestigious state-sponsored exhibitions. And you chastise yourself for your selfishness in the face of a crime not just against your gallery but art and history itself. But still."

I gazed at the watermark scarred on the building opposite and tried to picture how it all went down that night five years ago. The best my jetlagged imagination could conjure was a cheesy *America's Most Wanted*–style recreation. Camera pans down from a CGI-enhanced moon to find a lone figure clad like an urban ninja in cliché black hoodie and ski mask. He's drifting down the shadowy canal in a canoe, a rowboat, a kayak—nothing with a motor because of the noise, and he hardly would have swum. Police patrol the nearby streets on motorized rubber rafts, flashlight beams moving across the dark water, sweeping over the walls, bouncing off the windows. On this night the Little Venice moniker is for once fitting, with not just the Čertovka canal but all the narrow lanes and twisting byways of lower Malá Strana submerged in floodwaters. Electricity out, buildings vacated, no sounds but the water, perhaps the odd bullhorn or siren in the distance. Our figure navigates by moonlight, drifting silently down the streets until he merges with the canal. Gliding to a halt beside a pale blue building, he breaks the third story candy glass window with the hook and expertly ties the rope to the boat to keep it from floating away. The water is so high it's no climb at all to reach the window, and in one fluid, stuntman-enacted motion, he hoists himself inside.

He searches the room, locates the watch, and carefully wraps it in a plastic shopping bag, a nylon sack, something waterproof. This he slips it into a small backpack. He lowers himself back into the boat, cuts the rope with a cinematically large and shiny bowie knife, and drifts away, leaving the hook still lodged in the window frame. At some point north, between say the Charles Bridge and the Mánesuv Bridge, he goes silently to ground. A sinister looking man with slicked back hair emerges from the shadows, greeting my brother with an oily smile. In the final shot, the abandoned get-away vehicle washes downstream, and the camera pans up and fades on the moon. My father plays the tanned and vengeful studio host who steps forward and gives the audience a number to call if they have any information about Paul Holloway, considered highly dangerous to himself and those who by birth or misfortune care about him. In the background, Vera wears a telephone headset, manning calls on the tip line and then we go to commercial break.

Aside from piloting the boat, there was virtually no risk involved. The gallery was empty, alarms useless without electricity, all potential witnesses in the neighborhood had been evacuated, and the city was in a general state of emergency. Stealing copper wiring from a construction site was probably more dangerous. If my brother really had been a part of this, it was among the most well-thought-out actions in his entire life. Which made me suspect he wasn't the one doing the thinking.

"Whoever did it had to know the watch hadn't been taken somewhere else during the flood," I reasoned aloud. "They knew it was still in this building."

"And knew it was on the third floor," Gustav added, leaning halfway out the window as if addressing the water below. "And knew which room it was in. And knew where inside the room it was located. An inside job. That's what the police thought. I was one of the leading suspects for a time. Maybe I still am. Is that why you're here? Posing as a journalist to see if my story still checks out?"

I gave a chuckle. Tried to smile but my face wouldn't cooperate and my stomach went sick and twitchy. So I just chuckled again and it came out all wrong.

"I'm quite serious. You don't work for any newspaper." He turned to face me now, head tilting slowly back, eyes narrowing as if weighing the compositional merits of a photograph he didn't particularly like. "You haven't written down a word I've said. You carry no tape recorder, no notebook, take no pictures. You're wearing a decent suit. Wrinkled and oversized, but not the suit of an expatriate journalist. And while I'm perfectly willing to believe an American could live and work here for two years without bothering to learn Czech, it seems you would at least be familiar with the phrase asking if you had. At the same time, I don't think you're Interpol. And you're obviously not the local police. But maybe I should give them a call. They might be interested in who you really are. What you're really doing here. I know I am."

He took a phone out of his pocket.

I turned to leave and he grabbed for the sleeve of my jacket. I shook him off and was already hurrying away when I heard a stifled shout and his glasses clattering over the floor. As I got to the doorway, I glanced back over my shoulder.

The room was empty. The curator was gone.

I hesitated, then turned and bolted back into the room, inadvertently kicking his glasses and sending them spinning into the wall. I leaned out the window and looked down. The curator lay in crumpled heap on the pavement three stories below. He was less than a foot from the edge of the canal. His right arm was twitching, blood already pooling around his head in a red-black penumbra. I could hear him moaning. He still clutched his cell phone.

"Don't move," I yammered. "Hang on."

His one visible eye beaded on me, blinked and closed. I tore out of the room, hurtled down the stairs and out of the gallery.

The real problem started when I got outside.

With all the buildings jammed together, I couldn't just run around the side of the house—I'd have to circumnavigate the entire block the reach the back. I headed one way but dead-ended into some little plaza dominated by a turquoise statue of two men pissing in a fountain. There were plenty of people around—I could have asked for help, but I didn't. I had to get to him first, make sure he didn't roll into the canal. I reversed course, headed back up the block, ran all the way to the waterwheel near the base of the Charles Bridge, then raced along the canal bank behind all the little Hansel and Gretel houses.

I stepped in his blood before I realized he was gone. Aside from what was smeared at my feet, there was no sign of him. Nothing in back but an empty watering can and an overturned wheelbarrow edged up against the building. The canal water moved with undisturbed lethargy, its surface brackish and opaque. If he'd fallen in, the current wouldn't have carried him far.

I kicked off my father's shoes and dove in.

I swam to the bottom, groping blindly in the silty darkness. I came up for air, dove down again. The third time I started panicking, and when I splashed back to the surface, I was gasping for air, dizzy and sputtering. A woman was leaning out a second-story window in a building on Kampa Island and yelling something at me. I wanted to yell back for her to call for help, that a man had fallen in the canal, but I could barely breathe. I hoisted myself back onto the bank and she kept yelling. By my estimation, the curator had probably been underwater for between three and five minutes now.

"Police," I managed to croak. I made a thumb-to-ear, pinkie-to-mouth phone gesture. She made an ugly face and parroted the word back at me. I repeated it and she unleashed a stream of invectives. She thought I was taunting her, daring her to call the cops on me for taking an unauthorized dip in the canal. Then all at once her expression changed. She saw the blood. An instant later where she'd stood was only a yellow curtain fluttering in the breeze. All I could hear was a sloshing sound in my head. I put on my dad's shoes and rose, taking one last look for splashes or bubbles or any sign of the curator upon the canal's surface but saw only my own wavering reflection, hair plastered and dripping on my forehead, eyes blinking away thick drops of water. And then I was gone. The canal reflected only the sky.

INSIDE THE MIRROR MAZE—
PART III

AUDIO RECORDING #3113d

DATE: September 26, 1984 [Time Unspecified]

Subject: Eliška Reznícková

Case: #1331—Incident at Zrcadlové Bludiště

Interview session #8

Location: Bartolomějská 10, Prague, Praha 1

Investigator: Agent #3553

AGENT #3553: Let us summarize what you've told us up to this point. A man you'd never met, calling himself Vokov, no first name given, arrived at the Black Rabbit just before closing time on the night of Saturday, September 22.

REZNÍCKOVÁ: I saw him only after we had closed. I have no idea when he actually arrived.

AGENT #3553: This man then told you that he'd been followed by a plainclothes member of the police. He showed you an accordion case inside which were fifty copies of an illegal publication called *The Defenestrator*. He showed you a copy of this samizdat and said he was to deliver the accordion case to an unknown third party who would be waiting atop Petřín Hill the next morning. He then asked you to help him burn the copies in the tavern's fireplace, as he believed he was about to be arrested.

You not only refused to destroy them, but also volunteered to deliver the contents of the accordion case yourself.

REZNÍCKOVÁ: That is correct.

AGENT #3553: Remarkable. Let's resume there.

REZNÍCKOVÁ: Like I said, we decided on a plan. Vokov was to exit out the front of the tavern where he would, he was certain, be apprehended. Meanwhile, I was to take the accordion case and ascend to the first floor and take the back exit into the court-yard. By cutting across the open space and passing through the building on the other side, I'd eventually emerge one block over on V jirchářích Street, where with any luck, no police would be waiting. Early the next day, while Vokov was still in custody, I'd deliver the samizdat to a nameless man sitting atop Petřín Hill waiting with the keys to open the case.

AGENT #3553: Are you saying the case was locked? How was Vokov able to show you a copy of *The Defenestrator*?

REZNÍCKOVÁ: He'd taken it from his jacket. I told you.

AGENT #3553: But he didn't provide you with any keys to open the case yourself?

REZNÍCKOVÁ: My understanding is that only the unknown third man was in possession of the keys.

AGENT #3553: But how then could he have expected you to burn the documents, as he'd originally requested? Were you supposed to throw the entire accordion case on the fire?

REZNÍCKOVÁ: I don't know. Only after Vokov had limped up the stairs—

AGENT #3553: He walked with a limp? Why didn't you mention this previously?

REZNÍCKOVÁ: You never asked how he walked. And it was only after he'd gone and I'd closed the door behind him and picked up the accordion case and made it out the back, through the courtyard and safely to my apartment without being arrested, that I discovered the accordion case was fastened in three places by concealed locks. Even then, it wasn't until early the next morning that I realized Vokov could never have intended to burn the contents of the accordion case.

AGENT #3553: And you didn't find that sufficient cause for alarm? There could have been a bomb in the case, for all you knew.

REZNÍCKOVÁ: Unlike your sort, I don't immediately imagine the worst of people. Besides, in a few hours *The Defenestrator* would be in the hands of the other man and no longer my concern. Of course, I realized my worries didn't exactly end there. If Vokov had really been arrested without the all-important accordion case, it was only a matter of time until you people ferreted me out.

AGENT #3553: And that's when you began disposing of your writings, correct?

REZNÍCKOVÁ: My diaries such as they were, some poetic sketches, story ideas, incomplete novels. I tore them all up by the handful and fed them to the sewers. I don't imagine they were politically sensitive. But I've learned such things are a matter of interpretation and the rules are always changing. Politics don't interest me. It's like the joke about the man passing out leaflets.

AGENT #3553: What joke would that be?

REZNÍCKOVÁ: A man is passing out leaflets in Wenceslas Square. The police approach to arrest him but are startled to find the leaflets he's distributing are blank, nothing written on them. The police ask why he's handing out blank sheets of paper, and he says, "Why bother writing it down? It's all obvious anyway."

AGENT #3553: Was this then when you also got rid of the type-writer you were reportedly heard using at odd hours of the night?

REZNÍCKOVÁ: I got rid of that long ago, after nice old ████████ down the hall had mentioned hearing a *clackety-clack* at night and wondered whether I might be some sort of writer. An inno-cent enough question, except I knew no such thing exists. But I suppose if ██████████ really was your *fizl*[7], he never would have asked. He would just have continued quietly reporting me. Perhaps he was even trying to warn me.

AGENT #3553: What did it feel like, we wonder, flushing away your life's work?

REZNÍCKOVÁ: What did it feel like? I remember next door,

---

[7] "Weasel" was a term commonly used at the time to describe a police informant.

the neighbors were arguing about someone named Jitka who owed them money. From upstairs, I heard the *Major Zeman*[8] theme blaring from a TV. The idea of writing seemed suddenly ridiculous.

AGENT #3553: And yet you saved this Right Hand of God manuscript?

REZNÍCKOVÁ: It wouldn't flush.

AGENT #3553: What do you mean?

REZNÍCKOVÁ: I mean the pages literally wouldn't flush. I jiggled the handle. Tried a plunger. Took the lid off the back and mucked around inside. Nothing worked. Times like this it would be nice to have a husband, I suppose. The toilet would not refill with water, leaving the first page clinging dampened to the porcelain.

I flipped through the remaining pages, taking in a sentence here, a paragraph there. It wasn't terrible. Flawed, yes, and not the most original premise—but wasn't it Marx who said all property was theft?

AGENT #3553: Marx said no such thing.

REZNÍCKOVÁ: I just thought it was something that someone, somewhere might conceivably read. Though State Security wasn't the audience I had in mind. I gathered the Right Hand

8 *The Thirty Cases of Major Zeman* was a popular, heavily propagandized TV police drama that ran on state television beginning in 1975.

materials, removed the back panel from my television, curled the pages into a tight roll, and crammed them inside and screwed the panel back on.

AGENT #3553: Why the TV?

REZNÍCKOVÁ: Because it was so old and beat up I didn't imagine the police would be tempted to steal it.

AGENT #3553: You then boarded a tram at Kosmonautů station.

REZNÍCKOVÁ: Yes, yes. I got there however you say. It's not important. When I arrived at Petřín, the tram ascending the grassy slope was temporarily closed. A sign at the station said it was being repaired. Signs like this everywhere and yet no one ever seems to be repairing anything. Why is that? Churches and cathedrals cocooned in scaffolding year after year, buildings left paint-flecked and buckling under their own weight. Have you ever felt like this city is a ghost town everybody forgot to leave?

AGENT #3553: You had to climb the hill because the third man would be waiting at the top.

REZNÍCKOVÁ: The plan called for him to be sitting on a bench outside the Zrcadlové Bludiště, the toy castle housing a labyrinth of distorted funhouse mirrors. Halfway up the zigzagging path ascending Petřín, I turned and gazed down the hill. The path was empty. Barren trees and grass, fog hovering white on the poisonous river. Frost-tipped rooftops, rising spires, and the bleached-out beyond. Parts of what I saw I could not really be seeing, with my limited vision. Parts I must only have remembered from the days when I could see everything clearly.

AGENT #3553: Who was waiting for you at the top of the hill?

REZNÍCKOVÁ: Nobody. Nobody waiting at the top, nobody climbing the hill below. I took a seat outside the toy castle, placed the accordion case under the bench as Vokov had instructed, and watched my breath unfurl in the cold morning air.

I must've dozed off, for when I woke, a little girl was sitting next to me. She was no more than seven or eight, underdressed in a thin red gown rippling slowly in the breeze. She was barefoot, shivering. She sat there staring at me for what seemed like minutes. Big black eyes, face pale, empty. A strangely adult face. Grown-up features on a child-sized head.

"Don't you have any shoes?" I asked. She said nothing, just sat there, swinging her naked legs under the bench. I swiveled my head, looking for parents, a grandma, an older brother or sister. "You'll freeze," I said. "No shoes, no coat. Where is your mummy?"

She smiled. An ugly smile, her mouth like something cut with a knife. The girl had no teeth.

AGENT #3553: She was missing some front teeth?

REZNÍCKOVÁ: No, it wasn't like a couple baby teeth had fallen out. She had the shriveled mouth of an old woman. I cursed and began taking off my coat to wrap around the child. Now what was I supposed to do? Take the little vagabond to the police?

Risk missing my contact and walk into a police station carrying a case full of prison sentences? I decided I'd wait until after the exchange and then take the girl somewhere. But then how to explain what I'd been doing atop Petřín Hill when I'd found her? And besides, where had the little girl even come from? What if her parents came looking for her?

The girl suddenly spoke. "Someone is waiting for you," she said. She motioned toward the toy castle. I stopped removing my coat.

"Inside," she said. "Someone is waiting."

AGENT #3553: The Zrcadlové Bludiště is not opened until 10:00 AM. Wouldn't it have then been closed at this time?

REZNÍCKOVÁ: All I know is the door was wide open. I passed through and found myself in the labyrinth, a narrow passageway lined top to bottom with long mirrors framed by wooden columns. Not even the shivering child on the bench could've gotten properly lost in such a maze, but the mirrors were disquieting. Eliška now on the left, now on the right, in front of myself, behind myself, beside myself. Everywhere a multiplicity of Eliška, everywhere the blasted accordion case.

The maze ended in a small room walled with yet more mirrors, curved surfaces that elongated my chin, stretched my fingers, made my arms bandy and warped. Mirrors pressed my nose against my lip, squashed my forehead, ballooned my stomach. Here Eliška in monstrous caricature, taffy faced and leering, here Eliška as grotesquerie, caveman browed, giraffe legged, here Eliška growing from the head of Eliška. Eliška and Eliška, the Siamese twins.

At the end of maze hung an arrowed sign that read *To the Battle on Charles Bridge*. Another turn and the maze opened onto . . . well, I'm sure you've been there. Otherwise I wouldn't be here, would I?

AGENT #3553: Tell us what you saw.

REZNÍCKOVÁ: After the maze you're spit out into this somber little room featuring a diorama of the Charles Bridge under siege. A dusty model cannon, discarded muskets, and helmets sit foregrounded amid strewn rubble, while on the bridge in the painting beyond, the Bohemians fought back the advancing Swedes. Weird finding this at the end of a child's maze. Like reaching the conclusion of a Hloupý Honza adventure story only to discover the last page had been replaced with text from a history book.

AGENT #3553: And this is where Vokov's man was waiting?

REZNÍCKOVÁ: There was no sign of him. I put down the accordion case. My arm ached. My hand stayed curled in a half-fist, and only then did I realize how tightly I'd been gripping the handle. I stood and waited, looking at the diorama. On the Charles Bridge, a decapitated Christ statue was perched on his cross. A bit heavy handed with the symbolism, I remember thinking.

AGENT #3553: And then what happened?

REZNÍCKOVÁ: Nothing. I stood. I waited. I grew nervous. I got scared. It was possible the third man had already been arrested. That even as I passed the time staring at this stupid diorama, he could be in a little room like the one I'm in now. Talking to a person like you, telling him where *The Defenestrator* exchange was supposed to happen. While I stood gawking at the decapitated Christ and wondering where the head went, the police could be encircling the castle, preparing a siege. Like the Swedes in the diorama. Then I started getting angry.

I decided I was finished. I'd done my part and it never had anything to do with me anyway. I left the accordion case sitting on the floor and walked out of the castle.

[Silence—duration 5 seconds]

AGENT #3553: What of the little girl on the bench?

REZNÍCKOVÁ: She was gone. No sign of her.

AGENT #3553: Weren't you curious where she went?

REZNÍCKOVÁ: I imagine her parents had found her. Maybe they'd been at the nearby lookout tower or maybe wandering the rose garden. I had my own problems.

AGENT #3553: You're saying you never saw her except outside on the bench atop the hill. That you did not encounter the little girl in the maze.

REZNÍCKOVÁ: There was no one there but me. Me and my reflections. Eliška and the Eliškas.

[Silence—duration 4 seconds]

AGENT #3553: Comrade Rezníčková, it's in your best interest to give up this foolish story about some samizdat and tell us what really happened on Petřín. With the little girl. We might find our way to understanding what caused you to do what you did.

REZNÍCKOVÁ: I don't know what you're talking about.

AGENT #3553: We never arrested any man named Vokov. We never followed any man named Vokov. There never was any Vokov. Nor was there any samizdat called *The Defenestrator*. Certainly not in the accordion case.

REZNÍCKOVÁ: Then I suspect it's as I've been saying all along. We're talking about two different accordion cases. That's the only explanation for what you're telling me. Vokov is a real person. I sat across the table from him, just as I'm doing with you now. Except him I could see because no one had broken my glasses.

AGENT #3553: What kind of name do you imagine Vokov to be? Slovakian? Moravian? Russian?

REZNÍCKOVÁ: I don't know. I didn't think about it.

AGENT #3553: It's a made-up name for a man who doesn't exist. We listened because in our experience, all lies eventually lead to the truth. We're prepared to allow you to identify the accordion case now. Perhaps it's necessary to show you the gravity of the situation. Maybe then you'll stop indulging in this fantasy.

[Chair squeaks across floor, footsteps, opening of a door, closing of a door.]

[Silence—duration 9 minutes]

[Door opens, door closes, footsteps approach. A thump. Sounds like something being dropped upon the desk. Chair squeaks across floor.]

[Silence—duration 2 seconds]

AGENT #3553: Please describe, if you would, the object I have just placed upon the table.

REZNÍCKOVÁ: Lo and behold, the long-awaited accordion case.

AGENT #3553: Details would be helpful.

REZNÍCKOVÁ: It's brown. It's squarish. That's all I can see without my glasses.

AGENT #3553: Ah, thank you for the reminder. We'd nearly forgotten—the reading glasses retrieved from your apartment. Perhaps they will help. Please put them on and describe the accordion case.

[Silence—duration 7 seconds]

REZNÍCKOVÁ: It's brown. It's squarish. Upholstered in leather. It's got a handle. One corner is dented.

AGENT #3553: Please describe the object sitting to the immediate left of the accordion case.

REZNÍCKOVÁ: Keys. A key ring with keys.

AGENT #3553: We found them in your flat.

REZNÍCKOVÁ: That's impossible. I've never seen them.

AGENT #3553: Please open the case if you would.

REZNÍCKOVÁ: I don't know which key—

AGENT #3553: We're confident you'll find it eventually.

[Jingling of keys—duration 4 seconds]

[Metallic snapping sound of locks on accordion case being simultaneously released—less than 1 second]

REZNÍCKOVÁ: Fine, I got it opened, but that doesn't —[unintelligible].

[Sound of REZNÍCKOVÁ screaming—duration 3 seconds]

AGENT #3553: Could you please describe the contents of the case?

[Screaming/gasping—duration 4 seconds]

AGENT #3553: No? We'll describe them for you. Inside the case is a severed right hand measuring approximately 9.5 centimeters from the point of severance at the lunate to the tip of the index finger. The size and shape is consistent with that of a child six to eight years of age.

REZNÍCKOVÁ: Close it! Jesus fucking [unintelligible]

AGENT #3553: Blood tests and other forensic data link this detached appendage to the corpse of a female child identified as Dusana Malinová, six years of age, whose body was discovered on the morning of September 22 inside the Zrcadlové Bludiště. Do you wish to describe the knife?

REZNÍCKOVÁ: Oh my Jesus. Jesus oh my lord.

AGENT #3553: Then allow me—inside the accordion case, just to the left of the girl's severed hand, is a cutting or hacking implement commonly referred to as a butcher's knife. Blunted end one inch in thickness, blade end sharpened to less than a millimeter.

[Sobbing—female—continuous]

Blood samples taken from the blade match those of the deceased[9]. Fingerprints lifted from the wooden handle match those of the interview subject. All of this is detailed in report 752a covering

9 Given the state of forensic science at this time, the scarcity of top-flight laboratorial resources available to the StB, and the lack of corroborating evidence in the surviving files related to this incident, the UDZ believes it's highly unlikely AGENT #3553's assessment was an accurate representation of the state of the investigation. More likely he was exaggerating if not lying outright in order to manipulate the suspect.

the Incident at the Zrcadlové Bludiště.[10] Does what I said in any way contradict what you see before you?

REZNÍCKOVÁ: My God. You're him.

AGENT #3553: Your Right Hand of God manuscript is clearly evidence of a disturbed mind. We believe writing it provided you a dress rehearsal. A fantasy acting out of a child murder very similar to that which all evidence points to you committing on Friday night. As we cannot conclude that this was your only foray into violence, however, it is our recommendation that open homicide files with any similarities to the murder of Dusana Malinová be thoroughly investigated.

REZNÍCKOVÁ: You're Vokov. The beard is gone, you've a haircut. But you're him. Oh my God. Let me out of here—

AGENT #3553: Why you would return to the scene of your crime Sunday morning is an open question, but it's not an uncommon occurrence among criminals, and you're clearly delusional. This would explain your claims of having spoken with the girl on the bench two days after you'd killed her. It would explain this Vokov figure and the fact that you've somehow conflated your interviewer with a character completely of your own imagining.

REZNÍCKOVÁ: Why would you do this to me?

AGENT #3553: Given what you've told us and what we've read of your manuscript, we don't believe you are mentally competent

---

10 This report was not among materials recovered by ÚDZ. Whether or not it ever existed is unclear, as the name formatting cited by Agent #3553 (712a) is inconsistent with other documents recovered from the StB archives.

to offer a confession. Testimony in your current condition is unreliable. It's our recommendation that you be taken to the mental health facility for a thorough evaluation. The interview is to be suspended indefinitely pending their recommendation.

REZNÍCKOVÁ: You can't do this. Please. [sobbing]

AGENT #3553: We thank you for your cooperation. We will prepare your confession in hopes of revisiting the matter when your health improves.

[Tape concludes]

Eliška Reznícková and the Incident at Zrcadlové Bludiště—
Summary of Subsequent Events and Concluding
Recommendations

Subsequent to the interview transcribed herein, Eliška Reznícková was admitted to the Bohnice Psychiatric Hospital (see attached document 7a) on September 27, 1984. The admitting physician diagnosed Reznícková with acute paranoid schizophrenia and prescribed heavy doses of thorazine (her file also notes that, like many patients, Reznícková spent much of her time there in a caged bed).

Records show Reznícková's condition steadily deteriorated while at Bohnice. She held fast to her belief that AGENT #3553 was the same person she had met calling himself Vokov, and also said she believed he was the Right Hand of God killer of legend. While at Bohnice, she further came to believe that demons were communicating with her. Reznícková became particularly fixated on a figure she called Madimi, a demon she said took the form a little girl. She claimed this entity was sending her secret messages through books and paintings.

By her final year of treatment she had withdrawn completely, ceasing all form of communication with staff or other patients. More than four years after being admitted to Bohnice, on December 12, 1988, Eliška Reznícková died as the result of injuries sustained in fall from the clock tower of the asylum. Though most windows throughout the facility were barred to prevent such occurrences, the incident report (see attached 7b) notes she had surreptitiously gained access to this area by entering a wing of the hospital normally restricted to staff. There was no evidence reported by the hospital that would suggest foul play, and her death was ruled a suicide.

No further action was taken by the StB in the case of the Incident at Zrcadlové Bludiště. The investigation into the young girl's death was closed without officially being declared solved.

After a thorough consideration of the Zrcadlové Bludiště Incident, we have concluded that pursuing legal action against any state official or former member of the StB for actions taken against Eliška Reznícková would not be in keeping with the goals of the Office for the Documentation and Investigation of the Crimes of Communism (ÚDV). Though the fate suffered by Reznícková is regrettable to say the least, further pursuit of the matter is hampered by several factors.

AGENT #3553—This is the only individual associated with State Security who appears in the files surrounding this case. He not only authorized Reznícková's institutionalization at Bohnice, but apparently transported her there himself, as his agent ID is the only one appearing on the intake records. Without ascertaining his identity, further avenues of inquiry into the matter are unlikely to yield desirable results. At present, we are unable to find any other case files related to Agent #3553 and must assume they have been destroyed, as it is highly improbable an officer assigned to carry out an important murder investigation would have worked no prior cases of note (nor, indeed, of any description whatsoever).

Eliška Rezníčková's mental state—Statements made during the interview lead one to believe that the police may have had grounds for ordering that Rezníčková undergo psychiatric evaluation. A thorough search of government records reveals no evidence of a male figure in his mid-forties by the name Vokov (though, of course, such a figure could have given Rezníčková a false name). More problematically, no evidence has been found to corroborate the existence of a samizdat newspaper called *The Defenestrator*.

Lack of demonstrable political motivation—Crimes possibly committed by either the authorities pursuant to the Zrcadlové Bludiště Incident or Rezníčková herself don't appear to be politically or ideologically motivated. Though no documents exist to confirm our hypothesis, this case was likely handled by State Security rather than the city's police force because a) the magnitude of the crime and b) the fear that child murder rumors might cause panic among the citizens of the Czechoslovak capital or harm Czechoslovakia's international reputation. And while Rezníčková's treatment at the hands of the StB was certainly less than desirable, there remains no evidence that she was tortured or her basic human rights were otherwise violated (the destruction of her eye glasses notwithstanding). Any pursuant legal claims would then fall outside the realm of those normally handled by the Office for the Documentation and Investigation of the Crimes of Communism (ÚDV).

We therefore regret that at present, the ÚDV will be unable to contribute further efforts related to the StB's handling of Eliška Reznícková and the Incident at the Zrcadlové Bludiště. We have flagged AGENT #3553 as an operative in need of further pursuit, and in the eventuality that his identity comes to light, the case may be reopened.

Sadly, until such time, any role Reznícková may or may not have played in the death of the young girl will remain as unclear as it was in 1984.

Office for the Documentation and Investigation of the Crimes of Communism (ÚDV)

170 34 Poštovní úřad
Praha 7
Poštovní schránka 21/ÚDV

PART

TWO

CHAPTER 6

■

My face still felt stuck in a weird grimace and my stomach was churning something awful as I lurched off the subway. The air tasted like sweat and metal, and the walls enclosing the Florenc station escalator reflected a green industrial half-light that did terrible things to the human physiognomy. I looked over my shoulder to see if anyone was following me, just as I had ten or thirty times since leaving Malá Strana, my suit hanging heavy and dripping over my frame. Why I'd thought to remove my shoes but not my jacket before taking the plunge I don't know. In retrospect, there were a lot of things I would have done differently had I been thinking.

The escalator spit me into daylight.

Outside the station, people streamed from a dingy supermarket adjacent to the entrance while trams painted cream-yellow and red shuddered by on the street opposite. A group of anarcho-squatter kids with ropy dreads and pincushioned faces sat shipwrecked on the sidewalk. One of the girls had a pet rat, its white head poking out of the pocket of her army jacket, pink nose twitching, while behind them a high fence rimmed with razor wire enclosed a flea market encampment where Vietnamese sold trademark infraction apparel.

I should've called the police the moment the curator had fallen from the window. I knew this. Even after I'd left the scene, I could've grabbed one of the bored cops in black paramilitary gear hanging out by the Charles Bridge. No matter how often I told myself that surely the woman who poked her head out the window on Kampa Island had called the police, I was nagged by the possibility she hadn't. And what would she tell them? She probably had no idea what I was doing in the canal, didn't see the curator fall in. Of course all of this occurred to me too late. At the time, all I wanted was to get away from the little gnome houses and tangled little streets and knots of unfamiliar faces and their polyglot cacophony. Go somewhere I could reason everything out, put it together in a way that made sense. Now that I was almost back to the Hotel Dalibor, I realized such a place likely didn't exist.

I was half-amazed to find a payphone at the end of the block, but maybe it had been given historical landmark status in our cellular age. The local emergency number was even stickered on the unit. I dug some coins out of my pocket and picked up a blue handset practically writhing with graffiti. No surface was safe in this city.

I'd leave an anonymous tip. Tell the police what happened and hang up. No sooner had I slotted the coins than my chest cavity rattled in the onset of a major cardiac event. I dropped the payphone, hand shooting to my heart. Instead I felt the contours of my shirtpocketed cell phone quivering with an incoming call. I'd left the thing on vibrate/scare-the-fuck-out-of-me mode. Glad at least the plunge in the canal hadn't killed it. I took the phone out and glanced at the caller ID.

BOB HANNAH

Of course.

With everything that happened at the gallery, I'd forgotten that I'd called, left a message. This right before I tried to impersonate him with lethal ineptitude. Being other people is harder, more dangerous, than you might think. Even with that realization it took a good two seconds to understand why I had a sudden urge to curl up in a little ball on the sidewalk, squeeze my eyes closed, and scream obscenities.

Bob Hannah's business card.

The curator had it in his pocket.

The payphone receiver swayed on its cord, proscribing tighter and tighter circles while the cell buzzed in my palm like some polymer cicada. I wondered if it was possible to lift prints from a business card after it had been underwater. What else had I touched? The handrail going up the stairs. A doorknob maybe. Coins in the donation box. I'd kicked the curator's glasses. Shoe prints—could they get shoe prints?

I'd have to let Bob Hannah's call go unanswered. I'd call him back after I spoke anonymously with the police, after I got back to the hotel and booked a flight. I'd return Bob Hannah's call from Tahiti or Thailand or wherever some quick Google query told me had no extradition treaty with the Czech Republic.

Instead I answered.

"Bob Hannah calling," said the voice on the other end. He was American, had the flat, regionless intonations of a TV news anchor. "Received your message. We should talk. Face-to-face would be best. I'm on assignment much of this afternoon but perhaps you could meet me in, say, one hour? I'll be at the St. James Church, near Old Town Square. Can you find this place?"

"I have a map."

"Just the two of us. No detective."

Then he hung up. Another tram rattled by. One of the anarchist kids on the sidewalk shot me a look. His shirt had CLOWNING FOOL, a band I guess, printed in thick gothic letters. I slipped the cell back into my pocket and reholstered the payphone. Upon second glance the kid's shirt said DROWNING POOL. I stood rooted in place, weighing my options. The woman in the window on Kampa Island had either called the police or she hadn't. They'd either found the curator's body or they hadn't, he was alive or he wasn't. Tying me to him would take time. There was no reason to panic. I snatched my coins from the return slot of the payphone. From now on I would be all about leaving nothing behind.

My suit had apparently shrunken as a result of my diving expedition because taking *Prague Unbound* out of my inner pocket on the train back to Old Town turned into a silent comedy of tugging and pulling, jerking and twisting. The thing just would not come out, until it did, with sudden, mocking ease. More likely the book had expanded, the pages having soaked up water, though in truth they looked neither damp nor warped. On the subject of St. James Church, the guidebook had this to say:

If you insist upon visiting the Kostel sv. Jakuba (St. James Church), make your way to Old Town Square where twenty-seven noblemen were once executed in a single day, their severed heads then hung in iron cages on the Old Town Bridge Tower where they remained for ten years. Seek guidance from some agreeable local merchant. In absence of agreeable personages, you may wish to write the words Sv. Jakuba upon a piece of paper and hand it to one of the worthless shitsmelling vagabonds to be found on the benches encircling the Jan Hus monument. Offer him a small gratuity, or liquor if you have it upon your person (the cheaper varieties will do). If he refuses, threaten him with violence and spit upon him as you would a three-legged mongrel.

Not the sort of advice you'd find in Lonely Planet.
I went on reading.

The St. James Basilica was founded by minorites in the twelfth century before being rebuilt in the Baroque style after the fire that cleansed Old Town in 1689. Among its many attractions is the unrestful resting place of Count Vratislav of Mitrovice, accidentally entombed alive by dimwitted clergy in the fifteenth century. For three days and three nights the Count's agonized wails echoed throughout the church while palsied husks of men blinkered by their ignorance bowed their liverspotted skulls and shuffled in circles, mumbling in Latin. They cast holy water here and thereabout as the Count scraped and clawed at the walls of his enclosure, wearing the very flesh from his fingers until they were bloodied shards of bone and there was no more air to breathe and so he breathed no more. Of special interest is a severed, mummified arm that hangs inside the church's entrance. One night some four hundred years ago, a thief tried to snatch a necklace of pearls from a statue of Mary, but Our Lady held fast to his arm and would not release it even in the morrow until at length the executioner was called to hack off the appendage. After prison, the repentant, one-armed thief returned to St. James and the monks accepted him into their brotherhood, and he would late at night enter the church and gaze in reverie upon his own severed limb, which still hangs there to this day.

St. James is also acclaimed for its splendid pipe organ, said to be one of the finest in Europe.

Like many travel guides, I assumed this one had multiple authors and was edited on the cheap, but there was no "About the

Contributors" section to be found, and neither could I locate the name of any editor before the train pulled into Mûstek station. Getting the book back in my pocket meant running the whole jerking, tugging, shoving gag reel in reverse.

I was able to find St. James without bothering any shopkeepers or spitting on any homeless people. Saints and angels dogpiled in relief above the church entrance like some medieval version of the *Sgt. Pepper's* album cover. Inside, every lavish nook and gilt-edged cranny of the narrow church burst with iconography, as if these holy things had fled three or four larger churches and taken up refuge in this one. There was a St. James Church in Chicago, too. I'd been there for a wedding. It looked like a dentist's waiting room compared to this place.

At this hour the light from the clerestory above struggled to penetrate the lower reaches, leaving the dark pews and carved wooden pulpits in a twilight haze. A sign at the entrance warned that photography and cell phones were forbidden, but except for an older couple whispering along the aisle, the place was deserted.

A voice spoke my name from the darkness and I caught a flicker of movement at the left edge of the nave. As my eyes adjusted, I could just make out a man beckoning in the middle distance. I made my way down the center of the pews and as I neared the transept crossing, a hand extended into my face.

"Bob Hannah," the hand's seated owner announced. Judging by the hand, he was a big guy. The failing light obscured most of his face, but I could see he was somewhere in his mid-forties. Wavy brown hair. A head oversized and squarish plopped on rounded shoulders without the intercession of a neck. He wore a black suit much like my own (so much for the curator's theory that I was overdressed for a journalist), but his ballooned where mine slackened. We looked like Laurel and Hardy after a wardrobe mix-up.

"Apologies for the venue," he said as I shook his hand and settled into the pew next to him. "Not the church-going type myself, but I'm interviewing an organist who is giving a concert here as part of the festival. They say St. James has the second-most beautiful organ in all of Europe. Lucky guy that James, eh? Now that I've broken the ice with a penis joke, let me ask you—is this your first time in Prague?"

I nodded.

"A wonderful city. Magical even, though less so every day. How does the song go? '*In the days when you were hopelessly poor, I just liked you more.*'" He sat for a moment as if trying to recall the rest of the lyrics or maybe formulate another dick joke. "Truth be told, you ask me, there is no such thing as a beautiful organ. The noises they make. No coincidence organists are not happy people. Being subject day and night to those awful sounds, it does something to them. I've met my fair share. Their skin is universally horrible. Ashen, starved of B12. I feel for them, though, I do. Years of grueling practice, countless recitals in dismal churches, an ever-dwindling number of suitable instruments. Audiences shrinking, aging, growing every year more geriatric and indifferent. I imagine these organists alone in hotel rooms. They sit on bed corners, feet planted on the floor, ties undone and collars loosened. They stare at the walls and their heads are filled with awful sounds."

The church acoustics gave his voice a disembodied quality, and it was difficult to read his expression as he spoke. My eyes were still adjusting, struggling to pick out details in the half-light. Next to Hannah sat a white cardboard box roughly the size as an accordion case. In the distance behind him, several life-sized marble figures were draped over the hulking mass that must have been Vratislav's tomb. The Count would've needed a jackhammer to get out.

"Whenever an organist is late for an interview, I think the worst," Hannah continued. "Did you know organists have the highest suicide rate of any classical musicians? And they're not punctual, these organists. Not as a rule. The man I am speaking with today was supposed to be here two hours ago. I even brought him a cake," he nodded toward the box at his side, "A *bublanina* sponge cake. It has cherries. Are you hungry? We could eat the cake and he'd never know the difference."

I forced a smile and shook my head.

"Maybe we could just look at the cake? No—you're right, that would just make it worse." Hannah drummed his fingers on the box and then forced himself to stop with what seemed a supreme act of willpower. "Very well. So, your message. Your brother. Detective Soros. Let me start by saying I am truly sorry. I did not know Paul Holloway, but when I got your call, I felt a certain responsibility to set the record straight. Which is not to say I believe our detective friend is trying to mislead you. Not deliberately. Was he drunk when you saw him?"

"I don't think so, no."

"Good for him. But why did he have you call me?"

"He said I should ask about my brother's right hand."

Bob Hannah nodded. "The one they cut off."

"Cut off? As in severed?"

Hannah made a crude chopping motion, followed by a shrug.

"He didn't tell me that part. Jesus, nobody ever told me that part."

"Right Hand of God," Hannah pronounced, as if that should make everything clear.

"What's the Right Hand of God?"

"He didn't tell you that either? Maybe that's a good sign. Maybe he's getting better." Hannah checked his cell phone again, glanced at the cake box, grimaced. "The Right Hand of God is a local legend of sorts. Dates back to the seventeenth century, probably earlier. Has variously to do with a goblin or demon. Or gypsy or Jew. Or serial killer or psychotic Balkan gangster, depending on which era's boogeymen are being invoked. The Right Hand of God commits a murder each year. Late August usually, early September. He then severs the right hand of his victim. According to legend, this marks said victim as being unworthy of a seat at the right hand of God, meaning Heaven. Said victim is thus not only relieved of his mortal coil but damned for all eternity. I must say that sitting next to a cake can make you incredibly hungry."

"How do they know his hand was cut off? They never found a body."

"They don't know. All they had to go on was the rather impressive bloodstain on his right sleeve. And there was the timing. According to Soros's theory, your brother vanished just when the Right Hand of God was poised to strike again. "

How much of this had my dad known? Did he have any copies of the police reports? Would he have had them translated from Czech into English? I didn't know. Easy to curse the old man now, but back then I'd been reluctant to ask about details. It was half a decade too late to feel indignant about his possible lack of oversight.

"So the hand was never found?" I asked.

"I don't believe so. Does it make a difference?"

I supposed not—either way he was gone. Near the altar, vespers began lighting candles, the flames emerging colorless and fragile in the middle distance. Wherever I looked, eyes looked back at me, cherubs, saints, angels, Madonnas, and Christs staring out from the lusterless paintings and dark wooden statues perched on the balustrades.

"How did you get hooked up with Soros?" I asked.

"Started with an All Hallows' Eve piece," said Hannah. "Little thing I wrote about spooky local legends, ghost stories and such. Right Hand of God I learned about from the first landlady I had here. She was the superstitious sort. A sparrow flew through an open window and into my apartment once, and she was convinced it was an omen of death. So convinced she made me pay next month's rent early, just in case, though I think she was trying to drive me out because I could never get accustomed to the Czech habit of removing one's shoes at home. Said my clomping around was keeping her awake, ruining her floors. But then she died that fall, so maybe the sparrow *was* an omen. Anyway, I wrote a few sentences about the Right Hand of God, along with stuff about the begging skeleton outside the Karolinum, the headless coachman of Jánský vršek Street. Rabbi Löew and his obligatory Golem, Edward Kelley and other alchemists and black magicians who called Prague home in its heyday. A week later, Detective Soros phoned. He was very upset. You think he's salty in English, you should hear him speak Czech. Man can swear for half an hour straight without once repeating himself. He said the Right Hand of God didn't belong in my story, that it wasn't a myth or legend at all. People really were being killed each autumn, corpses showing up without right hands. He said he had proof. So I met with him. He gave me this."

The paper he handed me had been unfolded and refolded many times, its creases worn smooth from multiple backpocketings. It was a map of Prague. The Vltava River ran like a question mark down its center, crosshatched with a series of hand-drawn lines that connected yellow squared numbers at various points throughout the city.

"The squares show where bodies were found," Hannah explained. "The number is the year the alleged murders took place. According to the detective, this map shows every Right Hand of God killing that has occurred over the last twenty years. On the back is a list of victim names with street addresses corresponding to the year numbers."

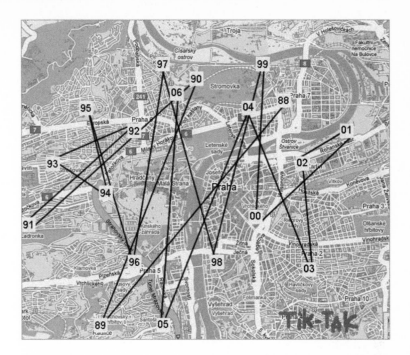

I flipped it over, eyes running down the list. Midway down the second column, there it was, sandwiched between a M. Husova in 2001 and a J. Macha in 2003—P. Holloway 2002, Křižíkova 60, 186-00 Praha 8-Karlín. I flipped back over to the map.

"What does this mean," I asked, pointing to the corner of the map. "Tik-tak."

"The sound a watch makes," Hannah replied. "*Tick-tock.* To remind himself, I suppose, that the clock was ticking. That it would only be so long before the killer struck again."

"And these lines?"

"Detective Soros said he was looking for a pattern. If he found one, I can't make sense of it. I was able to confirm that a handful, er, fair number of these names and locations do correspond to unsolved murders. As for the rest, I assume the detective is privy to information I can't access. I understand he still has friends on the force."

Through some trick of the light, the darker it grew, the more Hannah's body seemed to expand. His face looked inflated, features photoshopped ten pixels too large. Only his eyes looked normal, two small holes punched in afterthought at the center of his face. I think I was starting to hallucinate from adrenaline withdrawal and lack of food. The low light of the church and all the sad-faced statues weren't helping. Nor was the smell, a pungent, faintly sour odor that may have come from Hannah, may have just been air trapped for eons in the old building. May even have been the cake.

"A Czech reporter friend of mine who works for the *Mladá fronta* newspaper told me the hand thing isn't as uncommon as you might think," continued Hannah. "It became kind of a trend in the nineties among organized criminals. A gang from Albania or Serbia or somewhere used it as their signature. Then other gangs started doing it, whether because they thought it was cool or to throw off police, I don't know."

"But Soros says it isn't gangs behind these deaths?"

"The gangland calling-card explanation was created by the police department itself, according to him. A fabrication to cover up what was really happening. But then he says the same of any evidence that contradicts his Right Hand of God hypothesis."

"So you don't buy the serial killer theory?"

"I'm in no position to buy or sell," Hannah sighed. "I write about local documentary film festivals. New clubs, restaurants. Indie rock bands coming to town. Czech hip-hop, if you can imagine such a thing. And of course, the annual festival celebrating the wheezy organs of Prague and the miserable bastards who play them. Maybe the detective thought *The Stone Folio* would do a five-part investigative piece, make a big stink about him getting booted off the force, put pressure on the local authorities. But we're not that kind of paper."

"Kicked off the force? Soros told me he retired."

Hannah said it depended on how you looked at it. They'd moved the detective from working homicide to manning the non-emergency call center. He stuck around for a year hoping some big break in my brother's case would come along to prove his theory right, get him back in with the big boys. Eventually he decided he was better off working the Right Hand of God case on a freelance basis than fielding calls about fender benders and missing dogs. Plus, as an added bonus, working alone gave him more time to drink. Technically he may have retired, but he was forced out.

"Not that I ever confronted him on this point," said Hannah, looking again at the cake box. "I suppose I've been guilty of indulging him. Each year around this time he rings me up, convinced another murder is coming. Each August he's a little more desperate, a little less coherent. During our last conversation, he let slip that his wife had left him. At a point he became somewhat threatening. He said by not helping him bring this story to the world, I was as good as an accomplice. That I had blood on my hands. I was surprised he'd given you my card. That he might consider me his confidante is somewhat alarming."

"Do you think he's dangerous?"

Hannah considered. "I think he's alcoholic and sad."

"But you think he's right that my brother was murdered."

"I can't speak to that," Hannah said. "But given the circumstances, I thought you should know a little about the former detective so that any conclusions you draw might be better informed. As we say in our dying newspaper biz, if your mother says she loves you, check Wikipedia."

Just then Hannah's phone began buzzing. He picked it up and stared in puzzlement for several moments, his swollen head illuminated by the LCD glow. From the confusion on his face, I guessed it was the police. They'd found the card in the curator's pocket. I knew it would happen but figured I'd have more time. Hannah put the phone to the side of his head and muttered a few words and then clapped the phone shut with a sigh.

"Good thing we didn't eat the cake," he said, voicing a relief I suddenly felt for entirely different reasons. "The organist has put off his suicide for another day. He'll be here in five minutes. We should bring this to a close. I hope I haven't been too hard on Detective Soros. I don't wish to seem unsympathetic. When I came to Prague fifteen years ago, I was going to be a poet. Like pretty much every other American here then, I guess. As you can see, the universe had other ideas. Meaning only that few of us intend what we become."

After that, he recommended a couple good places to eat and gave me the name of bakery where I could get a cake just like the one he had. Sturdy boxes, too, he added. I thanked him for his time and made my way down the center aisle, back toward the entrance at the rear of the church.

I was nearly to the door when I saw what looked like a withered length of tree branch dangling from a chain attached to a metal rod that jutted from the wall fifteen feet above. I figured it was some splinter from the cross or other bogus relic. Then I recalled the entry in *Prague Unbound*, the part about the mummified human hand hanging inside the church for the last four hundred years as a warning to thieves. I couldn't tell whether it was the left or the right one.

· *The Cruel Geometry of Zugzwang* ·

March 12, 1938

My Dearest Klara,

As I write to you, the sun creeps over the horizon to render the city out-side my window as a study in charcoals, embellished by a dirt-streaked window in dire need of cleaning. You know I was never much for tidiness, and I'm afraid even rudimentary upkeep on this modest apartment is beyond me now. But at long last, I do finally have news to report. Such a remarkable day has finished that I scarce know where to begin.

The Black Rabbit is as good a place as any. I spend a fair deal of my leisure there these days, despite stern doctoral warnings against the foul airs of the tavern. The establishment is ill suited for a serious chess match, but it's the only venue our nephew Max Froehlich and I can agree upon. A neutral battlefield suspended in its own unmistak-able gloom, faces subsumed in the old shadows, conversations muted as if by the blanket of hovering smoke.

Let's begin with me at my usual table, me fumbling for my tobacco pouch, relighting the meerschaum pipe you gave me on our anniversary, my face rigid with mock concentration as I consider the chessboard. The elaborate pantomime is lost on our nephew Max, who is busy ordering another coffee to be put, as always, on Uncle Jan's tab. After a cha-rade of painstaking, brow-knit deliberation, I pick up my rook and send it the length of the board, capturing an unprotected white bishop and imperiling a knight. A bold move, improvisational audacity I dare say reminiscent of Alekhine himself. Max takes no notice. He is distracted *of late, preoccupied. He seems to subsist solely on coffee and paranoia, and all afternoon he's been wiping his spectacles and dusting off his coat like Emil Jannings in that film about the hotel porter.*

"Have you made a decision?" asks Max.

"I've decided to take your bishop."

"You know what I'm talking about."

I maintain silence, studying the board.

"Don't you read the papers, listen to the radio?"

"Let me guess. A recent spate of bad news?"

March winds rattle the upstairs windows as Max leans across the table, his face close enough I can see the wrinkles blooming at the corners of his eyes. It shocks me to realize he's thirty-nine years old, the same age as our Franz. No sooner do you reluctantly accept yourself growing old than the younger generation demands you acknowledge their aging as well.

"While you worry over these useless wooden pieces," Max says, "the whole world is poised for war. Slovakia is soon to declare independence. The Germans will invade the moment they do. Be sure of it. Then it will be too late for you. Too late for Franz, too late for Europe."

"So I was right," I grumble. "Bad news."

Max crosses his arms and pouts, but I know it won't last. His silences are brief and strategic. He never retreats, this one, only shifts his angle of attack. But for once, I must admit, our nephew's paranoia may be justified. The Little Mustache is on the march.

You'll recall my account from last September, when I wrote of fighting my way through the throngs in Wenceslas Square on the night news of the Munich betrayal broke, looking for Franz that night the country learned we were alone, orphaned at Europe's center (though "learned" seems disingenuous; how could we ever have imagined otherwise?). Since returning from the war our son can't resist a crowd, gets swept up in any peopled mass that winds its way near the little apartment we share on Bilkova Street. Workers' demonstrations, drunken Majáles spring revels, a parade for the World Cup runners-up, Masaryk's funeral — it's all the same to Franz, just another ocean of heaving humanity in which to throw himself.

You'll recall that September night he'd lost himself among those hurling invective against President Beneš for his surrender of the Sudetenlands, a crowd made mostly of angry students denouncing the French and British for appeasing The Little Mustache. You'll recall I eventually found Franz huddled in a narrow lane not far from the protest, propped against the wall like an unstrung puppet, imbecile grin slanted across his unshaven face as he clutched his tattered army coat around his shoulders and shivered against the cold. Twice in the last twenty-two years I've tried to throw out the jacket. Franz shrieked and wept hysterically on both occasions until I was forced to retrieve the ragged, soiled garment from the dust heap. Let none doubt his commitment to the Austro-Hungarian Empire, relic though it has become.

Our nephew Max breaks his petulant silence. In Austria, he says, they're dragging Jews into the streets. I remind him that just because we're in a coffeehouse doesn't make us Viennese. There was Czechoslovakia before Austria, there will be Czechoslovakia after. There will be Czechoslovakia after our chess match and Czechoslovakia after The Little Mustache, too.

Why does he allow himself to get so caught up in the narrative of world affairs? The world has but one unchanging drama. The setting may shift, the players occasionally exchange roles, but the story is always that of the powerful taking advantage of the powerless, with the Czech people typically cast in the latter role, and we Jews never cast as anything else.

Oh yes, Klara, I nearly forgot to tell you.

I am a Jew!

No joke. Not the sort to provoke a laugh, at any rate. Though I've never set foot inside a synagogue, don't celebrate Chanukah, and have long since ceased believing in any God whatsoever, I am now among His chosen people. You protest that I speak fluent German, barely passable Czech, know nary a word of Yiddish, and can scarce distinguish between Hebrew and Swahili? You argue that I converted to Catholicism years ago to appease your family, you note that our son Franz was baptized in the St. Nicholas Cathedral in front of God and everyone?

Still a Jew!

Max tells me when the Nazis take Czechoslovakia they'll impose some decree under which anyone with Jewish grandparents is racially impure. Because my mother's maiden name was Weil, if the Nazis come—abracadabra!—Franz and I metamorphose into Jews.

And the Nazis will come. About this Max is right. Europe's old axes are poised and our land ripe for the hacking. The end of our fledgling democracy leaves me with the same numb sense of inevitability as the death of a distant uncle long diagnosed with cancer. Too bad, certainly, but no great surprise. Last time it was the Austrians, this time the Germans, next time the Russians, the Hungarians, the Swedes, the Turks. Perhaps one day the Americans will invade. Perhaps one day I shall be transformed into a Hindi, an Aztec, an Eskimo!

If Franz and I are to become Jews, we will have a great deal of company. Refugees are already flooding Prague—German Jews, Austrian Jews, Moravians, Slovakians, all living in vast makeshift encampments on the city's outskirts. Inside the city they go door to door in peddler's rags, hawking pencil nubs, matches, used razors, and speaking with a rabbinical fervor impossible to credit.

Max now casually maneuvers his white knight out of danger and tells me he's spoken to his contact at the embassy (yes, that fellow again). He's like a love-struck schoolboy when he speaks of this man. Max tells me the embassy is overwhelmed, that five thousand emigration requests have been filed since Kristallnacht.

I try to concentrate on the game. Max's last move has forked my queen and bishop. The Black Rabbit proprietor plays an American Negro tune on the gramophone, one which I grudgingly tolerated the

first two dozen times I heard it but whose boisterous charms have faded
the three dozen times since. This is no dancehall, but people can't stand
silence now, must always obliterate their thoughts with music, the
more raucous the better.

A headache blossoms in my skull. How could I not have anticipated
Max's counterstrike? I'd have to sacrifice my bishop to save my queen,
leaving my attack in shambles. I'd captured more pawns, gained control of the center of the board, built an intricate defense, and yet was
suddenly at a disadvantage. No choice but to withdraw to the safety
of the back line. Across the room, an old woman begins coughing.
Looking up, I see she is not old at all.

"I'm leaving in three days," Max says.

"You can't be serious."

"There are Froehlings overseas. In Chicago. I found a family in
an American telephone directory at the Central Post Office. I've been
exchanging letters with them since last summer. I've convinced them
I'm their cousin. They've filed an affidavit on our behalf."

"You want to go, go. I can't stop you."

"Listen to me. They've submitted paperwork for you and Franz as
well. A document that pledges that you're not criminals, that you're
both able to work —"

"Franz work? What sort of work do you imagine him doing in
America? Rustling cattle? Fighting Indians?"

Max makes a horseshoe of his mouth and runs through his reper-
toire of compulsory poses. The Insouciant Slouch. The Double-Elbow
Hunch. Rodin's Thinker. Ankle Upon Knee. Reverse Ankle Upon
Knee. The Negro tune ends and soon Karel Vacek's voice is singing
about the fairy tale of our youth and how it will never return. I think
you would have liked this song. Dust particles dance in the failing light
,and time hemorrhages from unseen corners of the room.

And just when the game looks abandoned, Max takes up his rook
and swings it down the right flank, knocking out a black pawn. Thanks

to all his embassy blather, he's overlooked the obvious and my bishop is spared. Max realizes his error as soon as he's made it and hastily pushes himself from the table.

In four moves, the game will be mine.

"Three days," he says, buttoning his overcoat.

"Four words," I say. "Talk less, win more."

"And a word for you, Uncle Jan. Checkmate."

Max unleashes a withering smile rich with the condescension that has become his unfortunate trademark of late. My eyes dart over the board. Black is indeed in check—but checkmate? Surely not. Surely there is a way out. But Max is already up the stairs and through the door by the time the cruel geometry upon the tabletop forces me to conclude that, no matter what move I next make, the game is well and truly lost.

Maybe this isn't the place to begin.

Maybe I should begin after I leave the Black Rabbit and make my way through the streets that lead to our apartment. Begin with the lacerating wind racing down the corridors of Altstadt, knifing through the angled passageways with such violence that the very buildings seem to bow to its force, bending and twisting until the whole cityscape resembles the Old Jewish Cemetery with its layers of stone rising jumbled from the earth, a mouth crammed with rotting teeth where in days of old it's said the ghosts of children would at midnight emerge to make a terrible ruckus until the wise Rabbi Löew confronted them and learned they were but endeavoring to reveal the source of a plague afflicting the Fifth Quarter by dancing and playing about a tombstone showing the name of the sorcerer who had brought the pestilence upon them.

Perhaps we should begin when I reach Josefstadt—Židovské Město, Josefov as they call it now—the Fifth Quarter by any name not itself since it was razed by the government for fear it was a breeding ground

for disease. True, disease had long plagued the Fifth Quarter, the disease of poverty, incurable by sledgehammers and wrecking balls. I contend its destruction had little to do with those old anti-Semitic urges
now freshly fashionable as by the time of its annihilation, Josefstadt
was devoid of all but the most desperate of Jews. No, there was something else there, some nameless something in that teeming ghetto that
terrified the bureaucratic heart, something mutinous and ungovern-
able that laughed in the face of lofty notions like progress and order.
The poor were driven out, who knows where they went, but the rich never
moved in as planned. Towering art nouveau apartments now line the
widened rectilinear avenues, their immodest façades already maudlin
and timeworn. And yet still something of the old ghetto survives. Any
landlord in our city knows ghosts are the most difficult tenants to evict.

We begin our goodbye in Josefstadt then, begin with this old man
ambling through those emptied streets, conjuring phantom glimpses
of the vanished ghetto. Ulcerated wooden hovels piggybacked one atop
another, houses growing from houses like malignant tumors, streets
expanding ever inward, a maze with no exit. We begin our farewell
with an old man recollecting those sunless shrunken lanes, uneven surfaces with the pitch and roll of a troubled sea, streets rife with blind
turns plunging to sudden dead ends. As he walks he conjures disembodied faces floating gaunt and silent in the misshapen windows above,
the filthy stark-eyed children running riot below, the bearded junkmen
and shadowy soothsayers, the cadaverous whores and consumptive
drunks in a decaying labyrinth echoing with the music and laughter
of madness.

Now these streets all but empty.

Soundless but for the wind.

Yet amongst the faint scent of acacias, this old man's nose still
registers the stench of onions and sewage. He ducks now beneath the
sapling branches and recalls nowhere then were there trees, flowers,
nor bushes, nor even weeds, save for those in the untended cemetery.

Atop the walls still lingered broken coils of rusted barbed wire strung up centuries past, fragmented reminders that this was once a forbidden city-within-a-city, an impoverished funhouse reflection of the castle complex across the river.

This is the world the old man remembers, the world he'd found himself in when accompanying his father all the way from their home in the affluent Bubeneč suburbs to slum in Josefstadt for antiques. Afterward, his father would stop off for a beer at the Black Eagle tavern, while this boy would be left to his own devices in the nearby Valentinské market square, too frightened to do anything but remain frozen in the long-fingered shadows until his father wobbled out and they set homeward.

It's a world you never experienced, Klara, this vanished carnival, this sordid emporium. Streetcart chemists pedaled bottled cures for baldness, impotence, and bad luck. One mad cart pusher hawked patchwork animals, ravens painted as parrots, small dogs sewn into the skins of foxes. For years an old Turkish woman clad in flowing purple led a black bear by a chain attached to a thick ring through its nose. For a few ducats, the bear would perform a clumsy waltz, lurching on its hind legs, salivating great parabolic ropes from its mouth. One morning the bear arrived in Valentiské Square alone, the woman nowhere in evidence save for her left leg clutched between its jaws. It's said the bear was dancing when the police killed it, firing several rounds and wounding two of their own in the process.

Only slightly more respectable than the street vendors were the shopkeepers, a species cursed to lack powers of discrimination, habitually ensconcing their few worthy items amid stockpiled hordes of bent spoons, broken umbrellas, keyless locks, lockless keys, mangled birdcages, watches without hands, dolls without heads—it was as if they were amassing items willy-nilly inside their gloomy little shops in an effort to prepare for some coming catastrophe, or perhaps to memorialize the world as it existed before the last one.

It was here in the Fifth Quarter that I first contracted the disease of collecting, and so perhaps its no surprise that here I returned when your much crueler disease claimed you. Was it to my childhood I was retreating in coming here? No, my childhood was sun and tall grass, summer breezes and azure skies. And like my childhood, the dark mystery of Josefstadt is gone now, irretrievable no matter where I chose to live.

What ultimately drew me here was the lack of you, Klara. You were everywhere in our old house. Sleeping in the bed we shared, hovering over the stove, sitting under the willow tree, stacking jars in the root cellar. You in the sunlight pouring through summer windows, you in the crackling fire and creaking floorboards of winter, you in the dancing patter of spring rain upon the rooftop. You as if you never left. You reminding me you were never returning.

I find reminders of you strewn throughout the city. On the bench where we shared our first kiss that July afternoon, you wrapped in a thick towel after we'd frolicked in the river, me with wet hair clinging to my pale forehead. At the Three Foxes where we danced, in Weinberge Park where in autumn we'd stroll and talk for hours. I smile now and wonder what could we have possibly talked about, knowing as little as we did.

Nothing so precious as memory, nothing so useless.

Our Franz is unburdened by such recollections. To him, you're little more than a figure in a sun-bleached photograph that sits atop the corner bookshelf, one half of a happy young couple posed in front of a Marienbad hot springs resort. She in high-collared white dress, he in dark suit and bowler hat, both of them gazing out with unyielding, vexed expressions, as if unsure how best to arrange their features for the camera. I find our Franz staring at this photo sometimes. On such occasions I envy his lack of understanding.

If I am thankful for anything, it is that the Spanish flu claimed you when it did, that you never lived to see your only child return from the Great War with a hole under his chin and another out the top of his skull, the wounds mapping the trajectory of the pea-sized bead of shrapnel that effectively severed the twin hemispheres of his brain. Better you never heard the military doctor say it was God's own miracle Franz had lived. Better you never heard me curse a God capable of such miracles.

He's still strong as an ox, God's Miracle, but he has been rendered helpless and childlike in every other sense. He can bathe himself, dress himself, and use the lavatory, but much beyond these rudimentary acts frustrates him to tears. God's Miracle sleeps irregularly. God's Miracle throws tantrums. God's Miracle weeps inconsolably one minute, brays with laughter the next. But I can't bear to send Franz to an asylum, and so the two of us have lived mostly in silence these last twenty odd years, father and son, as together and alone as any two men can be.

But you know all this.

And you know that despite outwardly resisting my nephew's notions of escape, I've been pondering our future ever since last summer, when the Petschek family, one of the wealthiest in Bohemia, quietly left on train out of the country. If the rich don't like their chances, how are a penniless sixty-one-year-old and a mental cripple supposed to survive another war? Yet even if we make it to America, we shall arrive as ourselves. Which is to say a penniless sixty-one-year-old and a mental cripple.

Or so I thought before today.

But I race ahead of myself.

We begin then with a frigid blast scattering my nostalgia as I round the corner, the wind watering my eyes, tears blurring my vision so that I do not see the man standing in front of Murcek Curios and Antiquities until I am nearly upon him. He seems to materialize out of nowhere, gaunt and spindly, a figure from a dream.

The shop is closed, I tell him, but if he would kindly return in the morning, I will be more than happy to show him my wares. The man *makes no reply. He is dressed in a narrow-waisted Beiderbecke overcoat and a battered stovepipe hat that stays improbably in place despite the wind. Silvery hair falls over his ears and down his back while his face remains veiled in shadow. This human spire of a man wields a smart black cane capped by a solid gold handle in the shape of a bear's head. A man of no little eccentricity.*

I tell him I am truly sorry to keep a gentleman such as himself waiting, but as the sign on the door plainly states, my shop is in operation from 10 AM to 5 PM, and it is going on seven o' clock now.

"I'm told you repair watches," the man says.

"Repair them I do, however—"

"May we continue this conversation inside?"

Streetlamps still painted over from the September blackouts begin pulsing to life, casting a dull blue pallor over the empty streets. The man takes a step closer, and for the first time I gaze upon his face unobscured, a face neither old nor young, neither handsome nor ugly. The man doesn't look healthy, true, with his sallow skin and sunken eyes. Flesh yellow like an old bruise, eyes hard and luminous yet clouded, darkened with age. Still, there is no obvious feature that forces me to look away, though look away I do, nor any that compels me to dig through my pocket for the keys to unlock the shop, though unlock it I do.

The man enters and I shut the door behind us. He carries with him a smell, malodorous and sickly sweet, the scent of baked lamb left out too long after Easter. The man leans heavily on his cane, hobbling a slow clip-clop rhythm as he wanders the floor, surveying one item after the next with studied leisure. I notice he has a false leg. After the last war, I'd traded in all manner of prosthetics, crutches, wheelchairs. If our nephew is right, a new generation of broken young men will soon be limping through my door. But then if Max is right, I will no longer be behind the counter.

"My name is Doctor Kačak," says the man, stopping to gaze reproachfully at a mounted boar's head with splintered tusks. Seeing

my shop through another's eyes, I realize how much it has started to resemble those congested ghetto emporiums of my youth. Arabian camel saddle here, cracked scrimshaw figurine there, unstrung harp, musical snuffbox, dressmaker's dummy, glass eyeball, telescope, stroboscope, flotsam, jetsam — where had so many unloved things come from? Why had they all come here?

Suddenly weary and knowing Franz will be upstairs waiting, I regret opening the shop. "What can I do for you, Doctor Kačak? You mentioned a watch?"

"An old watch," he says. "Of little value beyond the sentimental, but I've grown as accustomed to its ticking as to the beating of my own heart. But it's ticking faster now, gaining dangerous speed, and I fear it may soon wear itself out. The watch, that is. Not my heart, knock wood."

Doctor Kačak raps the cane against his false leg.

"Time is critical as I may be soon be traveling," he resumes. "The watch must be returned in three days. You will, of course, be generously compensated for your expediency."

"Have you brought the piece with you?"

Doctor Kačak hooks the protruding bear's snout of his cane handle over his forearm and removes his stovepipe hat with a magician's flourish. Animated by static charge, wisps of fine, silvery hair spring from his scalp in every direction. The man reaches into the hollow of his hat and withdraws a bundle of black velvet cloth. Judging by the bundle's size, the watch is quite large, roughly the circumference of a tea saucer. He places this bundle gently on the counter, flashes his gray teeth, and then slowly unwraps it, fold by delicate fold, until the piece lies naked before me.

My eyes first land upon the exquisite ivory inlay, the heraldic White Lion gleaming upon the watch's case. My mouth goes dry; sweat beads my upper lip. How I wish to seize the watch, to flip it over and look for the telltale sign! But I resist, rummaging for words, any will do, but all I can summon is a weak cough. Maybe, just maybe, there is a future for me and God's Miracle after all. Doctor Kačak replaces the empty hat on his silvery head and proffers a showman's grin.

"You were expecting, perhaps, a rabbit?"

Several things happen in a blurred succession before this strange man takes his leave. He provides a down payment and I provide him a receipt. He gives me the watch and I am shocked to discover it still ticking, in fine working condition despite being, if my estimation is correct, more than three hundred years old. My amazement is surely evident because before I can utter a word, he insists the watch must be ticking when I return it. He further insists it must never cease ticking. As a condition of accepting this commission, I agree to repair the piece without allowing the watch to cease its movements for even a moment. He is deadly serious, and I have no wish to tell him what he is asking is akin to changing an automobile tire while motoring down a mountain road. I don't trust myself to say anything at all and can scarce even breathe until he clip-clops out of my shop, the door catching the wind and thundering closed behind him.

Here at last I've found the proper beginning of my long, final farewell. But alas, now the sun is fully risen, the day bearing down with important work to be done. I shall resume our correspondence this evening. And no more false starts, my darling. The next beginning, I promise, shall be the last.

Ever yours,
Jan

CHAPTER 7

∎

Wenceslas Square was not a square at all but a broad avenue hemmed by trees and spacious sidewalks stretching beneath the shadow of the huge National Museum. The towering nineteenth-century estates lining the avenue had since been gutted to house global retailers like Nike and Benetton along with luxury hotels and high-wattage casinos. Once the site where a student named Jan Palach set himself on fire to protest the Soviet Invasion of 1968, and later the gathering point of mass protests that brought down the Communists, it was now the city's biggest shopping arcade and swirled with a constant motion bordering on vertiginous. Starved beyond reason, I bought a sausage from a street cart and swore it was the best sausage I'd ever eaten in my life no matter what counter arguments my stomach might later make. At the far end of the avenue stood Vera's man-on-a-horse statue, a fifty-foot-high monument of St. Wenceslas planted at the base of the museum. Appropriate St. Wenceslas should be depicted atop his steed, as the area had been a horse market in medieval times, this according to *Prague Unbound*, which I'd been forced to carry by hand since the last time I'd tried to pocket it as the task had proven impossible. At least my suit had finally dried. No sooner did the thought arrive than it started raining.

I ducked into an arcade to wait out the downpour. A narrow hallway wound past an array of interchangeable strip clubs with identical purple neon lights running the perimeters of their black smoked windows. The air was nicotine stale and reverberating with a low bass that pulsed behind the walls while the floor was painted with arrows promising a casino just ahead which always failed to materialize. I found an Internet café before plumbing too far into the building's depths. Five old PCs lined up against the wall in a room the size of a mini-van. It was the kind of place I imagined Al-Qaeda operatives sending untraceable messages to each other between visits to the Atlantis Lounge and the Kitty Kat Cabaret.

I tried checking my work e-mail, but the server at Grimley & Dunballer Recovery Solutions kept rejecting my password. No matter; my job already felt like part of a former life.

Next I googled *Czech + News + English* and reached the *Prague Post's* online edition. The lead story was about Parliament postponing a debate on whether one of its members should be stripped of immunity as he was suspected of having tortured people while working as a prison guard under the former Communist regime. Sparta Prague was warning its fans against racist chants when the club faced Arsenal in an upcoming Champions League game. The price of poultry was on the rise. In the crime section, police were investigating the disappearance of an ATM in Kutná Hora. Six employees from a hospital in Litoměřice were being charged with organ trafficking. I checked a couple other news sites, but unearthed nothing about a Malá Strana art gallery curator found dead in the Čertovka canal.

Like Detective Soros, Bob Hannah hadn't mentioned anything about the Rudolf Complication. Made sense as most of his information about my brother's case came from the detective. More importantly, it underscored my suspicion that Soros hadn't tied my brother's disappearance to the watch theft. Meaning Vera's secret really was a secret. Problem was, my presence at the Black Rabbit last night had essentially cemented her link to my brother, and I wondered how long it would be until Soros started pestering her. Maybe it would be best to warn her about him before she decided I'd broken my promise. Or maybe it would be better to wait. She might not believe me, and I couldn't have her clamming up if I was ever to have a chance at finding out who this Martinko Klingáč was. And if I did find out, what then? Still seemed too remote a possibility to worry over.

Googling Martinko Klingáč yielded only links to an animated DVD of the Slovak fairytale and some rock band's outdated MySpace page. Thinking maybe the last owner of the Rudolf Complication might lead somewhere, I tried searching "Martin Novotny" and got about forty thousand results. Guess it was a common name. Narrowing that to news results only brought the links number down to four hundred. Sorting by date, I found what I'd been looking for, sort of. Two barebones paragraphs on the English language website praguedaily.com said a dead body discovered on the third floor of an abandoned textile factory in Strašnice had been identified as Martin Novotny, an unemployed twenty-eight-year-old man originally from Brno who had twice served time for burglary and petty theft. Nothing about him being the victim of a reverse defenestration, nothing about his previous "ownership" of the Rudolf Complication. The article said foul play was suspected, but the paper hadn't run any follow-up story, so I assumed no arrests were ever made. "Man Found Dead in Strašnice Factory" was just one of those stories about one of those nobodies that crops up, goes nowhere, and disappears. Not unlike "American Missing and Presumed Drowned in Karlín."

Clicking on the most viewed stories, I ended up on an article about the upcoming 650ᵗʰ birthday celebration planned for the Charles Bridge. Story said the bridge was founded in 1357 on July 9 at 5:31 AM, a date chosen as its odd primary numbers ran palindromically—1/3/5/7/9/7/5/3/1. I found it interesting, although I didn't know who I planned on impressing with this knowledge. The story was a couple months old now; the party had already come and gone.

Outside it had stopped raining.

I logged off and made my way to the statue.

There were lots of people hanging out by the man on the horse but not so many I worried I'd miss her. A few gangster slash pimp types were milling around near dodgy looking side streets. Some had greasy hair, but I could imagine none being nicknamed Martinko Klingáč. Somehow I was sure he wasn't just some street corner hoodlum. I kept envisioning a James Bond villain. Elegantly dressed, sitting in a wheelchair and stroking a cat, maybe a chinchilla. I was sure he wasn't that either.

With all the people-watching, I'd failed to notice Vera standing just a few feet away. I don't know how long she'd been there, eyeing me with a slightly startled expression, eyebrows inward bent, lips fractionally parted. She was looking straight at me, but it was obvious it wasn't me she was seeing. I'd encountered this same dazed expression on the faces of my brother's friends once or twice since he'd died. It took me awhile to realize they were just seeing Paul. Not the Paul they knew, but an older version, one of many possible Pauls now impossible. So it was with Vera. All at once something in her eyes receded and her mouth hardened and she was just seeing good ol' Lee again. There were no pleasantries though. She didn't say hello or anything else, just took my arm as if it was the most natural thing in the world and started walking.

A few minutes later we were inside another palatial shopping arcade, this one more upscale. Checkerboard marble floors, broad columns, high domed ceilings. Dangling suspended from the center of a giant stained glass skylight was another sculpture of St. Wenceslas on his horse. In this version the horse was upside down, hooves pointed skyward, head limp and dangling open mouthed toward the floor while King Wenceslas nonchalantly straddled his belly.

We moved up a sweeping staircase into a café on the second floor and took a table in the corner. Polished dark wood, waiters in immaculate white aprons. Vera removed her coat and I placed *Prague Unbound* in an empty chair. I'd thought the book's cover was black and was surprised to find it was actually a dark shade of green. Funny the things we misremember.

Vera and I both waited for the other to speak. Her eyes were glazed over as if she'd just woken, no jewelry, no make-up. Her hair looked lifeless, blacker and longer somehow than it had been the night before.

I pulled my jacket close around me, the too-long sleeves reaching past my wrists.

"I am prepared to speak with you for one hour," she began. "I will answer your questions, the ones I can answer. My hope is at the end of one hour you will no longer consider involving the police. But I can't prevent you. Whatever you choose to do, you must agree to one condition. We must never see each other again."

"Let's call it two hours."

"Ninety minutes. That's all the time I have."

"Okay, fine. How did you and Paul meet?"

"A pickpocket."

"Is this a long story?"

"I don't know. I've never told it before."

Turned out it was a long story.

"I was working at the gallery," Vera began. "One day this man bursts through the door. He's sweaty and his hair is long and sticks to his face. On his arm I can see a tattoo of a cartoon man carrying a big gun."

"Elmer Fudd."

"That's the one. What is the meaning of this tattoo?"

I shook my head. "People thought he sounded like Elmer Fudd when he laughed."

"Paul liked to laugh. He has his own sense of humor, I think."

"You'd have to with Elmer Fudd on your arm."

"Do you also laugh like this Elmer Fudd?"

"Mine is more of a Woody Woodpecker."

"Really? Let's hear it."

"I'm saving it for something funny."

She narrowed her eyes, studying me a moment before she resumed speaking. "Anyway, that day he is not Paul but only a man with an odd tattoo. He looks angry, this man. He says, 'Where the fuck is the fucking little prick hiding at?' These are the first words your brother speaks to me. I tell him I have no idea what he is talking about. He says, 'I'm talking about the little pickpocket prick who stole my wallet. The kid I just chased across the goddamn bridge. I know how it works. Kid comes running in here, you hide him in the basement or wherever like he's Anne fucking Frank, he gives you a cut of the take.' 'We're an art gallery,' I tell him. 'We have nothing to do with pickpockets or Anne Frank.' 'Get my wallet back, I'll double what he pays. Let me punch him in the nose, I'll triple it.'"

Her impression of him was uncanny, the hunched shoulders, the smoke-ravaged half-growl of his voice, even the Southside accent I'd somehow avoided. I'd already started forgetting what he sounded like. Vera clearly hadn't.

"Then your brother, he picks up a vase," Vera said, fiddling with her cigarettes. With only three or four left in the pack, she'd evidently gone into full relapse since last night. "Not an artwork, just a cheap thing for flowers, like something you would purchase at Tesco or Bílá Labut. He picks up this vase and says, 'If you don't bring him out by the time I count to three, I'm going to smash the living fuck out of this vase.' I cross my arms, stare at him. 'One,' he counts. 'Two.' He looks like a lost little boy. 'I'm serious here,' he says. A little boy who doesn't know what he is doing but who has gone too far to stop."

Summed up my brother's past troubles more than she probably knew. The way her eyelids practically fluttered at 'lost little boy' told me a lot too. Women were always thinking they could settle him down, straighten him out, give him some direction in life. Some of them even succeeded for a few months.

"A couple seconds pass," she resumes, "and then *WHAM!* He throws the vase to the floor. Big noise, pieces scatter everywhere. He stands looking around like he's not sure what happened. Then he goes running out the door without a word."

I checked to see how many of my ninety minutes have passed, noticed my watch was still set to Chicago time. Right about now I'd be figuring out how to kill ten or forty minutes on the Internet before heading out to lunch. Looking at my watch did me no good anyway because I couldn't remember when our ninety minutes started. Time did strange things here.

"The next day I told my boss that I knocked over the vase when cleaning. An accident. He tells to me a lecture about what it means to be careful. My boss Gustav, he likes to make lectures."

I felt a little sick. I thought of Gustav laying there on the edge of the canal, his arm twitching, blood pooled around his head. I felt a little sicker.

"A couple days later your brother comes back. Just before closing. He looks . . . what's the word? Like a sheep. Sheepish. He tells me that he has come to pay for the vase. I say this is not necessary. He takes a pile of money out of his pocket and spreads it on the counter. Like a card dealer. Its over thirty-five thousand crowns. Nearly what, two thousand U.S. dollars? Put it away, I tell him, it was just a mistake, a misunderstanding. He says to me if I won't take his money, will I let him buy for me dinner? So I agreed. What can I say, I thought he was funny."

"They ever catch the pickpocket?"

She lit a cigarette. "That's the best part. Your brother found his wallet in another pants, where it had been always. There never was any pickpocket."

Just then a waiter arrived. I hadn't even noticed that we'd gone unattended since being seated. Vera ordered for both of us and dispatched him without further ceremony.

"Two thousand dollars is a lot of cash," I said. "What did Paul do here? Where did he work?"

She dragged on her cigarette and frowned. "He was an ambassador, he tells to me. The Ambassador of Awesome. Or he would say he worked on behalf of the International Brotherhood of Kicking Ass. When I got tired of his joking and tried to make him be serious, he would get angry. Why it was important? People were not their jobs. As for money, he didn't always have money. Often he was broke."

Paul could never hang on to money. I knew he'd used my dad's credit card to buy his plane ticket to Prague, an act I would have caught holy hell for, but with Paul all was forgiven. Dad was always sure Paul could make something of himself, he just needed a fresh start. About every two or three years, as it turned out.

"Did my brother have many friends here?"

Vera considered. "He knew many people. Prague 1 or Prague 8, it didn't matter; when we went out people would know him. His mobile was always ringing. Paul would answer, say a few words, hang up. Or he would look at the caller screen and not answer. He rarely introduced me to people who came up to him in a club, or on the street. I thought there were reasons. I didn't want to know these reasons."

"Where did he live?"

"With me."

"With you where?"

"Is it important?"

"You said you'd answer my questions."

"In Smíchov. At my apartment. South from here, on the other side of the river. We'd only been together maybe two weeks when he moved in."

So I'd been right. They were in a relationship, a serious one from the sound of it.

"He had only one suitcase. But he would come and go. Like having a cat. Where he stayed when he wasn't with me, I don't know."

"Weren't you curious?"

"Of course." She looked away and snubbed out her cigarette. "Even now sometimes I wonder if we would have been together much longer. What would've happened to us."

"How long were you together?"

"Nearly one year. It seemed longer. Also shorter. Being with Paul, there was always something happening, you know? He had so much energy he didn't know what to do with. Like something was missing for him. Always he was looking for this something. And this can wear you out. It can wear out the people around you. They never know what you're about, what to expect. Does that make sense?"

"You're saying he was undependable."

"Not really what I meant. But yes, he could be undependable. But also dependable. Big things yes, little things no."

"So dependable or undependable, depending?"

"Paul would die for me," she said. "This I knew in my heart. This I know still. In this way I could depend on him. I could believe in him. But when he said he would meet me at the theater at 7:30? Or when he promised to pick up bread on the way over? This I could never believe. And normal relationships are full of little things like this, you know? More small things than big ones. Not that maybe our relationship was so normal. But I wanted it to be. I wanted to make us normal."

As she spoke I wondered whether he had in fact died for her without her even knowing it. I'd been thinking a lot about those bloodstains found on his shirtsleeve. Soros thought it meant Paul had been victim of some ritualistic serial killer who liked hacking off people's hands. But wasn't the blood also possible evidence that he'd been tortured? And why? Maybe because the mysterious Martinko Klingáč was trying to get Vera's identity out of him?

There was no way I could bring up this theory with Vera, just as there was no way I could tell her what had happened at the Galleria Čertovka earlier that morning or ask if she'd ever heard of the Right Hand of God. She was still my only real link to Paul, the only person who knew him as anything other than a disappeared body, even if she'd already determined our association would dissolve in less than ninety minutes. But I wondered if she knew about the bloodstained shirt. If so, why hadn't she mentioned it? If not, how could she be so sure that Paul was murdered in the first place?

The obvious answer was that she was in on it.

That she had set him up.

I didn't want to believe this. I couldn't rule it out.

"Whose idea was it to steal the watch?" I said.

She lit another cigarette. I found myself craving one even though I'd quit years ago when the price crept over five dollars a pack, reasoning you can only be expected to pay so much to kill yourself. "One day Paul came home with a page from the newspaper," she said. "This was not like him. Especially because this newspaper was in Czech, and he cannot read Czech. This is in May I think, maybe June. I remember it was before your brother's name day."

"His what day?"

"In Czech Republic everyone has a name day," she said. "Like a birthday. Paul's Czech name would be Pavel, so his name day is sometime in June. Anyway, he handed me the newspaper. It had been folded many times. Like he's had it in his pocket. One paragraph is circled in red. He hands the paper to me and says, 'This is where you work, right?' This newspaper story is about art shows for the fall and summer. The paragraph he circled is for something called *Rudolf's Curiosities*. I tell to him, yes, that's where I work, so what? Paul smiles and puts the newspaper back in his pocket."

A loud hiss issued from behind the counter as a barista heated milk, the steam rising and obscuring her face, rendering her momentarily headless. Vera went on to explain that two, maybe three weeks passed before he made mention of the Rudolf Complication again. Then one night riding the tram home after they went drinking with some of her friends in some unpronounceable Prague suburb, he asks what she would do with a million dollars.

First she laughs. He asks again. She says she sees no point in imagining impossible scenarios. But Paul tells her this question is not hypothetical. They could each have a million dollars—more than a million dollars—in two months. He knows a person who will pay $5 million dollars for a certain work of art. One that will soon be at the Gallery Čertovka. All they had to do was steal it, and half the money would be theirs.

I didn't know if $5 million was a ridiculous sum for the watch, and I'm sure Paul wouldn't have either. Pricing work for hire like this was probably tricky. Offer too much, the help will smell a rat, know they're going to be stiffed or worse. Offer too little, they'll consider cutting out the middleman and taking the piece on the open market. Or maybe if you're someone like Martinko Klingáč dealing with someone like my brother, you just pull a figure like $5 million out of your ass and watch the guy go all swirly eyed.

"I didn't take Paul seriously," Vera said. "We were both drunk and he is always saying some crazy thing. The conversation moved on and that was that. But a few days later, he starts asking questions. Do we have alarms at the Galleria Čertovka? Do we have security cameras? Are there cleaning people who come when we are closed? Does the door have an electronic lock or are there keys, do we have a safe, what are the busiest times? He'd write down what I said in a notebook. Notes and drawings in this child's notebook with a ridiculous cartoon mouse on the cover. Not a mouse, what's it called, a mole. Krtek the mole. It was an absurd game. I only started worrying when he brought home the gun."

"A gun? Where did he get a gun?"

"He said, 'I'm American, we all carry guns. For hunting wascally wabbits.' Always joking, your brother. But I asked was he planning on robbing the gallery with a gun? Because I wouldn't allow this. The gallery owner was a family friend and I would not let Paul put a gun into his face. I got very angry. Paul he says nothing, just listens. Finally he says, 'I'm not going to pull the gun on him. I'm going to pull the gun on *you*.'"

"And this was Klingáč's idea?"

She shook her head. "Paul's idea. Martinko Klingáč did not know about me, remember. He did not know Paul's accomplice was a person from the gallery. Paul swore to this, and I believed him. Whatever happened, he wanted to protect me."

"By sticking a gun in your face."

She explained the plan also called for a witness being inside the gallery when the robbery took place. Not Gustav—they'd

pull the heist during the late afternoon, when he was usually at
a pub called the Golden Weaver—but a customer, a tourist, best
case a lone female or an old couple. With a witness and a gun, it
wouldn't look like an inside job—either to the police, or just as
importantly, to Martinko Klingáč. Paul wouldn't tell her much
more about the plan because he wanted her to act natural, behave
like a person getting robbed. All she knew was that one day, a man
in a ski mask would burst in yelling in a language from *Star Trek*.

"*Star Trek*?" I repeated. "What, like Vulcan?"

"No, Klingon," she said. "That's what it was called, I think.
Because this way, if the witness was from Japan or Sweden or
Austria or the UK, it didn't matter. No one could know what Paul
was saying, and so they would only be able to tell to the police of
a man with a skiing mask yelling in a strange language. He bought
a book on the Internet and taught to himself a sentence always he
was repeating. God, I still remember it. *Fi tevakh ek yemtor*. I have
no idea what it meant, but for weeks he would mutter *fi tevakh
ek yemtor, fi tevakh ek yemtor*. He lives in Prague for two years,
doesn't speak five words of Czech. Instead he wants to learn some
language of TV aliens."

But the robbery didn't happen the way Paul planned, Vera said.
Martinko Klingáč insisted they wait for a sign.

"A sign? What kind of sign?"

"Paul didn't know," Vera said. "'Martinko Klingáč says there
will be a sign,' was all he said. 'When the sign comes, we'll know.
And then we must act. No hesitation.' Paul is drinking a lot at this
time, sleeping very little. He smokes like a fire and stops changing
his clothes, shaving, taking showers. And then there was his hair."

"What hair?"

"Yes, exactly. Always he had been bald since I've known him.
Always he kept his head shaved. But then he started growing his
hair. For eight weeks, ten weeks, he lets his hair begin to grow."

"Like as a disguise?"

She shook her head. "Klingáč, he does not trust people with no hair, Paul tells me. He will not even be in a room with a bald man. A superstition or something like this. And Paul always talking about Klingáč says this, Klingáč says that. Like Paul was in a cult. I say to him I don't want any part of this anymore. We had a terrible fight, our worst—and believe me, we fought all the time. We were passionate people, both stubborn. But in the end we reached a compromise, less from understanding than exhaustion. That's how it went. We would just go and go until there was nothing left. We decided if there was no sign within two weeks, he would give up the idea of stealing the watch. We would never speak of it again. Not the Rudolf Complication, Martinko Klingáč, none of it."

Two days later, one perfectly fine summer afternoon while waiting for my brother Paul to meet her for lunch at a café near the west bank of the Vltava River, she looked out the window to see dark clouds gathered low across the horizon. The moment she formed the thought rain was on the way, it had already arrived. No thundering overture, no cautionary flash of lightning, no drizzly prelude—just rain suddenly crashing down like a child's tantrum, too full of its own fury to last. Paul never showed up for lunch. She told me how she'd later waited for him at Andel station as she would sometimes, watching the crowds scurry out of the metro below and the big new Nový Smíchov mall above like confused mice flushed from their nests, women struggling with umbrellas, men angled against the wind, collars upturned on their raincoats. She told me how the rain kept falling for days as she waited for him to come home, to call, anything. How the low clouds moved across the sky, an endless conquering army flattening the cityscape, rendering it in blurred layers of gray, and how she'd watched the trees sway on the far side of the riverbank as tram after tram rattled across Palackého Bridge. How she'd allowed herself to believe that

Paul was in one of them, rehearsing apologies, how she'd believed he would soon appear at her door, bedraggled, wet hair plastered to his forehead, sheepish grin plastered on his face.

How the TV filled with images of the flood, shots of bleary-eyed tourists lugging suitcases through the maze of wet streets or crowded between the procession of stone saints on the Charles Bridge to marvel at the river below, now a thick, silty brown. Instead of tour boats and regal swans, the churning waters now ferried fallen trees, untethered rowboats, broken furniture, the odd discarded refrigerator. How the plight of an eighty-one-year-old elephant trapped at the Prague Zoo became the media focus, even as first thirty, then fifty, then seventy thousand people were evacuated, a process made more difficult as roads were washed out and tramlines severed. Thirteen Soviet-era subway stations were knocked out of commission, despite the fact that the system was designed to double as an impenetrable fallout shelter in the event of nuclear war. Busses transported residents to makeshift emergency shelters in school auditoriums while holdouts in the city center fortified their businesses, sandbagging doors, reinforcing windows, shuttling merchandise to higher elevations. Cash machines throughout the city were quickly drained, and canned food and bottled water disappeared from the shelves in ways not seen since the Nazi invasion nearly seventy years prior. How she'd called and called trying to reach Paul, and when her cell phone battery died how she'd slogged through the wet and abandoned streets to a pay phone outside the Nový Smíchov shopping mall. How an unfamiliar voice answered Paul's mobile, a voice she knew belonged to Martinko Klingáč.

"Who is this?" he'd said. *"Who is speaking?"*

How she'd dropped the phone, let the handset dangle and sway on its cord, the voice repeating the question as she backed away.

"Who is this? Who is speaking?"

How she'd run splashing down the hill and then up the stairs to her apartment, how she'd locked the door, how she hadn't taken her boots off until she'd turned on every light in the place. How all the lights had suddenly gone off, and the water too, as the flood swallowed the city. A perfect fairytale seven days had passed, she'd realized, since she'd last seen Paul. And then how lulled by the murky sonata of water cascading over the rooftops and streaming through rain pipes and spilling onto the streets, she'd finally succumbed to this wordless lullaby.

How later she woke from a dreamless sleep to find the rain had stopped just as it had started, suddenly, without warning. The clouds had parted and the sun was pouring through the window, and someone was pounding against the door of her apartment.

She was evacuated by emergency rescue personnel patrolling the area on rafts and taken to a makeshift shelter in a high school gymnasium where she slept on a cot for two days and spoke to no one. The water drained from the city and she knew Paul was gone.

"And I'll tell you one more story," she said. "This story is a Christmas story. From when I was little. But I think it is also a story about Paul. Each year at Christmas time, my father would bring home a carp and put it in the bathtub. Here it's tradition to eat carp for Christmas dinner. To keep the carp fresh, it would live in the bathtub until time came to cook it. When I was seven years old, I decided I did not want this particular carp to die. I decided to rescue it. Put it in a plastic bag, take it to the river—which was stupid because the river was so polluted then it would never have survived. But when I tried to catch the fish, it squirmed away. Again and again. I started crying and tried explaining to the fish that I only wanted to help, that terrible things would happen soon if it did not be still. But it thrashed and squirmed and raced around the bathtub, and I couldn't catch it."

By the time she'd finished we were well beyond the ninety-minute mark. She gave me a chance to ask one more question, anything I wanted, and then she really would have to go and that really would have to be the end.

I didn't ask her anything. I just told her I was sorry things turned out the way they did—not just for my brother, but for her, too. I said she seemed like a good person, and if Paul really had his mind set on something, there was nothing she could have done to stop him. More than once she looked like she was going to cry. More than once she gave me that look, like she was seeing Paul again. In the end she thanked me again for coming all the way to Prague, said talking with me had helped her more than I knew. Then she put on her coat and walked out the café, giving me one more hesitant glance as she disappeared down the stairs. I counted to forty and then got up to follow her.

CHAPTER 8

There's the truth and there's what people tell you. They're like a married couple laughing at each other's jokes in public when privately they've grown so far apart they can barely stand the sight of each other's socks. This assuming there is a truth, verifiable facts. The assumption makes life easier when you're dealing with, say, buying a used car, more difficult when dealing with questions of human motivation. Trickiest of all are the things you tell yourself, which in an ideal world would be outsourced for evaluation to an objective third party before you're allowed to act upon them.

All of which is to say there were a million questions I could've asked Vera, but I knew she had already told me everything she was prepared to share. Anything else I'd have to learn without her consent because as much as I wanted to believe her, she still hadn't answered the two most basic questions. One, why tell anyone that you were involved in an unsolved criminal conspiracy gone murderously awry—and two, why now? She'd written that letter to my father for a reason, and after talking to her for nearly three hours over the last couple days, I was no closer to finding out what that reason was.

After stepping outside she had taken out her phone and made a call, but she hadn't let the conversation slow her stride as she slipped through the throngs crowding the sidewalk. I'd nearly lost her when a bunch of Brits came stumbling drunkenly out of some bar at the corner of Vodičkova and was trailing some fifty feet behind her as we entered Můstek station. As I approached the ticket machine kiosk, I watched the top of her head disappear down the escalator. Stop to buy a train ticket and I'd risk losing her.

I walked right past the turnstile and hopped on the escalator, expecting beeping, sirens, some official someone putting a hand upon my shoulder, but nothing happened. Below the tube, walls were decorated in anodized steel a champagne color that made you feel like you were inside a Christmas ornament. The platform was crowded, and I took up a position just behind a marbled column, safely outside of Vera's sightlines. She rarely looked up from playing with her phone anyway. When the train came she got on, and I boarded two cars behind her.

Vera had told me she'd lived in Smíchov when Paul was around, but a glance at the subway map plastered above the train's doors told me Smíchov was southwest, on the yellow line. We were travelling northwest on the green line. Either Vera didn't live in Smíchov anymore, or she wasn't headed home. Staroměstská, Malostranská; at each stop I hopped off, looked for Vera, and then hopped back on just as the doors whisked shut, a move which evidently annoyed a woman opposite me with purple boots and a red streaked rooster hairdo like Keith Richards circa 1972. She spent most of the ride glowering at me while managing to completely ignore the teenage couple making out next to her. If the train ride lasted much longer, I might witness the actual conception of a little Czech.

Vera emerged at Hradčanská station. When I exited too, she started walking right towards me. She'd spotted me. She knew I was following her and was going to confront me, make a big scene right here on the train platform, probably scream "stalker!" or worse in Czech until the police came and hauled me off. Except that she hadn't noticed me yet. Everyone was walking my way. The only exit was located behind me. Ducking behind a column and circling behind Vera seemed too risky so I turned and rushed toward the escalator, trying to put some distance between us.

The ride up was excruciatingly slow. When I reached the street level I practically started running, a bad move as it attracted the attention of one of three guys dressed in black uniforms hanging out by the newspaper kiosk near the exit. Ticket inspectors. Two of them were already hassling some college kids, both of whom where digging around their backpacks and baggy pants in a transparent pantomime. The third one zeroed in on me. He stepped forward just as I was about to pass and held up a hand in the international hold-it-right-there gesture. Only when the rooster-maned redhead in purple boots unleashed a torrent of grievances did I realize the hand wasn't meant for me.

The darkening sky was crosshatched with tram cables and the rain had picked up, cars and trucks splashing by on either side of a narrow concrete strip where people stood waiting for trams and buses, looking miserable. It was oddly quiet outside the tourist zone, like being in another city entirely. I ducked behind a payphone and Vera emerged a moment later. She made another call with her cell, dialing and putting it to her ear, but she didn't appear to say anything. Could be the other party never answered, could be she was just checking messages. A tram pulled up and she slipped her phone back into her pocket and queued to board. I opted for the car behind her and got a window seat so I'd be able to see when she exited. We were on tramline 18, somewhere north of the city center and on the left bank of the river, but that was as precise as I could figure it. The tram could have been headed to some distant suburb for all I knew.

She got off at a stop called Ořechovka. With only three other people exiting, there was no crowd to blend into. I just had to hope she didn't see me. Luckily it wasn't the sort of weather for taking a leisurely stroll and having a look about. She tucked her chin to her chest and hurried through a gap in traffic across Střešovická Street. I watched her turn down a smaller street called Lomená, letting some distance build before I followed. If she saw me now, I'd just be some blurred figure across the road.

She kept up her hurried pace, staying on Lomená and marching past street names I tried to note for the way back. Západní, Cukrovarnická, Na Orechovce. Gone were the crowded, crooked ancient lanes where edifices crammed leaning one into the next. Here were empty sidewalks and high concrete security walls enclosing brick villas, estates, mansions replete with sloping green lawns lush with trees and shrubbery. I'd read apartments in the city center had price tags comparable to those in New York, and if that was true then maybe this was like the exclusive Connecticut suburb. Whatever the case, Vera's quarter of the Rudolf Complication money couldn't have bought a home here. Her portion and my brother's combined probably wouldn't have been enough.

Pondering the unknowns of the local real-estate market jarred loose a thought that should have occurred to me much earlier. Ever since I'd heard about the watch theft and the existence of Martinko Klingáč, I'd assumed that he killed Paul so he wouldn't have to pay him his cut. But then if he already had the watch, why torture Paul? I'd theorized Klingáč wanted to know the identity of the third conspirator, but I hadn't reasoned out why. To tie up loose ends? To keep an eye on her in case it looked like she might talk to the cops?

I hadn't considered the most obvious reason.

Paul didn't have the watch. Vera did.

By the time Martinko Klingáč had caught up with my brother, he'd already ditched the watch with Vera for safekeeping. Maybe as an assurance that he got paid. Or maybe they had just plain double-crossed Klingáč, had stolen the thing without ever intending to pass it on. They would sell it themselves, keep all the profits, double their money.

Vera stopped in front of a white, three-story, many-gabled house guarded on either side by twin pine trees rising above the obligatory red tiled roof. A BMW motored past as Vera stood outside the gate and punched her code into a keypad mounted on the fence. Amber lights blazed from inside the large picture window on the first floor, and I saw a fleeting silhouette move behind the glass as Vera closed the wrought iron gate behind her and started walking up the entryway. I hurried to the other side of the street for a better view.

Just as she was walking up the stairs, the front door swung open and a child rushed out. The kid was maybe five or six years old, barefoot and dressed in his pajamas. Vera chirped some mild admonishment, he giggled, and then she scooped him up in her arms. His face shone over her shoulder and even through the rain, from a distance of some thirty yards, I knew. Same broad nose, same mischievous turn to his lips. It was so much like looking at an old Polaroid that I half expected to find my younger self in the frame, posed next to my little brother in a snap button shirt and Tuffskins jeans from Sears circa 1977.

She carried the boy inside and pulled the door closed and then all was silence and stillness save for the pines moving in the breeze, their heavy limbs undulating as if dancing to secret music. Then a car roared up and came to a splashing halt beside me, and the driver rolled down the window and stuck out his head, red eyes bulging, teeth grinding inside his mouth so hard for a time he couldn't speak. He didn't need to. The first floor lights in a white house on a quiet corner of Lomená Street went off, and I stepped from the sidewalk, opened the car door, and slid inside.

· *The Cruel Geometry of Zugzwang—Part II* ·

March 13, 1938

My Dearest Klara,

You excelled at the abrupt departure, taking even your ultimate leave with but a few indiscriminate words, a parting to fit your lifelong abhorrence of the sentimental, the maudlin, that urge to say things more powerfully left unsaid. For me goodbyes have always been an agonizing, drawn out exchange, and I fear this farewell may yet grow more tortured.

And so let us now resume with my haggard face pressed to the smoked glass of my shop window, as I watch Doctor Kačak tottering down the street, afraid that any moment he will change his mind, reverse course, and come back toward me with his crippled spider's gait. Let us begin as he finally rounds the corner and I retreat from the window. Let us commence as I carefully swaddle the watch in its velvet cloth and steal down the groaning backstairs to the cellar that acts as my workshop, storeroom, and sanctuary, a cluttered enclosure that makes the shop's main floor appear a cheery paragon of organization and restraint.

Let you find me in the cellar where rickety shelves line damp stone walls, where rows of forgotten books form a vast mildew farm and cobweb skeins cling to every corner (curiously, I've seen neither spider nor fly in all my time there—perhaps they've fled to be with spider and fly relations in America). Upon the floor are strewn decaying wooden crates crammed with a hodgepodge of rolled maps, cases of old Victrola records, forgotten musical scores, rolls for player pianos. From a bent nail in the wall hangs an eighteenth-century rare Spanish Miquelet flintlock pistol. Broken gramophone, bladeless ice-skates, chipped Meissen figurines, brass candelabra, jar of preserved fetal pig, box of mousetraps, box of better mousetraps; for the thousandth time I pledged all must be gotten rid of lest they start crossbreeding and multiplying. Except now it appears they will remain while I'm the one who'll be gotten rid of.

But my narrative outraces my pen.

When Doctor Kačak had unveiled the piece, it was the exquisitely crafted ivory inset of the White Lion which first alerted me, nay, grabbed my lapels, shook me bodily, and roared, Wake man! Raise the alarms and rouse the guards, for I am no ordinary watch! Now in the privacy of my cellar, I am able to inspect it unencumbered, without fear that my mounting enthusiasm may betray me.

The watch's shape is the first sign of its authenticity, its tambour cylinder housing typical of watches made in the latter half of the sixteenth century. I find no anachronisms in the works—there is no minute hand, and the fusee cord consists of catgut rather than miniature drive chains. The escapement is of the verge rather than anchor, deadbeat, or lever variety and uses a primitive balance wheel but no balance spring. No suspect alloys, the delicate gears fashioned from hand-cut steel and everything held in place by pins and rivets rather than screws. Closing the watch's casement and turning it over, I discover upon its rear surface the obsidian symbol I almost dared not hope to find.

The self-consuming snake. The Ouroboros.

I re-swaddle the piece and set it down on my workbench as if delivering an infant into the arms of sleep. I need no further proof but still race to the bookshelf and scan the dusty leather and cracked vellum spines of my library until I've found Curiousities of Late Medieval Horology. Scarce do I begin thumbing through its yellowed pages of when my eyes land on the description in mid-sentence:

" . . . though many believe the ivory lion engraving on the watch's case had special significance for Rudolf II. Court astronomer Tycho Brahe had prophesized that Rudolf's fate was tied to that of his favorite pet lion, a declawed and toothless beast given to him by the Sultan of Turkey. An inventory of the Kunstkammer completed in 1595 also describes the case as featuring an inset of the 'Ouroboros'—the Greek name given to the circular symbol of a serpent swallowing its own tail, which alchemists used to represent infinity and primordial unity.

"Beyond its rumored link to nefarious court charlatan Edward Kelley, the origins and authorship of the Rudolf Complication remain murky. Jacob Zech, inventor of the fusee in 1525, likely had no role in its creation, though we can't rule out a skilled apprentice. Jost Bürgi is another name often put forth, but the Rudolf Complication predates the Prague arrival of the clockmaking genius and algorithm inventor by some years. If surviving accounts of the piece are to be trusted, the Rudolf Complication also far surpasses in miniaturization any known work by famed Rudolf contemporary Christof Margraf.

"Its ultimate fate remains murkier still. After Rudolf died in 1612, the unrivaled collection of art, esoteria, and naturalia that made up his 'Cabinet of Curiousities' was systematically looted over the next 150 years. His hated brother and successor Mathias took many of the treasures to Vienna, new seat of the Hapsburg Empire. Following the Battle of White Mountain, Bavarian conquerors hauled away some 1,500 additional wagonloads of precious works. During the Thirty Years' War, Rudolf's elderly Kunstkammer guardian, Dionisio Miseroni, was tortured into giving up the keys to occupying Swedes in 1648. What little the Swedes left behind was auctioned off by order of Emperor Joseph II in 1781. Unsold items were unceremoniously dumped into the Vltava River below the Hradčany, and the space which once housed perhaps the largest and most varied collection of art the world had yet seen was henceforth used as a storehouse for gun powder and cannonballs.

"As with so many of Rudolf's treasures, the whereabouts of the Rudolf Complication are unknown to this day. Sadly, this treasure must be presumed lost to history."

Emperor Rudolf II stares out from the page opposite, eyes hooded, wide, Hapsburg chin jutting above a disc of white frills orbiting his neck while the watch dangles at the end of its golden chain a gaudy albatross. A clever forger could have used this very portrait as a model of the watch now before me, but only the most diligent cheat would have known about the black serpent on the reverse side of the case.

I clap the book shut. Ouroboros or no ouroboros, the final, surefire method of verifying that Doctor Kačak's watch is the genuine Complication is to pry the back casing open and find the hidden clock face where time runs backwards, just as on the Hebrew clock adorning the Jewish Town Hall mere blocks from my shop.

Happily, I discover the complication intact, an ingenious reverse geometry built to send the indicator dial spinning the wrong way around the hidden face. In watches of this era, the movement was typically somewhere signed by its creator, but in keeping with its unknown origins, no signature is etched thereupon. Perhaps the watchmaker had a knack for self-preservation. The piece was, after all, delivered to Rudolf II under the pretense that it would give him eternal life. And when Rudolf eventually noticed that he was still getting older, still getting sicker, someone would be made to pay.

Two curious markings do appear etched in miniature upon the winding key, which Doctor Kačak has left in its arbor slot. Seemingly Hebrew symbols of some sort, they might as well be Egyptian hieroglyphs as far as this would-be Jew was concerned. Perhaps Grandfather Weil, wellspring of my pending racial impurity, could have transliterated the eldritch markings, but I find myself at a loss. The *important thing is that the key is there at all—had Doctor Kačak truly wished to prevent me from stopping the piece while I repaired it and then just winding when the work was complete, he need only have withheld the key.*

And so I set to work, opening the frontspiece to access the forward-turning half of the inner workings. The problem is readily apparent—the fusee cord is in tatters, scarcely enough catgut left to link the mainspring and escapement much less preserve the tension necessary to govern the watch's speed. Before removing the cord, I spend time digging through various boxes and drawers trying to find appropriate repair materials, mindful that replacing it with a length of wire would be simpler but may lower the piece's resale value when I take the Complication overseas (though perhaps I'm granting American antiquarians higher powers of discernment than they in fact possess). In the end I settle on an old lute string. It's not ideal, but the width and tension seem adequate.

But when trying to unhitch the old cord from the mainspring barrel, I find it too tightly attached. Forced to ignore Doctor Kačak's absurd instructions, I remove the mainspring itself, which will stop the watch movement. I'm inspecting the fusee and gauging the width of its spiral grooves (I know, Klara, that the minutiae of watch repair would bore you to death were you not dead already, but I go into such detail only to demonstrate that I have done nothing out of the ordinary) when it occurs to me that something quite extraordinary is happening.

The escapement is still working.

The tiny drive train gears of the Complication are still spinning. For several moments I listen to the half-dissembled watch tick as I stare dumbly at the piece, searching its exposed machinery for some hidden drive mechanism. Perhaps the backward spinning of the secondary, reverse mainspring somehow also propels the forward workings through a hidden cross-beat escapement? But even with epicyclic gearing—well, I'll cut to the quick.

The watch should not be working.

But it is working.

Each tick and every tock an affront to my expertise.

A mockery of the laws of physics.

An horological miracle.

At this my thoughts turn to God's Miracle, and I realize I've completely forgotten his supper. He will be up on the third floor, wondering what has happened to The Man Who Brings Him Food at Nighttime, and eventually he might make his way down the stairs and into my workshop, though he knows I won't allow him to enter. His clumsiness has cost me in the past.

Reluctantly I leave the impossibly ticking watch and make my way upstairs, sure that when I return with fresh eyes, the mechanism will be obvious. The ascent is one I must have made thousands of times since moving into this building. Up winding stairs to the apartment, down winding stairs to the shop, spiraling further to the cellar, helixing back up to the apartment, my world increasingly restricted to airless and corkscrewed vertical terrain. This is how your husband spends his days now. Up and down, down and up, serving as his own rickety dumb waiter until the end of time.

But Franz is not upstairs, which means he must still be wandering the streets. It often happens that he loses track of time, and so once again I must go hunt him down. Outside the wind keens and the streetlamps cast their dull penumbra. In the houses along my street, a few scattered lights glow opaque behind curtains, but most neighbors haven't bothered removing the blackout paper from their windows, measures taken when defense rather than surrender seemed imminent, and the city sought to cloak itself from the Luftwaffe. Now the blackout materials appear to issue a silent plea on behalf of their owners—take the country if you must, but let us sleep undisturbed behind darkened windows and heavy doors; let us withdraw into limitless interiors. Wake us when all your history making is done.

Walking in ever-widening circles for nearly forty minutes, I am unable to locate Franz until I reach the banks of the river near the Cechlův bridge. There at last I discover him in the company of a small girl. Both are laughing hysterically for reasons fathomable to only the young and the cerebrally compromised, but the girl stops laughing abruptly as I approach. No more than seven or eight years old, she is clad in a moth-eaten red dress; her face is fixed in an expression beyond her years as she twirls a grubby lock of hair around a grubby finger. She is no doubt one of the recent émigrés The Little Mustache has thrust upon us, and wherever she has fled from must be a desolate place. Never mind a coat, the wretch hasn't even shoes. And when she smiles, I can't help but recoil. The wretch hasn't even teeth.

Before I can inquire after her parents she is already gone, moving down the street with a disquieting sense of purpose, as if late for an appointment with her bank manager. Franz laughs all the way home. The sound scatters sparrows from the trees.

When we finally arrive suppertime has long since passed. While Franz sits at the table, I prepare rolls and a simple soup. No sooner is the meal complete than I turn to find God's Miracle face down, arms sprawled across the small dining room table. He looks somehow even larger when asleep, his body uncoiling from its inward slouch, shoulders loosened, limbs expanding in repose. The peaceful tableau is mitigated by his usual snore, an industrial cacophony of some machine beyond repair.

As he sleeps my mind turns to last May when a regimental commander came pounding at our apartment door, demanding that one Private Franz Murcek immediately report to his garrison for re-mobilization. I was about to spit in the man's face when Franz came lumbering into the room in his tattered army coat, braying and clapping his meaty hands. The chastened commander sized up the situation at once, apologized for intruding, and, before retreating down the stairs, congratulated me on having a son worthy of so many high military honors.

The medals are still there now, pinned willy-nilly all over Franz's filthy jacket. Their original owners often parted with them for less than the equivalent of two drinks at the Twice Slaughtered Lamb. In the twenty years since the Great War has ended, I have bestowed upon Franz the War Cross, the Commemorative Cross, the Medal of the Revolution, the Žižka Medal, the Order of the Sokol, and even the Order of the White Lion, making our son surely the most decorated soldier in all of Czechoslovakia. He seems to enjoy the way they jingle, how they twinkle in the light.

I saw my pipe and gaze out the window.

Beneath Franz's snoring, I begin to detect the faintest echo of another sound. A low, dull, quick sound like a muted heartbeat. I try to locate its source, but it doesn't seem to being coming from anywhere in the room. I cup my hand to the wall. The unwavering rhythm grows louder. The White Lion medal pinned to Franz's shoulder glints in lamplight, and I flash to the miniature ivory heraldic on Doctor Kačak's watch and realize what I am hearing.

Rudolf II's watch, of course.

Doctor Kačak's watch. My watch.

The Murcek Complication.

Across the room, Franz wakes with a start, hopping to his feet and swiveling his head in wide-eyed alarm. When he spots me his features slur into a grin, and he wipes the spittle from his chin. Call me a sentimentalist, but it warms my heart to know Franz is still comforted by my presence. How many fathers of my age are still needed by their sons? How many of my generation needed by the world at all?

"Report to bed, private," I say.

Ever the disciplined soldier, Franz ignores the sound, rises dutifully, and thumps down the hallway, lurching into his room and collapsing into bed without removing his boots. We bachelors have become more eccentric in habit and appearance in your absence, Klara. Let the outside world keep up its regimented charade of order and progress, see where it leads them. I pocket my pipe, walk down the hallway, and gently close the door on God's Miracle.

The ticking continues unabated. When I attempt to relight my pipe, I can't concentrate for the sound reverberating throughout the apartment. It has now grown loud enough to eclipse God's Miracle's freshly resumed snoring.

And then I realize it's not a ticking at all.

It's a knocking sound.

There is someone downstairs, rapping at the door to Murcek's Curios and Antiquities. My heart leaps throat-ward and my mind fixes on an image of Doctor Kačak tilted against the wind, wisps of silver hair dancing behind him as he beats the golden bear's head cane handle against the door with inhuman, metronomic precision. He has come because he has changed his mind. He has sensed my intentions. He is here to reclaim the Complication.

I move across the floor, extinguishing lights as I pass, and edge up against the window frame. With the store awning directly beneath my window, I can't even see the street below much less any figure who may be standing outside the door. I hold my breath and press my palms to my ears but it only amplifies the sound. The knocker will not go away.

It's impossible to say how the idea of killing Dr. Kačak first enters my brain, but once conceived, it's as if the notion had been there all along, just waiting to be discovered. I'm sure this revelation shocks you, Klara, but I have suffered enough cruel luck for one lifetime, only to have a last-minute reprieve fall into my lap. They say there is nothing so dangerous as hope, and maybe it's true because whereas only yesterday I was a hopeless but peaceful man, as I listen to the endless rapping, I know I'm prepared to do anything to protect the one chance Franz and I have left.

I will invite the doctor into the shop under the pretense of letting him warm up inside while I fetch the watch and return his deposit — disappointed at losing the commission, but understanding nonetheless. One good blow to the head with my weapon of choice and I can then drag him into the basement and finish the deed using any number of implements.

I scan the room for a suitable weapon, debating the merits of the butcher knife versus the heavy iron fire poker. In the end, I snatch up the fire poker, gauging the weapon's heft as I descend the stairs in time to the thumping at the door. As I get closer I detect another noise, a twinned sound of the Complication ticking in perfect time to the Doctor Kačak's rapping. Obviously he can also hear its ticking, even outside amidst the howling wind, and is making a show of keeping time with his treasure. The thought realizes itself ridiculous, but no more ridiculous than its thinker creeping down the stairs, fire poker in hand, poised to murder a stranger.

The glass eye of a mounted boar's head winks in the dark as I enter the shop and move toward the entrance. Behind my back my right hand grips the fire poker tight, my own thudding heartbeat now filling in the caesuras between the hammering from the other side and the ticking down below. I undo the lock and open the door.

A blast of inrushing wind nearly blinds me. For a moment I can make out only a silhouette, the form of a half-slumped man leaning forward, one arm braced against the doorframe. He raises his head and his eyes seek mine in the dark.

"Uncle Jan," the man says. Even with the wind, the smell of alcohol is overpowering. Our nephew Max tries to stand unaided and totters back a step before righting himself. Eyes glassy and distant, grin wet and smeared across his face, he's evidently been celebrating his chess victory ever since we parted at the Black Rabbit earlier this evening. "Did I wake you? I knocked as softly as I could. So soft, so soft. Did I wake Franz?"

My grip, my whole body loosens.

"What the devil are you doing?" I ask, pulling him inside. As I close the door he notices the fire poker I still hold in my right hand and lets out a laugh, freeing himself from my hold.

"When they come knocking you'll need more than that."

"You're drunk. What is it you want?"

"Why aren't you drunk? Why isn't everybody?" His head swivels loose on his shoulders as he takes in the shop inventory with a look of bemused disapproval. "You've become an old fool. I'm here to beg you anyway. Come with me. I won't ask again."

"There's no need. I've decided we'll go."

"I'm not going to debate you," he slurs, the alcohol stoppering his ears even as it strengthens his resolve. "The train leaves Wilson station the day after tomorrow. I've tickets for both you and Franz. I'll be waiting on the platform. And then I'll be on the train. And I then I will be gone."

He presses an envelope into my hand.

Once again I labor to explain that I've already made the decision to join him on this hair-brained expedition to America and that his besotted theatrics are as unbecoming as they are unnecessary, but he dismisses my words with a clumsy wave and yanks open the front door. "One other thing," he mumbles, his coat tails flapping in the wind. "There was a way out."

"What are you talking about?"

"This afternoon. In our match. You weren't beaten, not yet. There was a way out. Only you didn't see it. You know why?"

I nodded only because he'd tell me anyway.

"Because there is something in you that wants to lose, Uncle Jan. Something that yearns to be punished. And if you stay, you will lose. You'll lose everything."

With this he turns and rambles down the street without even bothering to close the door, leaving me standing on my shop floor holding train tickets in one hand and a fire poker in the other. A fresh gust of arctic air brings me to my senses, and I close the door.

The ticking sound has abated.

Maybe it was never there to begin with.

To begin with, beginnings, endings—I'm afraid I have once again failed to bring my farewell to a conclusion or even a suitable commencement. There is much more to tell, and in its telling I am racing to the end of me, even as I resist it.

Ever yours,
Jan

CHAPTER 9

■

The ex-detective Soros was wearing a stocking cap pulled down to his eyebrows, and his eyes beneath were bleary and red-rimmed in the rearview mirror as he ripped his tin can Skoda around the corner of the quiet residential street and merged onto the wider Střešovická. I was sitting in the back, taxicab style, but had no choice since the front seat was awash with papers. The car doubled as his office. Right Hand of God investigatory headquarters on wheels. I guess I should've been grateful he'd shown up when he did because the rain was coming down hard now, the sound like fevered applause as it pounded the roof of the car. For a while Soros didn't speak, preferring to roll his tongue around the inside of his mouth like a good opening line was located somewhere between his cheek and gum if only he could find it.

"You follow Vera," he said. "Why?"

"All due respect, it doesn't really concern you."

He growled something in Czech and leaned into the horn. A small truck in the road ahead of us was carrying a payload of unsecured copper pipes that rolled and bounced around in the back. One good bump, they'd come spearing through our windshield.

"Titass fuck thieves," Soros cursed. "You think those metal are belong to them? Last month they steal a bridge in Chleb. Whole fucking bridge—poof! Gone, taken for metal. Cockeats, from the mouth of their dog mothers they would steal teeth. Why do you follow Vera Svobodova?"

"I might ask you the same," I said. "Or are you following me?"

He reached in his pocket, extracted a bottle.

"Becherovka?" he offered.

"What's it, some kind of liquor?"

"No, magic piss. From the goat who is fucks on your sister. You want or no?"

I chose the latter. He unscrewed the cap, took a swig, and tucked it back into his jacket pocket. The stuff smelled like cough medicine mixed with grain alcohol. A Tweety Bird air freshener dangling from the rearview mirror did a jaunty little dance as Soros yanked the steering wheel sideways and hit the accelerator. Empty beer cans rattled around the car. As we pulled beside the truck carrying the supposed thieves, Soros rolled down the window and half climbed out, rain pelting his face as he spat obscenities at them. He looked like some crazed mariner chained to the helm of his ship, barking at the heavens, but I don't think the two guys inside the truck even noticed. Moments later, Soros sank back into his seat and rolled the window back up with one hand and wiped the rain from his face with the other, leaving the car to steer itself for a moment. Just as well. The car wasn't drinking Becherovka.

"Vera is not the person you think." He wrapped his hands around the wheel again. "You are in danger, man. Big danger. Today a man is attacked in Malá Strana. Beaten and thrown out a window. The police they find him under a wheelbarrow. Hiding from this man who tries to kill him."

I almost started laughing with relief. The curator was alive.

"The man suffers from a coma now," Soros said.

"Is it a bad coma, or—"

"No, good coma! Big tit coma!" spat Soros. "This man works at an art gallery. You know who works there five years ago? Vera Svobodova. She has a file. Criminal record. Friend with the police, he gets it for me. Drugs. Drug dealing. Big drug ring."

"When was this?"

"First we must be friends. Tell me of her, we can be friends. If no, fuck on you."

"I think you're barking up the wrong tree."

"What tree? How I am fucking like bark up a tree?"

"I don't think she's your killer. And I don't think she attacked anyone today."

"The man who does this," Soros slowly growled, "is the cock-fuck who is killed your brother. The gallery where this coma man is attacked? Today I learn it's five years ago robbed. During the flood, just before your brother disappears. Art stolen. Big art stolen. You know of the Rudolf Complex?"

"Complication. You left the booklet in my hotel."

"What booklet?"

So it wasn't him. And it wasn't Vera.

Unless he was lying. But then why would he be?

"Maybe you should drop me off. I get car sick."

"Did already you speak to Bob Hannah?"

"No," I lied. Because if I said I had, he'd want to know what we talked about, and I'd have to tell him the journalist thought he was mad as a hatter and that I agreed. Then I'd have to explain what mad as a hatter meant.

"We go to see Bob Hannah now," said Soros. "Talk like friends. Tell to me his address."

"I don't know his address."

"Address it's on card I give you."

"I don't have the card."

He locked eyes with me in the rearview. "Fuck on me. No card?"

"I left it at the hotel."

His tongue started probing the inside of his mouth again. He didn't believe me. Whether his distrust was based on anything more than general principle, I couldn't tell. How much had his police friends told him about the art gallery curator?

"We go to his apartment," Soros said. He started rifling through loose papers on the front seat, came up with a bent yellow sticky note. "Na bojišti 8 #414, Prague 2," he read. "We go. Have big talk. Make big friends."

Soros took another swig of Becherovka then tossed the bottle over his shoulder. It missed my head by inches, bounced off the headrest next to me then tumbled down the seat and landed in the empty beer cans with a clatter.

"Sorry," said Soros. "I forget you are there."

"What do you say we pull over? Wait out the rain."

He shook his head. "We see Bob Hannah. This man with a coma, police in his pocket find a business card. Card of Bob Hannah. Like the one I give to you. We find out how this card got to the man in coma. All of us talk like big friends."

"Isn't this something the police should handle?"

"I am police. Once police, always police."

Ahead gaped the large mouth of a tunnel. I guessed we were headed south, but couldn't be sure. Just before we went underground my phone started buzzing inside my pants pocket. I slipped it out and checked the caller ID.

BOB HANNAH.

Speak of the devil.

Soros was squinting at me through the mirror. He'd heard the phone. If I didn't answer it, he'd just get even more suspicious. "Jackasses in marketing," I stage muttered, making a show of staring daggers into the phone. "Leave for a couple days, fuck-sticks can't find their dicks to piss with." My words sounded nothing like me. Apparently Soros's swearing was contagious. I clicked open the phone and put it to my ear.

"Sorry to bother you," Hannah said.

"No bother, Jimmy."

"No, this is Bob. Bob Hannah. Is this a bad time?"

"Having a great time. Good food, great people over here."

"I wouldn't call if it wasn't urgent."

"I'm in a car, Jimmy. Going into a tunnel."

"I can hear you fine. Can you hear me?"

"Absolutely. With you one hundred percent. In a car."

He puzzled through it. "Whose car are you in?"

"Yes, we covered that issue earlier."

Silence for a moment. "Are you with Soros?"

"That's the ticket, Jimbo."

"What are you doing with him?"

"Just shoot me the text on over."

"Can he hear you?"

Inside the tunnel it was eerily quiet without the rain pounding the cab roof, so quiet I worried Soros could make out every word Hannah said. There were disadvantages to everybody knowing English when you couldn't speak a second language. Maybe my brother had been onto something with that Klingon idea.

"Just shoot me the text," I said.

"I'll make this quick," replied Hannah, not taking my text message hint. "Our chat earlier had me curious. I talked to that journalist friend of mine, the one from *Mladá fronta*. Turns out our detective didn't lose his job over your brother's case. He was dismissed over something that happened when he was StB back in the day. Secret police."

"That's an interesting development."

The tunnel lights turned Soros's face a sallow green and revealed a network of broken capillaries pulsing and spreading across his face like some cruel time-lapse montage. I had to look away to concentrate on what Hannah was saying.

"Yes and no," said Hannah. "Lots of police came from the StB. Police, politicians, entertainers, priests—everyone had ties to the StB. Half the country was busy informing on the other half. But our detective was no mere informant nor StB thug. He was a ranking officer of the most feared institution in the country. Details on exactly what he did are murky, but something in his past spooked someone bad."

The ex-detective and former StB man kept his eyes on mine in the mirror. I was practically shoving the phone up my ear canal in hopes of muffling Hannah's voice. If Soros had bothered to turn off the windshield wipers when we entered the tunnel he probably would've heard everything. As it was they screeched and whined against the glass, adding another layer of dissonance.

"It gets worse," Hannah continued. "Not only was Soros's dismissal unrelated to your brother's supposed murder—your brother hadn't even gone missing when it happened. Soros left the police in 1999."

"This news is not good, Jim."

"It gets worse."

Bob Hannah then told me how ex-detective Soros hadn't just sat around collecting his pension and obsessing about the Right Hand of God after leaving the force nearly a decade ago. Instead, he'd spent time working as a black sheriff. "Private security," Hannah explained, "thugs protecting bigger thugs. His boss was a Slovakian gangster. Con man, pornographer, drug dealer, pimp, arsonist, kidnapper, murderer. A trafficker of women and stealer of identities. Then he vanished. Just like that. The ÚOOZ— they're the national organized crime unit here, like the FBI—they don't even have a photograph of the guy."

"This party have a name?"

"Martinko Klingáč. A pseudonym. Means—"

"Rumpelstiltskin."

Soros's head jerked as if in recognition. We rocketed out of the tunnel and the rain came slamming down on all sides. Hannah said his journalist friend had dug up some documents I might be interested in seeing. He'd be home for the next couple hours if I wanted to come by and pick them up.

As he started to give me his address, I should have found some way to warn the journalist that the StB-turned-police-turned-black-sheriff and I were at that very moment headed his way, and maybe he ought to leave in a hurry. I should have told him that if the Prague police hadn't been in touch yet, they soon would be, because his business card had wound up in the pocket of a comatose art gallery curator.

But I never got the chance.

Soros had turned half around in his seat now, eyes glassy slits, mouth clamped in a shriveled hyphen, and I saw the shape ahead before he did.

In the middle of the road, maybe sixty feet distant, a small figure in red.

A little girl with a hackwork of stringy wet hair.

I pointed and yelled, and Soros just kept glaring and the car just kept careening towards her. She must've been crossing the intersection against the light, but now she was just planted in the middle of our lane, frozen by the onrushing headlights, dress dripping wet and hair plastered over her face. She opened her mouth to scream and revealed an expanse of black.

I reached over Soros shoulder and yanked the wheel hard left. The car lurched sideways, my shoulder slamming against the inside of the door, head connecting with the window a split second later with a dull crack before my body was sent sailing into the opposite door as Soros wrestled the wheel back from me.

I didn't know if we'd hit the girl or not. There was no time to wonder. We veered off the road, and I ducked and covered and heard splashing and screaming and brakes squealing and then felt a sudden weightlessness as I pitched forward. Then all sound disappeared. Time slowed. I was on a spacewalk, floating over the backseat as my shoulder dipped and my body rolled. Beer cans drifted slowly in the air around me. *Prague Unbound* came tumbling right past my head, the embossed gold lettering on its cover appearing to glow as it caught the light. Then my back slammed against the windshield and time stopped altogether.

· *The Cruel Geometry of Zugzwang – Part III* ·

March 14, 1938

My Dearest Klara,

The closer I get to saying goodbye, the more the moment seems to recede. A poet you admired (there were so many) once wrote that each second holds its own eternity, and maybe now I begin to understand his meaning. As I pen yet another farewell, time seems to move as if governed by the Rudolf Complication, backwards and forwards at once, resolution getting closer each moment yet remaining tantalizingly beyond reach. But this shall truly be the last farewell. Resolution is now at hand.

There is much to say. I'm not sure I can make the events comprehensible to you when even to their very author they seem fantastic, a progression governed by murky, unprincipled logic, but in recounting what has befallen me, perhaps some order shall reveal itself. I am doubtful.

We begin once more in my cellar. Having slept poorly after Max's drunken visit, I awoke still resolved to abscond with the Rudolf Complication and throw myself and God's Miracle at the mercy of America. My morning is spent trying in vain to discover what hidden mechanism has kept the watch in motion since I removed the fusee cord and mainspring.

The watch seems to be ticking more slowly now, a hypothesis I test against my modest wristwatch. Precise measurements are impossible as the Rudolf Complication has no minute hand, but there can be no doubt that the piece is losing in excess of ten minutes an hour. By my calculations, it shall cease functioning sometime early this evening. But then it should not be ticking at all. Not with half itself removed.

I'm no closer to discovering its secret, so on it ticks as I sit in my cellar, tinkering and worrying. I haven't bothered to open the shop and would hazard its closure shall go unnoticed among our fine citizens. Business has been poor. Antiques remind people of the past, and the only thing less popular than the past at present is the future. Children in gas masks, air raid shelters being dug in the parks, what kind of future can this be? For months people have been shuffling down the streets with stitched brows and wooden faces, thinking only of the war that's coming, the war that's over, the war that's already lost.

And yet my thoughts are of the future. Tomorrow we'll be leaving on a 9 AM train to Holland. From the coastal town of Flushing, we will make our way to Harwich, England, and then board a freighter ship to New York. Max will no doubt see my capitulation as a great victory, proof of his superior ability to peer into the shadowy crystal ball of Europe's future (I must bring the chessboard to ensure his sense of victory doesn't last across the Atlantic).

God's Miracle and I shall wash up on the shores of America, a two-man huddled mass. I'll need help, of course, to find a proper buyer for the Complication once we arrive, but I doubt it shall prove insurmountable. Even in these dark times, that country is said to compensate in wealth what it lacks in culture, and surely any self-respecting Vanderbilt or Carnegie or Rockefeller couldn't turn down a one-of-a-kind, late sixteenth century timepiece once worn by the Holy Roman Emperor himself. A watch not only preserved in its original condition but, miraculously, in complete working order. One lucky windfall, and Franz and I will live off the profits until the end of our days. Maybe there will even be something to spare for our meddlesome nephew Max. My ship has taken a long time to right its course, but at last it seems to be sailing towards providence.

Or so I believe until ten o'clock this morning, when my thoughts are bludgeoned into silence by a terrible racket above.

Crack! Crack! Crack!

Someone is knocking at the door of the shop, and it's not the measured rapping of our drunken nephew. My guilty conscience knows who it is, who it has to be. Crack crack crack, the cane rattling the whole building. I throw on my coat and make my way up the groaning staircase, trying to will my craggy features into a mask of innocence and servility as I stroll across the shop and throw open the door.

Doctor Kačak's shadow blackens the doorframe, his narrow body like an upright coffin. The cold air carries him and his sickly odor inside, and he shambles past me, only beginning to speak once he has clip-clop hobbled into the center of the shop.

"A change of plans" he announces. "I shall be travelling sooner than anticipated. I will be leaving the country by train at nine in the morning tomorrow."

The same time my own train will be leaving.

But then there must be many trains leaving in many directions. If he's fleeing the country, though, it will certainly be from the same Wilson station where Franz, Max, and I shall stage our departure. Scenes from a film unspool in my mind. The tophatted, silver maned doctor spotting our motley party on the platform, eyes set ablaze as he shoots an accusatory finger our way, THIEF!!! intertitled onscreen. The cheeks of a mustachioed policeman ballooning as he blows his whistle. Me cast as villain, my eyes darting in panic. NO ESCAPE!!! flash the intertitles. Franz grinning, dimly excited by the commotion as policemen rush through the crowd, truncheons raised overhead. Max as tragic hero suddenly realizing that he too will be implicated, that all his plans are in ruins. ALL MY PLANS—IN RUINS!

"Nine in the morning?" I parrot weakly.

"The repair must be complete by this evening."

"That may not be possible."

In a single electric movement, he bounds forward and swings his cane in wide arc. I try to avoid the strike but it is too late. My eyes slam shut and teeth gnash anticipating the blow. None comes. When I open my eyes, the polished golden bear handle shimmers inches from my skull. The hard, sunken eyes of Kačak gleam in the gray morning light.

"Then you'll just have to return my watch," he calmly states, dropping his arm and rapping the cane against his false leg for punctuation. "Along with my money, minus a fair sum to compensate you for your time. I'm not an unreasonable man. I would, of course, greatly prefer it if the repair could be completed. If it's a matter of money—well, of course it's a matter of money. It always is with your sort."

"My sort, sir?"

"You're a Jew, are you not?"

"I'm afraid you're mistaken."

"About Jews I'm never mistaken." In swiftly linked movements he removes his stovepipe hat, reaches inside, and produces a thick envelope, which he summarily jams into the waistband of my trousers. His eyes are inches from mine, the malodorous scent of him at such close quarters so pungent I nearly gag. "These funds should speed your progress."

My tongue is a dead thing in my mouth.

"I'll return for the watch this evening," he announces, replacing the hat with a flourish. "You have until 8 PM to complete your work. Don't disappoint me."

Doctor Kačak turns on his heel and hobbles out the door. My eyes fall upon the fire poker, still sitting against the wall where I left it after last night's encounter with Franz. I stare at it for a long time. Then I shove the doctor's money uncounted inside a desk drawer.

Franz has again spent the chilly, sunless afternoon outdoors. Before he left I told him I didn't want him playing with that strange little girl I found in his company yesterday. She looks sickly and may be carrying any number of fearsome diseases. I worry over the fact that God's Miracle wears his keys around his neck (he often manages to lose them nonetheless), and she has the desperate, larcenous face of one fully capable of duping him into handing over the keys in exchange for a bouquet of weeds or a dead mouse.

Whether my warnings register in his divided mind is unknowable. Even if he understood, an hour later he'd be likely to forget my instructions entirely. Besides, the thieves could help themselves for all I cared. Aside from the Complication, some clothes, my pipe, the chessboard, and your photograph, all will be left behind. My own little Kunstkammer to be plundered by conquerors.

Back in the cellar, my diligent work toward discovering what drives the watch movements is rewarded with equal portions zilch and nil. My nerves are frayed and concentration is difficult—there's so much left to do. Packing our bags, settling my meager account at the bank, deciding how to kill Doctor Kačak. If only the man was leaving one day later, if only his train did not depart at the same hour as my own. For all I know he'll be on the very same train, in the very same car. The risk is simply too great, and after Doctor Kačak's show with the cane this morning, I fear a fire poker may be inadequate for the job at hand. Kačak is quick, even with his false leg. He's surely stronger than I am, and something in his manner tells me he is no stranger to physical confrontation. Tells me he would perhaps relish it. I find it difficult to explain why he disturbs me so, whether it's the bruised yellow pallor of his skin, the unyielding expression in his eyes, or even that faint but decidedly foul odor that calls to mind spoiled meat. Maybe its is none of the characteristics he possesses. Maybe it's that essential part of him that seems lacking.

The watch has meanwhile slowed to such a degree that it ticks only once every eight or ten seconds. Less out of any wish to adhere to Doctor Kačak's demands than a desire to make sure my investment shall still *be in working order when we arrive in America, I decide to give the winding key a turn.*

To my astonishment, the key won't budge.

I remove the key and re-insert it in the slot, but the mechanism holds firm, as if fused into place. At a loss, I examine the strange symbols etched in miniature on either side of the key. Perhaps they are not merely decorative but contain some kind of instructions? A warning maybe. "Caveat" on one side, "Furtificus" on the other?

And so to the bookshelves I go, extracting any volumes that might conceivably contain information on Hebrew, Aramaic, Sanskrit, Chinese, Arabic—the eldritch symbols could come from any number of languages living or dead. I tear through my library, scarce discarding one book before I've cracked opened another, painfully aware all the while that such a rudderless expedition into this depthless swamp of quasi-scholarship is wasting precious minutes. The ticking of the watch has grown so irregular now that each time the sound startles me afresh.

Two fruitless hours elapse before I stumble upon an annotated epic poem in a worm-eaten journal published in 1881 by the Department of the Occult Sciences and Speculative Arts at Prague's own Royal and Imperial German Charles Ferdinand University. The poem is called "The Ballad of Edward Kelley," its author the mad poet Otto Rentner—one of your favorites I believe, but then all your favorites were mad.

I wait for the sound of another second passing.

I allow myself to indulge in this poem concerning Irish lowlife Kelley who came to Prague centuries ago—his story is also an immigrant's story, after all, one in which I may find a cautionary lesson—but I am chiefly concerned with a reference to the Enochian Keys, an alphabet reputedly transmitted to Kelley and Dee by an impish spirit called Madimi. This little sprite was said to be six thousand years old but took the form of a small girl when she appeared to them to help unlock the angelic language in use before the Fall of Adam. Herein might be a clue to the symbols on the winding key. My diligence pays off, for in appendix I find reproduced the entire known Enochian language. Pulse quickening, my fingers race through the pages and sure enough, the symbols I seek appear all but leaping from the page. I check them once more against the winding key to be absolutely certain. They match.

One the one side of the key, TELOAH.

Death.

On the other, AZIEN.

Hand.

Death's Hand? The Hand of Death? Fingers of Death? Death Fist? My body trembles with the thrill of discovery, but the fervor soon cools with the realization that this ancient bit of nonsense contributes precisely nothing to helping me unravel the twin mysteries now causing me a high degree of anxiety; the unfathomable ticking, the inoperable winding key.

I soon find myself returned to the ballad, somehow certain that in their stanzas all shall be revealed. Looking at my watch, however, I discover there is no time to pursue it until its end. Doctor Kačak will soon be returning to reclaim the Rudolf Complication, which I realize with sudden alarm has not sounded for over an hour. As if conjured by the very thought, its emits another click, a dull note that rings on and on.

Then an explosion of noise from above.

Someone is banging on the door.

Him, of course.

He's come early, hoping to find me unprepared. I am clearly not to be trusted. And with a sinking feeling, I understand that hours or days later would still find me unprepared for what needs doing. Had I been truly intent on murdering the doctor, would I not have been scheming how best to accomplish the deed rather than losing myself in the long-forgotten saga of John Dee and Edward Kelley?

The man above cries out, calling my name perhaps, cursing me, but it reaches my ears only as a low moan, the words themselves carried away by the wind. I slump over my workbench, listening, waiting. I can't bring myself to go upstairs. His smell, his yellow skin. I stare at the gears of the Rudolf Complication still turning against all physics. Maybe he'll go away. Would it not be plausible that I might've had to leave my shop unattended in order to seek out supplies for the repair? The knocking continues for a few moments longer and then all is silent.

I can't kill the doctor, yet can't risk encountering him tomorrow at the train station. I could leave tonight, Franz and I steal away on any train headed anywhere. I could get word to Max somehow, meet him in Holland or in England before heading to America. This would be entirely feasible had I money, but even with Doctor Kačak's generous advance, I lack funds for lodging and two continental train tickets, all of my other monies tied up in this shop that is to become my mausoleum.

Sometime later Doctor Kačak returns and kicks down the door with a single blow. I hear it crash to the floor above me with a great boom, and dust rains from the ceiling. I leap from my stool, swaddle the watch in its velvet cloth. His footfalls above thunder across the shop's floor.

I slam shut the door adjacent the stairs just as he begins hurtling down them. Hands atremble, I manage to secure the lock before his mass crashes against the door like a cannon shot. Back I stumble, struggling to keep my feet beneath me. Again Doctor Kačak hurls his weight, the knob rattling, wood bulging and groaning. Two, perhaps three such assaults and the door will splinter and he will be upon me.

My eyes flit around the room, scanning for some forgotten window or miraculously appearing exit. Another crash at the door, the walls shiver, the air roils with dust. My eyes fall upon the old Spanish pistol dangling from the bent nail. I can hear Doctor Kačak, his breath coming in animal bursts.

Somewhere is a leather ammunition pouch with gunpowder and three lead shots. For one panicked moment its location escapes me, until

I spot the battered metal footlocker stored beneath the workbench, one filled with Franz's childhood playthings. I snatch the pistol from the wall and rush toward the footlocker. Metal hoops and whipping tops, jackstraws and Jacob's ladders, I rummage through them all before finally discovering the pouch underneath a one-eyed Golliwog doll.

The room shudders with another assault on the door.

I pour the black powder into the muzzle. I drop one cloth-wrapped lead ball inside and remove the thin jamming rod from the underside of the barrel. Packing the shot is an easy matter, not so priming the flash pan. A puppet of Prince Bayaya stares up at me from inside the trunk, wooden grin knifed into his face. The pistol is loaded.

Another crash and a piece of the door splinters loose and clatters to the floor. Gripping the weapon I rise quickly. Too quickly. My legs go wobbly and objects start losing solidity. I reach out to steady myself and lurch through the dusty haze toward the door.

From the other side comes a series of low groans. I now stand directly in front of the stairs, some eight feet back from the door. Through the narrow three-inch slit where a splinter of wood had been dislodged, a flicker of movement. He is preparing another attack. I cock the hammer, take a deep breath, and level the pistol. From this distance there can be no missing.

A rush and the door bursts shattering open and I close my eyes and squeeze the trigger just as the man launches himself into the room. An explosion of sound and a thick black cloud fill the air. The gun's recoil jams my arm up into my shoulder socket, and the man is lifted off the ground and looses a terrible cry. He lands in a heap at my feet and makes no further movement.

The air is heavy with the acrid smell of gunpowder. My ears are ringing, and when I look down and my eyes first land on the shiny little lion glinting through the haze, I think it must be a mistake. The Order of the White Lion. And next to it the Commemorative Cross, the Medal of the Revolution, the Žižka Medal, the Order of the Sokol, all *showing in their dulled glory upon the moth-eaten army jacket. God's Miracle is sprawled arms akimbo, eyes opened and fixed at a point beyond reach.*

He is certainly with you now, Klara. Happy and whole again as you knew him. Now that my farewell letter is nearly complete, I shall be joining you both. In truth, this manner of resolution has occurred to me many times over the years, but I've always resisted. Nothing in this world now remains to keep me from your side.

I had hoped penning these words would allow me some better understanding of what has happened. But there is no understanding. I held Franz in my arms, just as I'd done when he was a child, until he was gone. As I first tried hopelessly to staunch the blood, I couldn't help but notice that his keys were no longer around his neck. He'd lost them and then come knocking. When I didn't answer, he panicked and broke the door down. Perhaps in his disjointed thoughts, he even believed me to be in danger, was coming to rescue his old man. Maybe one day he can tell us both how it happened. Maybe he'll have no memory of it at all. If there is a world better than this one, he'll have forgotten the last twenty odd years.

It is nearly 9 AM. Our nephew Max will be waiting at Wilson station. When Franz and I miss our appointment, perhaps he too shall come calling. I will leave this letter and the others upon the workbench so that he may find them. And Max, if you are reading this now, let me spare a few words to say you were right. Perhaps there was a part of me that yearned to lose everything. And perhaps having lost so much already, it was inevitable that this part would eventually win out. The battle raging within me has long ceased to be a fight among equals.

But maybe Max won't come. Maybe after checking his watch one last time, cursing his obdurate uncle and shaking his head, he will reluctantly board the train to Holland and eventually make his way to America, never to return. I hope it is so.

Perhaps it will then be Doctor Kačak who finds me. As he has not yet returned to claim his cursed watch, I can't help but think his travel plans must have changed. It's unfathomable that he could now be standing on the platform at Wilson, readying to leave without the Complication. Though I feel he and his nefarious watch were in some shadowy way complicit in my downfall, I should spare a word to thank him for speeding my deliverance, for ending these decades of life suspended. I have become a fly trapped in amber, like those the street peddlers of old Josefstadt used to sell when I was a boy.

Having spent my last days removed from the outside world, it occurs to me too that perhaps The Little Mustache has already arrived. Perhaps our city is even now echoing with the cadence of heavy boots over the cobblestones, the saints on the Charles Bridge gazing down on a procession of German tanks crossing the river. Here then one less Jew for The Little Mustache to worry over.

My only hope is that my next shot from the old Spanish pistol may ring true as the last. If whosoever reads this is one faint of heart, look no further about this place but summon the authorities. Tell them to listen for the ticking of the Rudolf Complication. They will find me in the corner, my face filled with flies.

Ever yours,
Jan

PART

THREE

CHAPTER 10

■

Time started up again in a hurry.

My eyes roamed a rippling underbelly of clouds, blinking against the rain. I could smell car exhaust and feel the pavement beneath my hands and hear the sound of car doors opening and closing. Turning my head, I saw my cell phone lying in pieces just beyond my reach. *Prague Unbound* wasn't far from it, lying open and facedown with granular bits of shatterproof glass rising embedded and glittering like jewels from its spine, its leather cover the unglossed gray of a dead fish. A large woman with a black umbrella was suddenly standing over me and saying words I couldn't understand. She wore a pair of big rubber galoshes redder than anything I'd seen in my entire life.

I let her talk for awhile then pushed myself to a sitting position. She started shaking her head like crazy, speaking twice as fast and twice as loud. "Look at my boots!" she said. "Look how red my goddamn boots are!" Only she couldn't have been saying that, was probably saying stay down, don't move, an ambulance is on the way. My whole upper body hurt like hell, and my brain surged against the inside of my skull like rioters against a police barricade. I was soaking wet, the shoulders of my coat were shredded, and blood stained my shirtsleeves and cuffs. But I could feel my arms at least. I could feel my legs. No bones were sticking out anywhere. I swiveled my neck and winced, blinded by headlights only a few feet away. When I struggled to my feet the woman started backing away, her eyes pleading, blubbery lips moving a mile a minute, voice echoing and garbled like she was underwater. I touched my cheek and my hand came away bloody. Red the color of galoshes. There was a gash beneath my left ear. The woman wrestled a phone from her handbag, punched numbers with the bleached carrot end of her thumb, said something indistinct and shrill.

The ex-detective's Skoda had jumped the curb and was bent around the wrecked bus stop shelter that prevented us from smashing into the side of the building. There was a gaping hole in the middle of his windshield where I'd been ejected. I'd bounced off the hood of the car and tumbled maybe another twelve feet across the rain-slicked pavement. Had we been going just a little bit faster, had I sailed just a bit further, my head would have been cratered against the wall a couple yards away. As it was, there was still little reason my skull should be intact.

Soros was alive too, still in the driver's seat, though I couldn't see anything but his arms pinwheeling on either side of the deployed airbag like he was being attacked by a giant marshmallow. A few beer cans had flown out the windshield and were strewn across the pavement.

I couldn't recall much of how this had happened except that someone or something in the road had made Soros swerve, but now there was no sign of who or what it might have been. Traffic was stopped and a crowd had begun to gather on the other side of the street. I took a few halting steps toward the car. I retrieved *Prague Unbound* and my broken cell phone. Next to it was a yellow sticky note reading "Na bojišti 8 #414 Prague 2." I wasn't sure what it meant, but something told me I should take that too. Then I heard sirens and hightailed it out of there.

By hightailed I mean staggered off in the opposite direction of the crowd.

The big woman on the cell phone barked in dolphin speak and even trailed me for half a block or so but then disappeared. The streets were making me dizzy, never mind trying to read signs with their clusters of unpronounceable consonants, their hooks and diacritics. I came across what looked to be a large park. I followed a dimly lit footpath along which empty spaces were dotted here and there with trees, the odd statue. Too many statues in this city, everywhere you looked the face of some dead someone staring back at you, giving you a look like *haven't we met somewhere before?*

Five minutes or two hours later I stopped at a bench next to a misshapen tree. Nearly trunkless, grown out rather than up, as if some force were pressing it down. Nearby was a withered garden with a sign poking out of the ground whose English translation said *No pets step on.* I picked pieces of glass from the cover of *Prague Unbound*, tossed them in the grass. I closed my eyes, felt the world merry go round. Then I started throwing up. The Wenceslas Square sausage proved less delicious in reverse. I wiped my mouth with my wet jacket sleeve, and while I was at it tried to rub some of the blood from the side of my face. Then I kicked my feet up and stretched out on the bench. The tree looked like an inverted octopus. An albino octopus planted head first into the ground. I needed to gather my strength, figure out what to do next. Needed to stop worrying about what the tree looked like. Two, three minutes, I'd be back on my feet.

Later I woke to a full-scale mining operation inside my head. Tractors, drills, big union guys with jackhammers and picks and shovels tunneling through my gray matter. The rain had stopped. Some fifty feet away, five or six sketchy looking dudes were drinking from large cans of beer. Their cigarettes flared orange in the dark like fireflies in a slow, drunken waltz.

I noticed I was only wearing one shoe. The left one.

I wondered if the sketchy dudes had taken my other shoe, but what the hell would anyone want with one shoe? The state of my sock told me I'd lost the shoe in the accident. I promptly took off my other shoe. You see a guy with no shoes you think, well there's an eccentric fellow. One shoe, the guy is just fucking crazy. I took my socks off too.

Then I fell asleep again.

When I woke the second time it was drizzling, and the sketchy park hobgoblins were long gone. There was a yellow sticky note in my pocket reading "Na bojišti 8 #414 Prague 2." I stared at it a long time wondering what it meant. Then I remembered. Bob Hannah's address. He'd said he had documents I needed to see. I needed to warn him that Detective Soros would be coming for him.

What I needed was to get back to the hotel. Take the mother of all hot showers, put on a bathrobe. Order room service, send my suit for intensive dry cleaning, and ask the concierge where I could get a decent pair of shoes and a CT scan. I couldn't remember the name of the hotel, though. It was pink. Kinda orange. Orangey pink, like what's it, that fish grizzly bears eat? It would be good to figure out where it was, make my way back to the general area. Karlín, that was the neighborhood I needed. My hotel was distinctive-looking enough I was confident I could recognize it.

No sooner had I thought as much than I noticed a hulking building at the end of the square painted the same vibrant salmon color. It wasn't my hotel, but I made my way over to it anyway, feet slapping puddles on the footpath.

A copper plaque on the wall said *Faustův Dům*.

A landmark. I could at least find out where I was.

I had trouble consulting *Prague Unbound*—the pages kept fluttering about, forcing me at length to pin the damn book against ground to keep them still. When I did, this is what it said:

This baroque mansion in Charles Square was reputed to be the dwelling place of the legendary Doktor Faustus, a fourteenth-century scholar who famously sold his soul to the Devil in exchange for knowledge. There is said to remain to this day a hole burned in the roof through which the Devil whisked the doomed scholar off to Hell, though the hole was in reality not a Beelzebubian exit but the result of an alchemical experiment gone explosively awry. This experiment was not conducted by original owner and alchemist Prince Václav of Opava, nor latter occupant Ferdinand Antonin Mladota of Solopysky, nor astrologer Jakub Krucinek—whose younger son murdered his own brother over treasure hidden in the house—nor nineteenth century eccentric Karl Jaenig, who commissioned functional gallows to be built on the premises and slept in a wooden coffin and specified in his will that he be buried face down in order to see where it was he was going (as might you be, if we're being frank here). Instead the hole was created by a certain Edward Kelley—forger, adulterer, duelist, occasional necromancer, mountebank, bad credit risk, accomplished bullshitter—but not, despite such obvious qualifications, a famous artist.

The best account of former occupant Edward Kelley's unhappy time in Prague can be found in "The Woeful Saga of Kelley and Was-Kelley," included in these pages for your edification.

The Faust House is currently closed to the general public. But they will gladly make an exception for you, you wascally wabbit.

Even by *Prague Unbound*'s standards, the passage baffled to the point that I couldn't be sure how much was the actual text and how much attributable to my concussed head. I tried rereading it under the diffuse light of a streetlamp but the text wouldn't sit still, words writhing across the page like halved worms. Colors appeared behind them, as if someone had indiscriminately high-lighted passages in pink or green or yellow, and random words pulsed and flickered like a neon sign on the fritz. I'd look away, turning my eyes to the Faust House or the clouded moon, and when I looked back the text was normal again, at least for a few seconds, until the next wave of nausea started building.

And when last I glanced up at the Faust House, I couldn't help notice a single lit window in its uppermost story. Silhou-etted there was a lone figure, unmoving as he looked down on me below. Dark clothes, long hair, what must have been a beard. Just to show whoever it was I knew he was watching, I gave a little wave. The gesture was not returned. I waved again, this time with both hands over my head. Nothing. Suddenly angered that he would pretend he didn't see me when it was so painfully obvious he was watching every move, I began jumping up and down and frantically pumping my arms. This is I did for some time before realizing how insane it might look to someone unaware of the man in the window. I managed to get a hold of myself, and as my fury slowly subsided, I had a strong desire to get as far away as I could from the Faust House, from the deserted square.

I looked up Na bojišti Street on the map at the back of the book. Bob Hannah's apartment was just blocks away, and there were few people around to double take on my naked feet as I passed. The building was indistinguishable from any of the other Hausmann-style apartments lining the street, block-long, four-story units with entrances lit by dusky lamps modeled on old gas lanterns. Hannah's name wasn't listed on the directory by the bat-tered metal buzzer, but I punched #414 and waited. In response came a sound like a robotic goose, and then the door clicked open. The elevator had an old-fashioned iron grillwork door, was roughly the size of a phone booth. The way it lurched and jolted on the way up made me picture a hunchback in the basement tugging on a frayed rope. I wondered if the cops would be waiting in Hannah's apartment. If that's how it ended, so be it. They'd be able to give me a new set of clothes at least. Some paper slippers, maybe a nice new straightjacket.

The fourth-floor hallway smelled like cabbage and stale tea, was unpeopled and noiseless save for the occasional TV murmuring behind closed doors. It must have been around midnight, most of the building's tenants asleep. I reached 414 and found the door slightly ajar, dim light from inside spilling out into the hall and onto my feet.

I knocked.

I called Hannah's name.

When there was still no answer, I pushed the door open and stepped inside. A pair of black dress shoes sat in the foyer. The hardwood floors were pitted and scarred and cold underfoot. I could feel the breeze even before rounding the corner. A gauzy curtain billowed into the room, and a double window opened outward onto a Juliette balcony overhanging the street. For one sickening moment I thought of the art gallery curator's plunge, but as I moved into the living room, I saw Bob Hannah sitting at a kitchen table. Its surface was empty but for an accordion folder stuffed with papers and laying on its side. Hannah had his back to me. Slumped forward, shoulders bunched. He somehow looked smaller asleep, his body coiling inward, limbs receding inside his black suit.

"Hello?" I called. "Door was opened."

When he didn't reply, I moved closer and was just about to give his shoulder a gentle shake when I stepped in something warm and sticky. Scrambling sideways I lost my footing, and my hand shot out for his chair to try to regain my balance. No such luck. I fell, and the chair toppled backward and Bob Hannah tumbled out of it, landing next to me with a muffled thump. I would have been eye-to-eye with him, his face just inches from my own, except Bob Hannah no longer had a face.

Bob Hannah no longer had a head.

I kept staring at the space where it should have been, sure that I was looking at everything wrong somehow, that it was a trick of perspective. That all those dark shapes pooled on the floor around me were shadows and not blood. I crabbed backwards and heard a low sound somewhere between a mumble and a growl. The sound rose to a shriek, and my head swiveled to locate its source before I understood its source was me. Blood was all over my suit, my pants, on *Prague Unbound*, on the bottom of my feet. Still viscous, warm to the touch. Whoever killed him couldn't have done it long ago.

Meaning the killer was still in the apartment.

I started for the front door and my hand was on the knob when I stopped. If whoever did this was still here and wanted to kill me, the time would've been either when I first walked in the room or when I was flailing around in Hannah's mess.

But that's not why I suddenly realized they'd left.

There was cake on the floor, next to the shoes.

A spongy cake with cherries, about half of it left. *Bublanina* cake, Hannah had called it.

The cake box was nowhere in sight.

Before consciously formulating the thought, I realized what had happened. The killer had buzzed me in then left down the stairs as I came up the elevator. Now he was somewhere on the streets below, walking around with an innocent looking cake box under one arm. Bob Hannah's head was no longer in the apartment—it was in that cake box.

I must say sitting next to a cake can make you incredibly hungry.

I put on the shoes left by the door, figuring I'd track less blood around that way even though my prints were already everywhere. And just in case I was wrong about the killer being gone, I went to the kitchen and started looking for a knife or some other weapon, but all the drawers and cupboards were empty. I spotted a heavy iron poker standing next to a small fireplace in the living room and snatched it up, gauging its heft as I started moving through the apartment. Making a sweep of the place didn't take long. Besides the kitchen and living room area, there was only a bedroom and small bathroom. Bob Hannah had lived modestly to say the least. No TV, no stereo, just a small alarm clock at his bedside blinking 12:21. No actual bed, just a pillow and an Army Surplus sleeping bag with strips of duct tape suturing its nylon wounds. Bob Hannah had hung no wallpaper, framed no pictures, magneted nothing to his refrigerator door, stacked no mail on the kitchen counter. In his bathroom, a single bar of soap on the sink, one hand towel on the rack, one full roll of toilet paper in the dispenser. No bath towel, no shampoo, no toothbrush. Not even monks lived with this level of austerity.

Something was wrong about this whole set up.

Scrawled in heavy marker on the brown accordion folder on the table was the outline of someone's right hand. Pages crammed inside were separated by tabs labeled with bizarre, obtuse headings—*Revenge Upon Don Julius and The Slime of Revolting Passions . . . The Skeleton of Jánský vršek . . . Inside the Mirror Maze . . . Death Beneath the Blossoming Hawthorn . . . Murcek Curios and Antiques . . . Edward Kelley Chronology.* There must have been fifteen or twenty such dividers, but aside from the name Edward Kelley, none held any meaning for me. If the killer was Martinko Klingáč or one of his henchmen, why would they have left this behind? Maybe they'd searched everything and found what they needed. But still, why waste time rifling through the contents of the folder? Why not just take the whole thing?

None of this was making sense.

Then came the sound of screeching brakes, doors being slammed, rushed footfalls on the pavement below. I moved to the opened window and looked down just in time to see five policemen come dashing into the building. There was a sixth one too, but he'd given up dashing sometime after he gained pound number two hundred and seventy-five.

I shoved the accordion folder down front of my waistband. *Unbound* I shoved in the back, the remaining glass granules from Soros's windshield raking against my skin. I took off my jacket and lashed it around my waist to keep everything together, and then pushed aside the balcony curtain. Green and white police cars were parked at angles in the middle of the street, lights spinning overhead, the cars themselves empty.

I stepped out on the faux balcony, an outcropping that protruded nearly a foot and was fenced in by a thin iron railing that rose to my waist. Looking down, an identical balcony stood outside the apartment beneath. Hoisting myself over the gate was clumsy going with all the printed matter I had girding my midsection, but in a few seconds I was on the other side. I crouched as low as I could, and then kicked out my feet, letting my body dangle. At full stretch I was still six or seven feet above the balcony below. From there, I'd have to drop two stories to the street. The police started pounding on Hannah's door. They yelled a couple times and then came a crash like a cannon shot as they kicked the thing in. I closed my eyes, opened my fingers, and dropped.

The Woeful Saga of Kelley and Was-Kelley

Glaucous and fixed in the black firmament of a midnight sky, the moon alights upon five dead men and one dead woman and a dead child of indeterminate sex, their bodies piled haphazard and lime dusted at the bottom of an open pit outside the gates of the village Most. The earth is hard with frost, and scant soil has yet been heaped upon them. A plague is upon the village, and the gravedigger who left his task unfinished is at this hour drunk and insensate, asleep under a mantle of untanned sheepskins inside a derelict construction at the edge of the makeshift cemetery.

Into this night's congealed blackness, a figure of apparitional white clamors out of the earth, emerging from the burial pit and falling to the ground, trembling like an infant yet to draw its first-born breath. His garments and closecropped hair are streaked with quicklime and are incandescent under the moonlight. Moments after his materialization, he rises to his knees and commences to brush and shake the substance from his person, and a cloud forms about him as if he were dissolving into the ashes of his creation.

The man has for two days been dead.

A suicide formerly known as Edward Kelley.

One of his legs is wooden below the knee and the other recently fractured in three places above the ankle. The encasing flesh is swollen and discolored, and the poorly set bone beneath has yet to commence knitting itself whole. Two of his ribs are broken, and the left side of his face is blackened with alkaline burns. Where his ears should be are shriveled whorls of purple.

What he is now is yet to acquire a name.

What he is now may best be understood as Was-Kelley.

The man crawls over rocks and sodden leaves, over fallen trees, over bracken and frozen mud and through the darkness of the forest until he reaches the edge of a highway not two carriages wide and deserted since day's close. Exhausted he lies prostrate and cold, a cold like he has never known but that will remain in his bones forever more, day or night, in sun or shadow. Under the fixed glaucous moon, he lies delirious and whispering a single name as if in blasphemous prayer.

Madimi. Madimi. Madimi.

Fifty miles distant, Prague awaits. Fifty miles distant, the Rudolf Complication his to reclaim. Was-Kelley watches the stars above recede, watches the road and the forest and waits for a sign from Madimi, the little spirit girl who has chased him from his home, who has earned and lost him a fortune, who has engineered his rise and his downfall, become his salvation and his damnation alike. *Madimi, Madimi, Madimi.* The little girl who is now his master.

Was-Kelley cannot remember when first he laid eyes upon her. It happened some fifteen years previous while gazing at Dr. John Dee's shewstone—a slab of convex, polished obsidian plundered by the Spanish from the Aztec race, an instrument of murderous pedigree. Other spirits had answered their call—Uriel, King Camara, Prince Lasky's guardian angel Jubanladec, Medicina and Galvah, Gabriel and Nalvage and Zadkiel—but it was Madimi who came most often, appearing as a six-year-old girl but announcing herself a six-thousand-year-old angel who spoke every tongue known on Earth and some long vanished from it. Was-Kelley no longer remembers those startling visions Madimi revealed—four sumptuous and belligerent Castles, out of which sounded Trumpets thrice. Three Ensign Bearers, each with the ancient name of God writ upon their banners. An East the red of new-smitten blood, a West green like the skins of dragons. Eleven Noblemen in Rich Sables. Seventy-two White Lilies with bowed heads, a Man on Fire and naked unto his paps, an Italian Bishop carrying an iron chest containing black wax and a dead hand.

Kelley knew then this spirit Madimi was no angel.

But still he heeded her words as Madimi drove Kelley and Dee from English soil, warning the crystal-gazers that their friends in Elizabeth's court were but worms in the straw who conspired mightily and were preparing to arrest them on charges of witch-craft. The animated corpse that is now Was-Kelley lacks power of recollection to summon the night Mortlake was stormed by an angry mob incited by tales of the dark happenings inside. He cannot recall how finding the crystal-gazers gone they had turned their wrath onto John Dee's instruments of divination, destroying his alchemical lab and his astronomical apparatuses and burning down his library.

To Bremen, to Lubeck, to Lask, and to Krakow they fled, a harsh winter forcing them to hire five and twenty men to clear the icebound road ahead. During their journey, Madimi revealed a vision of Mrs. Jane Dee dead in her petticoats, her face bat-tered in, and of maid Mary being pulled from a pool of water half drowned. She summoned Dee's stillborn children and made of them marionettes engaged in dances whimsical and lascivious. Dee would endure these horrors in hopes of unraveling cabalistic mysteries at any cost in his quest to unite the manifold sciences of Nature, still believing this spirit whose counsel they had gained was an emissary of God.

In Prague they'd gained favor of the pale, wanton King by promising him the Philosopher's Stone. When they'd failed to deliver, Dee hastily fled back to the ruins of Mortlake, but his skryer Kelley was captured at an inn in Soběslav, imprisoned in the castle Křivoklát, manacled and fed horsemeat pushed through a fist-sized hole in the wall while he awaited questioning by Master Executioner Jan Mydlář.

If there be any mercy in Was-Kelley's resurrection, perhaps it is that he doesn't remember those three days with the Master Executioner. Locks shorn so as not to be enmeshed in the gears of the rack he was stretched upon. Prodded by hot iron poker, invaded by pear of anguish, all the while the rack's wheel revolving notch by notch like the gears of some infernal clock. Was-Kelley doesn't remember those long weeks of solitary and starved convalescence in a dark oubliette afterward, only to learn that six months hence, the Master Executioner and his dread instruments would return.

It was then Kelley had tried to escape from a high castle tower, tearing what remained of his clothes to fashion a crude rope measuring some twelve feet in length in hopes of lowering himself seventy feet to the ground. His pathetic conveyance snapped, and Kelley had plummeted before landing with a calamity registered by none save the rats scurrying through the heaped refuse at the tower base. His left leg crumpled beneath him, and blood issued through every orifice. Moonlight pooled in a shallow puddle of his own micturition. Edward Kelley had begun to pray.

Madimi, Madimi, Madimi.

She answered his call. She revealed to him a vision, a plan with which he might win the King's favor afresh and prolong his own wretched life. She told him he may yet be spared, but it would come at a price. She demanded he aid her in unleashing onto the world a miraculous timekeeping instrument that granted its wearer eternal life. Thus in a vision of blood and shimmering piss was conceived the Rudolf Complication.

Upon seeing Kelley's splayed form the next morning the guards first guessed him dead, but the castle physician found no major damage had occurred save to his left leg, whose bones were broken in so many places the flesh was rendered a gangrenous mass in need of immediate amputation. The limb was sawed off and cauterized, replaced with a length of wood. Six months later he was again placed upon the rack, albeit with one less limb to be secured. *I know not the secret of the Philosopher's Stone*, Kelley confessed when the Master Executioner began the session. *But perhaps I can interest his Majesty in a watch?*

Morning and the sun rises pale and distant over rolling hills of snow-dusted trees. The resurrected Was-Kelley lies shivering and waiting for his sign from Madimi, and soon enough it comes. A gypsy caravan pulled by an emaciated horse with ashen hide scarce sufficient to cloak its bones arrives juddering down the narrow highway. The carriage makes slow progress through the forest, but the driver cracks no whip and issues neither threats nor entreaties into the ears of his skeletal nag. The sound of its hooves falling upon the frozen road is muted by the thin mantle of snow thereupon, and naught else is audible for miles. All at once the mare stops and the caravan creaks and groans as it is brought to a halt. The horse stands in contemplation of the obstruction in the path before him, and his nostrils send bursts of vapor into the cold winter air.

Was-Kelley looks up at the gray underchin of the nag. He takes in the caravan and the driver upon it. The motionless rider sits with a damask stitched of many cloths covering his head and a moth-eaten crimson blanket wrapped around his frame. Aside from a mossy black beard hoary with frost, his features cannot be countenanced. Only his hands are visible, the wagon reins lashed and knotted around one wrist, while his opposite fingers bear rings as large as goat eyes and cling to a lump of stale black bread.

Was-Kelley brushes against the horse as he struggles to his feet, and the nag lurches and whinnies as if snake bitten. Was-Kelley tries to calm the animal but it rears, front legs wheeling at the sky. When the horse comes down, the reins jerk taut, and the gypsy driver is tumbled from his carriage perch. He lands in a graceless heap but does not cry out nor attempt any movement. One naked eye gazes skyward, the other already picked clean by carrion. Beneath the beard the man's face is swollen and his neck black with buboes. A victim of the plague. Inside the carriage, his passengers are likewise unmoving and silent, and Was-Kelley understands they have been travelling dead upon this road for hours or days, understands that Madimi has brought them here. Like him they have become her servants.

Was-Kelley searches the man's garments and finds a stag horn–handled dagger lashed to his waist and a sow's ear coin pouch around his neck. He takes both into his possession and then wobbles to a stand with the aid of the high wagon wheels. Peering inside the coach he finds three women so withered and wild in their attire that they look not like inhabitants of the earth and yet are on it. Each corpse is swathed in a refulgent pandemonium of color, and each looks more lifeless than the last, as if the bodies had been arranged by the hour of their death. Was-Kelley opens the caravan door, climbs into the vacant carriage seat opposite these fellow travelers, and settles in for a long journey. The whitish sun moves unhurried across the sky as the gray nag snorts and the cart shudders into motion. Fifty miles distant, Prague awaits.

CHAPTER 11

∎

My brother broke his leg when he was seventeen, the year my mom left us. Fractured his fibula just above the ankle. Paul said he and some of his friends had been playing football, that he went up to catch a pass and just came down wrong. It was a Saturday night in late December while we were on Christmas break, and there were six inches of snow on the ground. Not the fluffy kind, either, but the week-old, frozen-solid and sculpted-by-the-wind variety. Snow nobody in their right mind would play football on. And though my brother's friends were often not in their right minds, they would never be out tossing a pigskin around in December when they could be holed up in somebody's basement, huddled around a bong while listening to Soundgarden.

The football story was bullshit, but whatever really happened had spooked Paul. He spent Christmas break and most of the month that followed hanging out in his room acting sullen and withdrawn. In the Christmas pictures from that year, Paul is mostly absent but where present, his leg cast gleams an overexposed, ghostly white. He wouldn't let anybody sign it, kept a sock stretched over the thing at all times. But when he got the cast sawed off and the halved plaster was lying in the garbage can at the hospital, I saw he'd written something on it. Magic markered in plain block letters were the words:

The abyss also gazes into you.

I imagined him lying down in bed, hands clasped behind his head, cast foot propped on pillows, meditating on the phrase in between staring at the ceiling listening to his headphones or watching *River's Edge*, a film he was obsessed with that year. I didn't understand what these words meant to him, didn't know how to bring something like that up to my little brother. In a college philosophy course two years later, I came across the quote in a unit on Nietzsche. It's a safe bet my brother wasn't reading Nietzsche. Where he saw the quote, what it meant to him, and how he really broke his leg, are just a few of the hundreds of things I'd never know.

We contain multitudes, went some other quote.

We are each one of us a gathering of strangers.

Somehow I managed to land on the street beneath Bob Hannah's apartment without breaking any bones of my own. I'd escaped with only a sprained ankle, nothing too bad, but I knew I'd be limping for a couple days when I got back to the States.

Because that was the plan. Go straight to the airport, get on the next available plane. Given that two of the last four people I'd spoken to were now either dead or comatose, I liked my odds better picking through the contents of the accordion folder back in the Windy City. If there was anything useful, I could always come back, make inquiries through the proper channels. I was done playing sleuth.

The plan had one problem, though. My passport was still back in the safe at the Hotel Dalibor. I had just enough cash for a cab and caught one near Můstek station. When we reached the hotel, I paid the cabbie but told him to wait, that I'd be right out. He nodded and smiled in kind of a blank way, and I hadn't even made it to the hotel entrance before he sped off. I limped through the lobby toward the front desk to ask the clerk to call me another cab, but he was busy checking in some visibly irritated couple laden with enough suitcases to stage a small-scale invasion, so I just headed for the elevator.

Its interior had too many mirrors, and none of them had kind things to say. I forgot which floor I was on for about four seconds then remembered and punched the number three button. The doors had nearly closed when a hand knifed inside. The doors whisked opened again, instantly filling the cab with the smell of alcohol and cigarettes. The new occupant didn't bother hitting any buttons but just slumped against the back wall of the elevator. I shuffled sideways to make room and looked down at my shoes. My dad's shoes, that is. No wait—Bob Hannah's shoes. It was difficult to remember whose shoes I was in at any given moment.

"Who was he?" said the person next me.

Vera's mouth was slanted, her eyes half closed and glistening. Her cheeks were flush, and her head visibly wobbled as she leaned against the mirrored back wall, awaiting my answer. She must have been in the hotel bar, sitting where she could monitor the entrance.

"Who was who?" I said.

"You followed me. You got into car with a man. Who was he?"

"Nobody you want to know."

That is if she didn't know him already. I watched the numbers light up above the doors. They stopped on three, the elevator opened, and I stepped out. Vera lurched after me down the hall. The ankle was going to be worse than I'd thought. Halfway down the hall she started yelling.

"You lied to me!"

"People are trying to sleep," I mumbled.

"You promised!" She latched onto my shoulder, taking a fistful of my jacket, trying to spin me around and ripping the fabric in the process. It didn't take much—what with diving in canal, going through a windshield, getting pelted with rain, and serving as a girdle, it had been a tough night for Dad's last black suit. Vera lowered her voice. "You said you would speak to no one. *You promised me.*"

"That was before certain facts came to light."

"Oh? Just what is it you think you know?"

I shook her off, kept moving down the hall.

"He is a policeman, isn't he?"

"Used to be," I said. "Not any more."

"I've seen him. At the Black Rabbit. *Ježíš Maria*, I knew he was a policeman."

"That a criminal thing, knowing how to make cops?"

"What do you mean?"

"You've had some scrapes with the law, no?"

"Scrapes? What did your policeman tell you?"

"Does it really matter at this point?" We reached my room. I shifted the accordion folder and *Unbound* under my arm as I dug through my pockets to find my key card.

"What did he say?"

"That you were involved in a drug ring."

"A drug ring? My God, no. Just some stupid friends when I was young. It's absurd to call this a drug ring. What else did he say?"

I slipped the key card into the slot and the door clicked opened and I went inside. Part of me wanted to slam the door in Vera's face. Paul had been dead for five years, and I'd done just fine with his death being an accident. Done fine without the Black Rabbit or the Rudolf Complication or the Right Hand of God or Martinko Klingáč. I had Vera to thank for all of them, and I'd have done just fine without her, too.

She followed me inside as I groped around for the light, my hand skittering moth-like over the wall. Vera moved past me and emerged on the other side of the room, pushing aside the curtain, bringing in the moonlight, the murky sonata of water cascading over the rooftops, streaming through rain pipes, spilling onto the streets. Maybe she was checking to see if I had been followed by the cops. Maybe it was a signal to someone below.

Come up in ten minutes.

Bring an empty cake box.

She stood silhouetted at the window, so thin she was nearly an abstract shape. I found the wall switch and threw it on and Vera winced against the light like it had insulted her. It hadn't. She'd look good under a floodlamp or inside a sensory deprivation chamber, which just irritated me more. I made my way to the metal safe containing my passport and valuables. I couldn't remember the combination.

"You want to know about this . . . this drug ring?"

"Not especially." 12 left . . . 07 right?

"When I was at the university, my boyfriend brought some ecstasy from the Netherlands. Five or six of us were going to go camping in Frymburk. Just hang out by the lake all weekend, have a good time."

09 left, 27 right . . . 71 left? Nope. Denied. I'd always used birthdates for setting combination codes—mine, Paul's, my father's—but with Vera nattering on, I couldn't keep the numbers lined up in my head.

"But it started raining just before we left. They said it was supposed to rain all week, and we decided let's stay in the city. So five of us, we went to a club instead."

"You don't have much luck with rain, do you?"

She gave me a wounded look. "What are you saying?"

"Nothing. What happened at the club?"

"My boyfriend at this time, Josef was his name, he was high. We were all high, but he was *really* out of his head. And he decided wouldn't it be funny to sell some of the pills? Let's pretend we are drug dealers! A joke, you know. A game. It was funny then, I can't say why."

"Maybe because you were on drugs?"

"Could be," she said. "So he sold ecstasy to some kid in the bathroom. And then the second person he tried to sell it to was a policeman. End of drug ring." Vera finished her story with a one-note laugh. "God, Josef was an idiot."

I don't know which numbers did it but the safe popped opened. *Absurd. A joke.* The same kind of language she'd used describing my brother's watch theft scheme, and yet she'd gone along with that, too. I didn't know if she was lying to me or just herself, or if she really was the perpetual passive victim-accomplice she came across as. I didn't care anymore. Everything in my wallet looked to be in order. All my dad's credit cards were there, along with two hundred dollars American and about two-thousand Czech crowns. I shoved all of it, passport, wallet, *Rudolf's Curiosities* exhibit booklet, and *Prague Unbound,* into the accordion folder now doubling as my suitcase.

I heard a dry click and spun to the sound. Vera held a lit cigarette in one hand and a gunmetal lighter in the other. She'd opened the window and was blowing smoke out into the night as the curtains flowed around her, her body entirely still, a statue of itself.

"Close that fucking window."

My tone jolted her. My tone jolted me.

"I thought because of the smoke—"

"I've got a thing about open windows."

"Alright, fine. Fine. *Ježíš Maria*."

"This room is no smoking anyway."

"So call your policeman. Have me arrested."

"Five years later your tracks are all covered, huh?"

"What are you talking about?"

"I know where you live, Vera. I saw your house. It's a nice house with a nice car in a nice garage. Nice big yard for kids to play in. That's an awful lot of nice for someone whose last job was as a part-time art gallery worker five years ago."

"That's what this about? My house?"

"Will you please close the window?"

"You don't know what you think you know."

"I'm an uncle. I know that."

That stopped her. I stomped across the room, pain emanating in waves from my ankle, and I must have looked crazy because she recoiled as I neared, moving off to one side, eyes not leaving mine for a second. I slammed the window shut and did the latch. As I moved away, she buried her face in her hands and started shaking her head and mumbling something over and over in Czech. Or maybe it was Klingon.

"His name is Lee," she finally said.

I turned around.

"My son. He's four years old and his name is Lee."

"You've got to be fucking kidding me."

"His middle name. His first name is Tomáš, after my grandfather. They call him Tomášek, or Tomík. Means like little Tomáš. But his middle name is for your father. Most Czech children don't have middle names, you know."

No, I didn't know. Ever since I got here, people thought I knew what I didn't know.

"But Paul once said if he had a child he would name it Lee," she continued. "And now Tomáš doesn't want to be called Tomáš because already there are already two other Tomáš' in his class. So we call him Lee. I was six weeks pregnant when Paul died. He didn't know. He never knew."

I couldn't muster a response. I went to the bathroom to grab my shaving kit and Vera trailed behind me. I realized I hadn't brought any shaving kit and bent over the sink and splashed water on my face. My wet face in the mirror a cruel caricature.

"Why are you so angry?" said Vera.

"I'm not angry."

"I'm the one who should be angry."

"So be angry. I'm going home."

"To America? It's nearly two in the morning. No planes will be leaving now. I don't even think the airport will be opened."

"Of course it's open. It's an airport."

"There's blood on your shirt."

There was. And looking down, more than I would've thought.

"What happened?" Vera said. "What is going on?"

I pushed past her, went into the main room to grab my things. I glanced at the painting on wall, *The Unmerciful Geometry of Zugzwang 1938,* with the grumpy old pipe smoker and his arrogant young chess opponent and all the faceless patrons in the smoky café and all at once pictured myself in an airport security line. Unshaven, disheveled, and baggy-eyed, a cut by my right ear and a rip in my suit jacket. Dried blood on my collar and shirtsleeves. Pants torn. I fast-forwarded to the part where I had to remove my shoes—whoever's shoes—and the security guy sees I'm wearing no socks. Sees the soles of my feet covered in a suspiciously reddish substance. Notices I have no carry-on luggage, save for a dog-eared book embedded with glass, and a giant folio with a black hand scribbled on its side. I had a better chance of being crowned King of Wallachia than I had getting on an airplane.

But that didn't mean I was going to stick around and wait for

Soros to show up. And as long as Vera was with me, well, there was one less person out there plotting how to kill me or frame me for killing someone else. *Keep your friends close and your enemies closer,* the saying went. I envied its originator for being able to tell the difference.

"We're leaving," I said.

"Leaving? To where?"

"I don't know. But we're not safe here."

"I'm not going anywhere until you tell to me what is happening."

"I'll tell you inside a cab."

She weighed this for a long time. Hers wasn't what you'd call an expressive face, but it moved through a number of frustrated variations only to arrive right where it had started the very first time I'd seen her, when I'd spotted her across the room at the Black Rabbit, looking beautiful and exhausted and resigned to the notion that whatever happened next could be no worse than what had already occurred. She was gazing into something also gazing into her, and each was waiting for the other one to blink.

CHAPTER 12

∎

Instead of a cab we took Vera's car, a BMW model maybe eight years old that she'd parked in the three-car lot opposite the Hotel Dalibor. There was a child's safety seat in the back, and when she turned on the ignition, some high-pitched cartoon voice started singing in Czech to a John Jacob Jingleheimer Schmidt melody. Vera turned off the stereo and took out her phone as she maneuvered the car out of the lot.

"What are you doing?" I said.

"I'm calling to say I won't be back tonight."

"Calling who?"

"You must relax."

"Don't tell anyone where we're going."

"Relax. I'll tell them what I tell them."

"I'm relaxed. Where are we going anyway?"

"You said not to say." A cutting smile. I didn't like it, but what was I going to do? I couldn't check into another hotel, not without using a credit card, which meant Soros and his former friends on the force or his newer friends in the Martinko Klingáč fan club would be able to track me down. I could've asked Vera to get a

room, but they knew her, too. As she spoke in hushed tones to
what must have been an answering machine, I tried to think what
I would've done in similar circumstances in Chicago. Go to that
twenty-four-hour Korean restaurant on Lawrence? Just drive up
and down Milwaukee Avenue all night until I ran out of gas? It
was a moot point. I wasn't in Chicago, and I wasn't in charge of
what happened next. Ever since I walked into the Black Rabbit, I
really never had been.

One of the hard parts about being in a foreign country is losing
your cultural signifiers. Back home, a woman talks a certain way,
wears a certain kind of clothes, and you can more or less gauge
the type of job she might have, her education level, who she votes
for, what TV shows she probably likes. With Vera, I had no idea.
What did it mean that she drove a BMW? What did it mean that
she'd gone to Charles University, that she'd been busted trying to
sell ecstasy in a club, that she smoked Marlboro Reds, or that she
spoke English as well as she did? What did it mean that, as far
as I could tell, she had no job? What did it mean that she lived
in Ořechovka? She had money—that much seemed obvious—
but was it old money, new money, earned money, stolen money?
What did it mean she'd had a child with my brother out of wed-
lock? Was this frowned upon here, or was it commonplace, no big
deal? If she was American, I could have sized her up and answered
all these questions without even having to consciously think
about it. And maybe my answers would have been wrong, based
on stereotypes and assumptions, all those snap judgments you're
not supposed to make by the book's cover, but at least it would've
been a start.

She finished her call, speaking a few phrases in Czech that
could have meant anything, and then hung up with a look of
relief. Outside the window the fabric of the night lay densely
woven over the tiny streets, the empty churches, the torpid river

and low stone bridges stitched across it. As Vera drove southward, the adrenaline left my body and my muscles lost their tension and I felt myself drifting.

Next thing I knew we were parked on a street canopied by trees growing on an adjacent grassy embankment. We were on the other side of the river now, the west side, perhaps only thirty yards from the water's edge.

"Wake up, wake up," Vera monotoned.

She got out of the car and slammed the door. I followed her. We walked past a blazing Erotic World porn shop that was better lit than most of the films they sold, then stopped at a door around the corner. I watched Vera's pale hands as she flipped through her keys. Fingers so thin a paper cut might hit bone. She opened the door and we ascended a dingy stairwell, vanishing in the gloom and reemerging onto a carpeted third-story hallway. She was now several yards ahead of me, jostling another key inside another lock. I found myself studying the back of her neck, her spine like a string of pearls stretched taut under her skin.

Then I saw the man in a black suit at the far end of the hall advancing with halting strides. When he saw I'd noticed him he stopped walking. For several moments we stood motionless regarding each other, and I felt a rising panic as I blinked against the light, trying to focus on his face. The man blinked too, and all at once I realized I was staring into a mirror, one mounted in a frame at the hall's end, placed above a little table with a vase and a few fake flowers. Couldn't blame me for thinking the guy suspect. Just look at the miserable bastard.

Vera pulled me by the crook of my arm into the room and turned on the light. She took off her shoes and motioned me to do the same. I waited until she'd moved into the living room lest she look too closely at my bloodied feet. Something about removing the shoes made me shudder, but I was unable to translate the sensation into actual thought. I stared at the shoes for awhile, but it didn't help. My neurons were misfiring from exhaustion.

The living room was sparsely furnished, a small TV in one corner, a beige sofa pushed up against a wall. There was a bookshelf whose lower reaches were filled with kids' stuff—coloring books, DVDs, and VHS tapes. Nearby sat red plastic storage containers jumbled with stuffed animals, trains, a Spider-Man action figure.

"*Vítáme vás*," said Vera, spreading her arms mock grandiose before letting them fall to her sides. "Means welcome. Something to drink?"

"This is your place?"

"Yes, for now."

"What about that place this afternoon?"

"That belongs to my parents. Tomáš and I go there for dinner every Friday night, and he often stays with them during the weekends."

"I thought you called him Lee."

"Tomáš, Tomášek, Lee." An exasperated shrug. "You seem strangely interested in the house, so I'll tell you a story. My grandfather bought it in the late 1930s. He then owned Czechoslovakia's largest textile factory. But when the Communists came to power, they took the factory, kicked his family out of the house, made it state property. My mother was one year old then. Twenty-one years later she married my father, who was a member of the Party and would become the Minister of Agriculture. And guess what house was designated for the Minister of Agriculture? So my mother moved in again to her childhood home. But then in 1989, the Communists were kicked out and we lost the place again. So we moved around for two years before my mother could prove that she was the rightful, pre-Communist owner. Now she's lived in the same house three different times, under three different regimes. Is there anything else about my living arrangements you'd like to know?"

I shook my head, and she turned and made her way into the kitchen. I don't know why I didn't consider that the place might have belonged to her parents, but then how could I have known? She was one of those people it was hard to imagine even having parents. That she evidently hadn't bought the mansion in Ořechovka with proceeds from the Rudolf Complication hardly meant she was above suspicion. Then again, there was no one else left to trust. Bob Hannah was dead. Soros was a black sheriff for Martinko Klingáč.

And trusting myself? Seemed like a clear conflict of interest.

On the other side of the room, a large window looked over the river and the bridge running across it. This must have been where Vera had sat watching tram after tram rattle by in the flood's early days, hoping against hope that Paul was in one of them. Be hard to continue living here with that kind of memory. Hard to live anywhere with a miniature version of Paul running around with his little Paul grin. Since my brother had died, there were days, not many but some, when I could forget about him completely, when nothing forced my memory into a place he occupied. But this couldn't have been true for Vera.

She returned with something clear in a glass with ice for herself and a beer for me. Alcohol was probably the last thing I needed, but I'd never needed a beer more in my life. She took me by the arm and led me into the living room, pushing one of Tomáš Lee Svobodova's storybooks to the floor in order to make room for us. We sat drinking on the couch. When she finally spoke, her voice was a measured hush.

"On your feet," she began. "Is it blood?"

I looked at my bloodied feet, nodded.

"Is it your blood?"

I shook my head. "Someone else's."

"Is this someone else . . . alive?"

I tossed up my hands and mumbled. Her eyes flitted away and she took another sip from her drink while she considered my feet and the origins of the substance upon them. "This is to do with Paul. And the man who killed him. Martinko Klingáč."

I nodded.

"Did you kill him?"

I shook my head.

"Your feet must be cold."

I said they were, a little.

She placed her glass on the coffee table, hand alighting for a moment on my knee as she rose and walked out of the room. On the table was some art magazine opened to a photograph of a large painting hanging on a white gallery wall. The painting depicted a man in a pea green military uniform sitting at a table upon which was placed a squarish case of some kind. It was a photorealistic painting, the details of the small, ugly room rendered with grimy accuracy, but where the uniformed man's head should be was only a diffuse smear of green. The painting was titled *The Interrogation* and was part of a controversial retrospective featuring artworks by inmates from mental hospitals throughout former Communist states. A pair of balled socks landed on the magazine. Men's socks, white. I thanked Vera and put them on. They were worn thin, and I wasn't about to ask whose feet had done the wearing. Vera slid onto the couch next to me, closer than before. She'd changed into a long gray T-shirt that hung loose on her frame, her contours beneath veiled save for the hard jutting line of her collarbone and the twin points of her nipples. Her legs were bare and coltish.

"Better, no?" she asked.

"My feet thank you."

"You're a lot like him, you know. Like Paul. Not just how you look. The way you move. How you carry yourself. When you are angry, your face is like his face."

I shrugged uneasily, not sure where she was going with this.

"Are you still going to leave tomorrow? To go back to Chicago?"

"I don't know. I think so."

"You should go. You should not have come. The letter wasn't meant for you. Don't take it the wrong way. It's nothing against you. But I wrote the letter for Paul's father. I wouldn't have asked you. It's different for brothers."

"What do you mean?"

"Brothers are always competing in everything. Like children fighting over toys. They always want what the other one has and it makes them do stupid things."

"You think my brother and I were rivals?"

"You're too much alike not to be."

"Is this based on something Paul told you?"

"He didn't have to tell me anything. Just like you don't have to tell me anything. I can see how you look at me."

"How I look at you?"

"Don't be angry."

"I'm not angry. You keep saying I'm angry."

"I imagine this happens often with brothers all the time. What you are feeling is natural."

"Oh? And what am I feeling?"

"That you wish to sleep with me."

I bit the inside of my lip and studied her dispassionate expression for any fissures while trying to assemble a response that didn't sound false or overly composed, one that matched her matter-of-fact delivery, as if we were merely two people discussing the train schedule. But when I spoke the words became decoupled before they'd even left the station. Deep down, I knew she was right. Not just about wanting to sleep with her—most guys would—but about my brother, too. I was only stunned that it was so obvious to her.

"If tonight, if I gave you the impression—"

"Not only tonight. Always."

"Whatever impression I gave, tonight or previously, I think maybe our signals got crossed. Which is to say I never intended to give you that sort of impression."

She smiled. "I never said you intended it."

"All I'm interested in right now is finding out who killed my brother."

"Martinko Klingáč did. I told you already."

"Yes, but why? How? Who is this person?"

She finished her drink. "Why does it matter?"

"Because he's my brother, Vera. Paul was murdered. You told me so yourself. This is the father of your child we're talking about. It matters."

"Don't you dare bring my son into this."

"Why write the letter, Vera? If you don't want to do anything. If you don't want anything done. If it doesn't matter. It makes no sense."

"A moment of weakness," she said. "Paul is not coming back. Nothing you learn, nothing you do, can make him alive again. And look at yourself. Running around in torn clothes and no socks. Blood on your shirt, on your feet. Carrying some folder you think has all the secrets. You're not bringing Paul back, but you know this. Because it's not really about him. It's about you."

"You don't know what you're talking about."

"You're only angry because it's true. Can you even hear how you sound?"

"Like Paul? Is that what you're going to say?"

"Yes, like him." She was talking faster now, and louder too, her composure slipping by degrees. "I shouldn't have told you anything, but you're the one who failed. You broke your promise. You talked. Whatever happens now is because of you. Because of what you did. Not because of the letter I wrote."

"Right. Has nothing to do with anything you did or didn't do five years ago. It all started with me, never mind that I've been here less than forty-eight hours."

"Stop lying!"

"Lying about what? Just what have I ever lied to you about, Vera?"

She closed her eyes and held both hands out in front of her. "What always I say is there is no winning against a person like Martinko Klingáč. All that can happen is you will be hurt. Or you will be killed. Go home while you still can."

"Always you said this? So you warned Paul about Martinko Klingáč?"

Stonefaced, she threw back some of her drink.

"Even though you didn't know who he was?" I pressed. "That's what you said earlier, right? That you had no idea who Martinko Klingáč was. That he was just some mysterious someone Paul met. Some guy with slick hair and a fairytale name who was afraid of bald people. So how, Vera, could you warn Paul if you didn't know anything about him? If you were so completely ignorant of all things Rumpelstiltskin?"

"I didn't know anything. I knew he was a gangster. Everybody knew this. You need sleep. I need sleep. This talking is absurd."

"I need answers," I said. "Nothing you tell me is making sense right now. Nothing you told me has ever made sense. You want to know what I think? I think you and this Martinko Klingáč knew each other before my brother ever set foot in this charming city of yours. I think you met Paul Holloway and said here's the fucking dupe we've been looking for. Here delivered unto us is the big-eared, grinning American idiot of our prayers."

She drew in her shoulders, recoiling and hardening. Whereas my words moments previously were stuttering and disjointed, now they issued forth in an unregulated torrent. I accused her of using Paul to steal the Rudolf Complication, intending all along to double-cross him once the heist was complete, to split the loot with Martinko Klingáč and leave Paul high and dry. And how was it that Soros the black sheriff just happened to be at the Black Rabbit the very night I came to visit? How was it the booklet for the *Rudolf's Curiosities* exhibit just happened to wind up in my hotel room? How did he just happen to be waiting outside her parents' house when I followed her from the café on Wenceslas Square? Too many events didn't add up, and she was a part of all of them, going all the way back to five years ago when my brother disappeared.

As I rambled on, she just sat there on the sofa, listening impassively, face betraying nothing. I don't even know if I believed half the things I said, but I knew they needed saying, and when I finally finished, she put her empty glass upon the coffee table, edging forward on the couch until her face was only a few inches from my own. Her voice was barely above a murmur when she spoke.

"Are you saying," she began, "that you think I had a hand in killing him?"

"Bad word choice. But yes, I'm saying I can't rule it out."

"You can't rule it out. The father of my child?"

"Don't bring your son into this."

She glanced away, eyes moist and blinking. Then her arm wheeled back and she slapped me. Her aim was a little off and she missed my face, her open hand walloping me on the side of the head, or maybe that's where she'd been aiming all along because she caught me just above my ear, where I'd been cut flying through Soros's windshield. But she wasn't done. She hit me again, same place and harder. I winced and jerked my head back. When next she swung there was blood on her hand and it was no longer opened but balled into a fist. I intercepted it in midswing, grabbing her forearm. She went for the glass on the table with her other hand and swung it in an arc at my head, but I ducked and she lost her grip and the glass plonked off the wall and then shattered on the floor. I let go of her wrist and planted the heel of my palm into her chest, shoving her down onto the couch. As she gasped I took up the accordion folder and started heading for the door.

Her voice was a whimper. "Paul, no."

No sooner did I stop to wonder if I really heard what I thought I heard than she rose and launched off the coffee table. She landed on my back, one arm going around my neck as she grabbed fistfuls of my hair with the other. Her legs wrapped around my midsection and squeezed tight as I wheeled, trying to shake her. I lurched and stumbled, dropping the folder and watching its contents flutter and spill across the floor, then I felt a shard of glass slice into the flat of my foot. I went sideways and Vera came loose and clutched at the left sleeve of my shirt as she fell and the fabric tore with her weight as we toppled.

Then we hit the floor and she rolled away, still clutching my now severed shirtsleeve as she stopped to gaze up at me, nostrils flaring, eyes jumping from my face to the exposed flesh of my forearm and back again.

"My God," she mouthed.

Then a moment of stillness before her lips starting trembling and her face began to twitch and she launched herself from the floor. She landed on top of me, knee going into my thigh, her hands ripping at my exposed chest. The mass of her hair slid across her head and then fell off altogether to reveal the unstubbled skull beneath, the skin of it beaded with sweat and almost translucent blue. Her baldness came as such a shock I stared a moment before I knocked her hands away and rolled free and she latched onto my waistband as I struggled to my feet and then my pants were halfway down my thighs and I was on my back again. She was upon me, flush with tears and howling and clawing. I grabbed her wrists and forced them to her sides and she writhed and kicked and pressed her face hot and sobbing into my neck.

My head was turned, eyes fixed on the wig lying a few feet away in a heap like some lifeless animal.

I held her still and her sobs relented but her tears never stopped coming and after a time she unburied her face and found my mouth with her own and pressed the entirety of her body flat against mine. Moments later she wrested one hand free of my grip and reached into the slit of my boxer shorts as my hands moved under shirt, fingers lacing the notches of her spine while she pulled aside her underwear to expose the full heat of herself and in a single movement bore down upon me until I was inside her.

Was-Kelley marvels not at the sooty black immensity of the New Tower Gate nor the transgressor's skulls rising gapemouthed upon pikes around its perimeter as he and the caravan of dead gypsies are ushered through the most formidable of Prague's thirteen points of entry. Without cloaking intercession from Madimi, this gruesome coach pulled by a skeletal nag would never have made it past the sentries, even at this predawn hour. Without intercession from Madimi, there would be no Was-Kelley, only a pile of bones at the bottom of an unconsecrated, lime-dusted pit. Without Madimi, there would be no Rudolf Complication that he has come to repossess.

The caravan halts, and Was-Kelley nods to the three withered dead women who have escorted him to the city, but they only gaze back eyeless and slackjawed as he hobbles out of the coach. He reaches out to pat the horse, but the nag lurches to avoid his touch and drags the caravan away. Later the coach and its rotting freight will by terrified Prague dwellers be discovered in the Old Town Square, the vessel arriving like the wooden horse of Troy to spread death and disease among them. The horse will be slaughtered and burned outside the city gates.

By sunrise the malformed streets are already alive with the cries of merchants, the bleating of sheep, the clatter of hooves upon the cobblestones. With half-closed eyes, Was-Kelley knows himself in Prague by its smell alone, one of acrid smoke and reeking offal as he limps to the edge of the street where a gathering of urchins stand in loose congregation about a fallen calf. They squeal and kick the dead animal in the mouth and tumble over each other to snatch up its bloodied teeth as if some soothsayer has declared these items fortuitous. Was-Kelley looks beyond the dogpiled urchins to the Rathaus adorned with Master Hanuš's horologe, to the Týn Church whose dark spires tower over the square like a congregation of magicians. They inspire no memories in him. The Hradschin Castle complex looms on the hill beyond the river, but he turns his face to the rising east, to a sun whose warmth is now powerless against the chill in his bones. The world entire angles askew as he staggers with lopsided and shambling gait. Dogs whimper or snarl as he passes, cats scurry at the mere sight of his shadow. Mothers look upon him with apprehension and pull their children from the path of this mad and earless cripple, this pale Lazarus crazed by daylight as he hobbles toward the House of the Black Rabbit where he knows Madimi will be waiting. Madimi will guide him to the Rudolf Complication. After that it will be up to Was-Kelley to put the cursed watch in motion.

Was-Kelley has no memory of creating the Rudolf Complication, cannot summon all those nights after the bemused King had freed him that he had spent alone in his meager study at a table edged up near the window where, lacking shewstone, he would fill a shallow silver bowl with water and wait for moonlight to pool upon its surface. Madimi would appear and for hours dictate how the Complication must be fashioned. Soon the mirror and the moonlight were no longer necessary, and she would reach him through paintings, through street signs or graffito scrawled upon walls. Most often she came to him through books. Kelley could open any volume upon his shelf and find her words written therein, for she was then so much with him she could no longer be said purely a spiritual entity and yet neither was she corporeal.

Was-Kelley can no longer remember how when among the living he would for days and weeks on end sit entranced by Madimi's words, one hand feverishly filling books with notes and diagrams, the other idly picking splinters from his wooden leg.

Trusting none to keep secret the apparatus of his devising, when its design was complete, Kelley commissioned three separate watchmakers—one to create the forward mechanism, a second the backwards, a third to construct the watch housing with the engraved ouroboros and heraldic lion. This third artisan also produced the winding key with Enochian symbols Madimi revealed during skrying sessions long ago with Dr. Dee. Kelley lacked the curiosity to inquire as to the meaning of these symbols, an oversight he would in time, and indeed throughout time, profoundly regret. Knowing the Emperor to be enthralled with the Cabbala and all things Hebrew, Kelley sought the assistance of the esteemed Rabbi Löew. Löew, a wise man of high estate, would have nothing to do with the known charlatan and necromancer. But Jacob Eliezer, an Italian known as the Black Rabbi, would. He conveyed during secret meetings at the Black Rabbit how the Cabbalistic sciences might be purposed to prolong the ticking of the watch far beyond its natural mechanical limitations.

Nearly three years after his release from Křivoklát Castle, exhausted and penniless and earless and half legless, Edward Kelley at last completed the Rudolf Complication. On the eve before he was to deliver the watch, in his study Kelly conducted one last test to vouchsafe the instrument's mechanisms. To his horror, when he placed the key in the winding slot, he discovered that it would not budge in any direction. A watch that could not be wound would not tick. A watch that would not tick would surely anger His Sovereign, move him to imprison and torture Kelley once again if not have him drawn and quartered. As Kelley in panicked vision imagined his body being fastened by ropes and torn asunder by charging steeds, he fell bodily upon the floor. Only then sweating and gnashing his teeth did he notice the black scrawled graffito on the ceiling above, the vehicle by which Madimi had chosen to reveal the Three Laws governing the Rudolf Complication:

1. For so long as the hands of the Rudolf Complication turn opposite each other upon time's twin faces, the wearer of the watch shall remain immune from the ravages of time.

2. Just as all life depends upon death, so the Rudolf Complication cannot be wound by the hand of any man living. Once each year, the winding key must be turned by the severed right hand of one so newly perished their soul still awaits Judgment.

3. Should the hands of the Rudolf Complication cease their movement, the heart of whosoever possesses it shall do the same.

Can this truly mean that once each year the watch must be wound by the right hand of a dead man? Kelley cried out. *A right hand that must be severed, no less?* Why had she had not previously made a single mention of these three damnable laws? How was he to explain these ghastly conditions to the Emperor? How could he present His Majesty with a contraption whose very engine ran on murder, whose perpetuation depended upon the desecration of corpses? One that while granting life everlasting also promised death and damnation?

Madimi vouchsafed no answer. But Kelley knew.

Madimi was, after all, no angel.

Days later, Kelley was summoned to the castle under the cover of night. Upon his reaching the Kunstkammer, the guards took their leave, abandoning him inside the colossal hall whose windows

had been walled up and whose torches had been extinguished, a
maudlin, sepulchral chamber illuminated solely by candles flickering here and there upon endless shelves. Inanimate faces from
innumerable paintings and the disembodied heads of mounted
beasts looked down upon Kelley as he wandered the Cabinet of
Curiosities in search of the King. After some time, Kelley heard a
whispering behind him and turned to find two large dull eyes glistening in the dark. This beast was not mounted—it was Rudolf's
famed lion, the animal standing not ten feet away, watching Kelley's
movements with languid curiosity. Kelley had heard tell of Rudolf's
pet lion, said to be a toothless old beast. This beast was neither
aged nor lacking of tooth. Neither was it clawless, its massive front
paws sheathing weapons sharp and curved like scimitars. Kelley
remained fixed in place unable even to breathe or blink until at
length the animal twitched its tail and returned into the darkness.

Moments later Rudolf materialized a much-diminished figure,
clad in black and pale of skin, eyes clouded and milky. His trembling hands gripped a candelabra with but two wax cylinders
burned down to nubs. Rudolf had taken up a position next to
Kelley, the light from his candelabra only then revealing to Kelley
a large mirror throwing back darkened reflections of the King and
his subject.

*At great cost I commissioned this mirror from the finest glassmaker in
Bohemia,* the King meekly intoned. *And yet anon I fear to gaze upon it
lest I find some flaw. In the glass itself or what it reveals to me? I'll leave
you to speculate. You've yet to speak. Are you a ghost? We've a scourge
of ghosts here already. Ah, but no. You're the Englishmen. The one with
no ears. Waste no more of my time. Show me the thing. A watch, wasn't
it? We've a scourge of watches too.*

Kelley drew a deep breath and slowly unfolded the velvet cloth
to reveal the watch inside, face up to show the heraldic white lion.
Rudolf's eyes were at once set ablaze. Without uttering a word, he

snatched the piece and draped it about his neck. His expression darkened.

It makes no sound, said the King. *It has no movement.*

Kelley sought to assuage the Emperor with a sawtoothed smile. The watch, he explained, had not yet been set into motion. It would first need to be wound using a specially crafted key with the magical symbols—

Wind it, speaks Rudolf. *Wind it, man.*

Kelley here played his final gambit, one he hoped would secure him the funds to flee Bohemia before the King discovered what fueled the Complication's infernal mechanism. Kelley gainsaid the King that presently he did not have the winding key upon his person. It was, he assured his Majesty, in a safe place, ready for delivery at the shortest notice. But having gone into great personal debt to have the watch produced, before Kelley relinquished it entire, he believed it only prudent to seek assurance that his efforts would be justly compensated.

Have you seen Otakar? interrupted the king. *My lion Otakar? He's here somewhere. He likes to hide but I can hear his heart beating.* The king put a finger to his lips, commanding Kelley's silence. *Can you hear the beating of his heart?* Kelley heard nothing until moments later Emperor Rudolf began coughing. When his fit had passed, the king reached into his cloak pocket and withdrew a small hand bell whose silvery brightness razored through the gloom. A delicate motion of his wrist and two sharp notes tolled in rapid succession, their overlapping sounds still echoing through the chamber as Rudolf turned on his heel, the watch hanging around his neck already forgotten. Guards emerged as if from the darkness itself and descended upon Kelley. They wrestled him to the floor and clapped manacles upon him and secured a sackcloth over his head. Kelley was in some measure relieved. He'd feared the bell was for summoning the lion.

Again imprisoned, this time at Hněvín Castle in the faraway village of Most, Kelley was ostensibly confined for amassing outstanding debts, his house nonetheless by royal troops ransacked from top-to-bottom, no object left untouched as the soldiers searched in vain for the winding key. Those few earthly acquaintances left to Kelley were called before the Imperial police and made to answer arcane horological queries understood by neither party. Their houses too were turned out, every inch scrutinized. Kelley was shaved bald and stripped naked, his body's every declivity explored by gaolers hands. The winding key was not found. In terror, Kelley awaited the visit from Master Executioner Jan Mydlář.

But a year later, the Master Executioner still had not been summoned, and only then did the portents of Mydlář's absence dawn on Kelley. Rudolf had given up on the Complication. Dismissed it as another amusing but useless geegaw, one among uncounted thousands already in his possession. Edward Kelley was no longer worthy of the rack, the pear, the hot iron poker. Nor even the gallows, nor drawing and quartering. Rudolf had sentenced him to slowly starve to death in obscurity.

Near two years into this second imprisonment, Kelley attempted self-murder. Mirroring his disastrous plunge at Křivoklát, he again sought escape through a tower window. Though he'd calculated a plunge from such heights would be sufficient to kill him, calculation was not among his talents. Kelley broke two ribs, and as if to complete the cruel twinning jest, shattered his other leg.

Madimi. Madimi. Madimi.

Kelley implored her to bring Death swiftly, but she had determined it still possible to purpose the Rudolf Complication and its creator to some nefarious deed. Rather than permit the watch to gather dust in the gloomy depths of Rudolf's treasure storehouse, would it not be better to loose the instrument upon the world as an agent of bedlam and malevolence?

Madimi proposed the terms by which she would aid in Kelley's escape from Hnĕvín Castle. Madimi said she would see to it that the Rudolf Complication would be awaiting him back in Prague. The watch would be his and would be governed under the same Three Laws of the Rudolf Complication. But should the watch ever cease its movement, regardless of who possessed it, Madimi would be loosed upon this earthly realm to claim Kelley. Was-Kelley would remain Madimi's servant for all the time left him. She would aid him in his endeavors until the day he failed, and then she would turn her full wrath upon him. Engineering his earthly destruction, she would harvest his soul. This harvesting might occur immediately upon the watch's cessation, or it might happen in a year, two years, five years, ten. Madimi had nothing but time. And could not time itself, properly wielded, be an instrument of torture?

Was-Kelley reaches the tavern at the House of the Black Rabbit where while alive, he had secretly convened with the Black Rabbi Jacob Eliezer, the Italian Jew who would sneak from the sequestered Fifth Quarter to tutor Kelley in the rudiments of gematria. Then as now, the tavern is no more than a lugubrious cellar with torchlit walls of clay. Two large beer casks, three long tables, and six benches rest upon a dirt floor at all times muddied by quantities of spilled libations, the innkeeper the same cloven-lipped oaf of yesteryear. At this hour only four other patrons are present. Two are engaged in a card game seemingly without end or purpose, hand after hand played sans wager or commentary, while the other two fervently whisper in low tones as if plotting murder or commercial venture. One man loudly remarks upon the sudden terrible stench, and swiveling his head to confront its source finds Was-Kelley sitting alone at a corner table. The conspirators and card-players fall silent and come to a sudden decision to hastily take their leave. Moments later the innkeeper himself has followed them, the fat man stumbling up the stairs and holding his scream only until he reaches the front door. Was-Kelley fingers the stag horn dagger taken from the dead gypsy.

Was-Kelley waits.

At length there appears before him a small figure dressed in a ragged gown of flowing red. Tangled black hair of varying length clings to her forehead. He has never seen Madimi as corporeal being, has only experienced her presence through the shewstone or shimmering water, has only heard her voice as something dis-embodied or speaking to him through books and writing. But Was-Kelley knows this little figure in red can only be the demon Madimi made flesh when he sees her black wormhole of a mouth, diseased and ravenous and smiling.

■

CHAPTER 13

Before I even opened my eyes I knew Vera was gone. I woke blinking against the harsh light flooding through the window as the sun rose above a serrated horizon into a raw blue sky. Below, the river was veiled in mist. I was on the couch, naked under a stiff white sheet like something draped over a corpse, corpselike being fair description of my general state that morning. While I slept, Vera must have swept the broken glass from the floor and picked up all the papers that had spilled out of the accordion folder. What was left of my clothes lay neatly folded on the coffee table next to a powder blue bath towel.

I gulped down two glasses of water in the kitchen. The digital oven clock read 7:47 AM. Taped to the refrigerator was a crayon drawing of someone in a striped shirt kicking a lopsided soccer ball. Tomášek's work. Paul always hated soccer, said no kid of his was going to play it, so I couldn't help but smile. Inside the fridge I found a few vegetables, yogurt, some goulashy looking muck. I was hungry, but I had my limits.

Inside the bathroom I turned the shower as hot as it would go and tried not to dwell on the images of Vera that arose every time I closed my eyes and even when I didn't. The water stung the gash above my ear and leached the dried blood from the cut on my foot in diffuse coppery tendrils. Even after vigorous lather-rinse-repeat cycles, I could still smell Vera. I didn't want to ponder what last night meant about me or about her or what should be done next. That she left at the crack of dawn meant she didn't much relish sifting through the aftermath either. It's one thing to wake up godknowswhere and creep down the backstairs, but to abandon your apartment to a stranger was black-belt-level avoidance behavior. Except I wasn't exactly a stranger.

I got out of the shower and toweled off and looked for a razor. Her bathroom drawers were a muddle of female implements, make-up and hair gels, lotions and soaps. Behind the mirror was a medicine cabinet overflowing with prescription bottles. The prescriptions were all printed in Czech, but there must have been fifteen or twenty different kinds of pills and capsules and liquids. All the dates were recent and bore the same Lékárna U Anděla brand pharmacy label. Maybe all these medications explained the wig. Maybe they explained a good deal more than that.

I gave up on the razor and headed back to the living room. Nothing more deflating than putting on dirty clothes after a good shower. I thought about digging around Vera's room to see if I could find some men's wear in her closet—she'd had the socks after all—but going through her medicine cabinet was bad enough. Besides, Vera could've just run out for coffee, might return any minute. Except I knew she wouldn't. I could wait there all day and into the next and I wouldn't be seeing her again.

It was time to leave, and once I got back to Chicago, there would be no returning. In a few hours I'd be on a plane, and in a few hours more I'd be home and this would all be a fever dream, a falling nightmare I'd woken from an instant before hitting the ground. A few thousand miles away and Martinko Klingáč would be nothing but a name from a fairytale. Soros the black sheriff and Bob Hannah the dead journalist and Gustav the comatose curator, all would be gone and forgotten. The Right Hand of God and the Rudolf Complication likewise. The Black Rabbit and the Hotel Dalibor and the Galleria Čertovka. The Vltava River and Čertovka canal. St. James Church, the Astronomical Clock, the Faust House, they could all burn to the ground tomorrow, and it would impact my life not one iota. Edward Kelley and John Dee, Rudolf II and his Kunstkammer, *Prague Unbound*, its cryptic and insane entries—all were things that would play no part in my future.

But I owed it to Bob Hannah to at least have a look inside the accordion folder. Whoever had killed the journalist had surely gone through it, but maybe they'd missed something. Right now all I had was he saids and she saids from parties I couldn't trust. What I needed was tangible proof. I'd check the folder, and if there was nothing good, I'd go to the airport and let time and distance work its forgetting magic.

Except I couldn't. The accordion folder was gone.

And with its departure returned all those muddled suspicions and unanswered questions about Vera I thought I was leaving behind. My mind started kicking back into paranoid mode and I felt my muscles tense and my jaw set hard and my pores yawn open, and I was right back to where I'd been eight, twelve, twenty-four hours ago.

But I was spent, emptied out.

My jaws unclenched and my face slackened.

And so fuck whatever had happened to Paul.

Good riddance to Malá Strana and its quaint pastel houses. Good riddance to the flood-scarred edifices of Karlín, to stately Ořechovka, to riverside Smíchov and the vague moonlit world of Charles Square. Fuck this city Prague and fuck my dad for keeping Vera's letter, for buying the plane ticket, and fuck him for dying. Fuck Vera for writing the letter in the first place. Fuck her for birthing little Tomášek-middle-name-Lee and for ever getting involved with my brother. And fuck my brother Paul and his short, meaningless life.

And most of all, fuck me.

Because when I reached into my back pocket and only came up with the annotated map Bob Hannah had given me and then frantically rifled through my other pockets and found them likewise empty, then and only then did I remember that last night I'd put both my wallet and passport inside the accordion folder, figuring they'd be safer there than in the pockets of my rapidly disintegrating suit.

And so fuck Lee Holloway most of all, the imbecile who'd misread every situation and made every wrong choice. There was no leaving. The city was not finished with me. The little mother still had me in her claws.

My cell phone was history, *Prague Unbound* had gone the way of the folder, and the map Bob Hannah had given me was so scarred with creases, inked circles, and crisscrossing pencil lines that it would have been no help in trying to find Vera's parents' house even if it had included street names and tram lines, which it didn't.

I had no address and no money for a cab and ended up pilfering train fare from a jar of loose change I found in Tomášek's bedroom, a space so tidy and well-organized that it was hard to believe it belonged to a five-year-old much less one descended from my brother.

I ended up going all the way across the river to Můstek station, then back across it to Hradčanská, onto tram 18, off at Ořechovka, and through the wide pristine streets and to Lomená, just like I had when following Vera. The sky was a faultless blue immensity, and the neighborhood looked even more pleasant by the light of the morning sun. Dignified without being imposing, the kind of retiring, unassuming place where you could imagine yourself leading the uncomplicated life of someone in a home furnishings catalog.

I strolled right up the bricked walkway, past a neat lawn polished by last night's rain, and into the cool shade of the trees flanking the front door. I rang the bell and stood around inhaling the scent of pine needles. A few moments later the door opened to reveal not Vera but an older version of her, a quizzical woman with gray hair in an unruly pile atop her head. She audibly gasped, one hand reaching for her chest, her mouth contracting in a withered pucker. She was looking at Tomášek's father. There wasn't a doubt in her mind.

I asked if Vera was around. She fishmouthed a moment longer and then yelled something over her shoulder. Deep in the recesses of the house someone yelled back. Mrs. Svobodova hollered again, louder and with a lot more words, and moments later a small old man in thick glasses tottered around the corner. He was wearing a gray sweater and a permanently harried look. As Vera's mom gave him an earful, he looked me up and down and didn't seem to reach any conclusions one way or another. When she finished he addressed me.

"What can I help?" he said in a leaden accent.

"Sorry to bother you. I'm looking for Vera."

"Vera is not here."

"Do you know where I might find her?"

Before he could answer, his wife unleashed a barrage of verbiage, each volley prompting him to sigh or shrug or issue terse rebuttals that did nothing to slow her attack. They carried on like this for what seemed an eternity, neither so much as glancing at each other, both keeping their eyes focused on the unshaven object of debate. Then all at once they were taking turns saying the same phrase, and I realized it was directed at me.

"*Ona je v parku Stromovka*," mumbled the man.

"*Stromovka sady*," she repeated.

"Stromovka park," the man clarified. "Do you know where is this place?"

"I'll find it," I said. "Thank you very much."

I walked back down the pathway and they resumed arguing behind me. Eventually one of them shut the door, but I'm sure that didn't end the discussion. I didn't know if Mrs. Svobodova wanted to pummel little Tomášek's father for leaving him and Vera to their own devices for five years or whether she was flustered with excitement because meeting him meant maybe there was a chance he had returned for good. Maybe he even had a certified check for a half a decade's worth of child support payments. Vera said she never spoke about Paul, and her parents must have wondered all these years who'd fathered the kid. Too bad I didn't speak Czech, or we could have had tea and coffee and compared notes on all the things about Vera and Paul we didn't know.

Thirty-five minutes later I reached the dense green stillness of Stromovka, an expanse sloping upwards into the distance as if here, exactly here, was where the city ended and beyond lay untrammeled wilderness. The illusion was quickly dissipated as I entered and saw couples holding hands along the rain-softened gravel footpath, people out walking their dogs, mothers pushing baby strollers, and all those other things civilized people do on a normal Sunday morning, but it was still jarring after the time I'd spent in the old parts of an old city whose every inch was layered in old stone.

After a few minutes wandering I was getting some idea of the immensity of the place. It would take hours just to walk its perimeter, not to mention all the grounds inside. I took out my

map and sure enough, Stromovka covered more territory than
all of Old Town. The chances of randomly stumbling upon Vera
and Tomášek were about the same as my chances of finding the
Rudolf Complication hung suddenly ticking about my neck. I'd
hoped the map might give me a hint as to what the park's attractions might be other than birch tree groves and slopes of patchwork grass, but all it showed was what looked to be a pond at the
park's center. A yellow square on Soros's map showed that it wasn't
far from where one of the Right Hand of God bodies was found
in 1990, if Hannah's reading of the document had been correct.
And as I looked at that yellow square, all at once those crisscrossing
lines made sense. Soros hadn't found some bizarre pattern, though
he was looking for one. By penciling directional arrows on the
lines he'd drawn, I now saw they were connecting the body sites
chronologically, starting with 1988 and finishing at 2006.

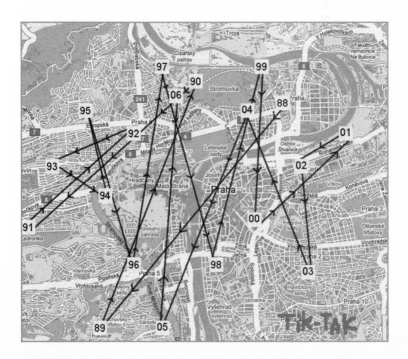

On and on the lines went, slicing across the city to connect the victims in chronological order. If these markings actually corresponded to real-life crimes—and Bob Hannah seemed to think at least some of them did—then what had Soros been hoping to gain by showing this to Bob Hannah? If he'd been under the employ of Martinko Klingáč, then why had he approached Hannah after the Right Hand of God article? He'd been interested in me and Vera because of Paul and the Rudolf Complication. But where did Hannah fit in?

I put away the map and tried to put these questions out of mind. With no idea where in the park to look for Vera, I ended up just following some lady pushing a two-year-old in a baby stroller and yapping on her phone some thirty yards ahead of me. She had a kid; maybe she was going somewhere kids go. I don't know where she and her little tyke ended up because after five minutes I spotted Vera and Tomášek in the distance adjacent one of the footpaths. Lee was climbing some orb-shaped and spiny piece of old playground equipment that looked like a Sputnik satellite. Vera was sitting on a bench not far away, her back to me as she unscrewed the cap of a thermos. She was wearing a purple scarf tied tight around her head, buccaneer rather than babushka style, no wig beneath.

She never saw me approach. I sat down beside her, watched the steam rise from her thermos. Tomášek had climbed the ladder and was inside the orb, peering out from the oval-shaped opening. On the other side of the orb, a rickety plastic slide descended to a muddy landing pit filled with several inches of standing water. We were sitting next to an empty swing set, and behind us was a merry-go-round painted fire engine red.

"Where's the folder?" I said.

Vera jumped. Coffee spilled onto her sleeve.

She didn't look at me. "Gone."

"What do you mean gone? Gone where?"

"In the pond." She screwed the lid back onto her thermos. Tomášek was sticking his foot out of the hole now, wiggling around a yellow rubber galosh. Vera took a tissue from her pocket, dabbed the spilled coffee on her sleeve. There was another kid inside the Sputnik too, one sticking a red sleeved, pale hand through the same opening. The sound of Tomášek giggling reverberated inside the orb.

"You threw the folder in a pond. Here in the park?"

"That's right."

I flashed to an image of papers floating across its surface. Me diving in, gathering what I could salvage. But after my dip in the Čertovka canal, I'd had enough swimming for one trip.

"Why?" I asked.

"Because you wouldn't."

"Especially not with my passport and wallet inside."

She shrugged. "You'll figure something out."

"Did you even look inside before you tossed it?"

She looked away and didn't answer. I barely had enough energy left to heave a proper sigh much less get worked up into a righteous fury. Itchy thoughts about Vera's latest action all but proving there had been something in the folder to implicate her I left unscratched, lest my whole brain get inflamed. What was done was done. I just wanted to get out, go home. Which would now mean a trip to the American consulate, wherever that was. Concocting a story about my lost passport and wallet. Copious amounts of alcohol, a band of pickpockets, a transexual prostitute skilled in martial arts. Whatever lie I told them was bound to be more feasible than the truth.

A little girl in a red dress came down the slide. She launched off the end and sailed through the air, her stringy hair fanning out behind her as she landed just beyond the puddle. Tomášek followed. He didn't fare as well, coming down with a muddy splash that set them both giggling as they ran off towards the merry-go-round.

"We used to come here," Vera said. "Paul and me. Not to the playground, but Stromovka. In the summer we would bring some beer and just lay around on a blanket drinking and talking. Or not talking. Doze off under the sun, wake up beneath the moon. You can still see stars at night in Stromovka. I remember one afternoon, Paul, he took off his shoes and when he woke up he could only find one. We searched everywhere in the dark but the other shoe was gone, vanished. He had to walk home without it." She smiled a little. "You went to my parents' house? This is how you found me?"

The little girl in red darted out from behind a tree and Tomášek followed in squealing pursuit, but he didn't have a chance. She leaped into a fenced-off flowerbed, leading Tomášek right into the thick of it, both of them trampling rows of daisies. Vera yelled and her kid froze guiltily in place, then gave her a smile that asked how much trouble he was in and how much the smile could get him out of. Next to the flowerbed sat the same sign I'd seen last night in Charles Square. *No pets step on.*

The message read the same backwards and forwards. A palindrome, of all the useless things to notice.

"Vera, I need to ask you a question."

"Aren't you tired of questions?"

"Listen, I know you're sick."

Her eyes met mine, slid away. "That's not a question."

On the path next to us, a pair of guys came by on mountain bikes, and Vera waited until the sound of their tires crunching over the gravel had passed. "Cancer," she said. "I'm sick with cancer. I don't know the English for what kind. Tumor on the brain. Very special, very rare. My last treatment was four months ago. The results were not what was hoped. Soon I start another. If this one doesn't work, well, that's that. Not many people survive. But then almost everyone who has this cancer is very old. Or they have HIV." She slowly unscrewed the lid of her thermos, watching for my reaction before showing me a wan smile. "Don't worry, I'm very special. Very rare. I don't have HIV or anything else you can catch. You're safe. At least from me."

The coffee had gone cold now, giving off no steam as she raised it to her lips. I didn't know what to say.

"Assuming the treatment goes well . . . " I started.

"The cancer leaves and I get better," she finished. "Otherwise, I have a few months left. With luck maybe longer. But it will be months, they say. Not years."

So there it was, the reason for her letter and its timing. She was dying and wanted to unburden her conscience about the watch heist. About her role in Paul's death. She didn't want to involve the police because, well, who wanted to spend the last months of their life dealing with cops and lawyers? More importantly, she wanted my father to know about what Paul had left behind when he disappeared. She wanted him to know about Tomášek. She wanted him to meet his grandson.

"Vera," I said, my voice just audible over the whispering trees, "why didn't you tell me about Tomáš that first night at the Black Rabbit? Or in the letter you sent. It would've saved us both a lot of trouble."

"Second thoughts," she said with a tired shrug. "Always so many second thoughts. And third thoughts. For years I wanted to tell your family. Always waiting for the right time. But there is no right time. Only the time we have. Does this make sense?"

It made sense. Not perfect sense, not even good sense. Just the kind of sense left to people like Vera and me. The kind of sense that remains when someone up and disappears. The kind of sense

I could live with as long as I didn't have to try to explain it to anybody else. And who else was left?

"When does your next treatment start?"

"Day after tomorrow. Tuesday it all begins again."

In her letter she'd pledged to be at the Black Rabbit every day for two months. The time between her treatments, the only functional time that remained to her.

"You must be scared," I said.

"Yes, I must be."

I could think of nothing else to say.

Two figures on a bench under blue skies and the shade of old trees. I reached out a hand, put it on top of hers. She let it stay there. After a few moments she intertwined her fingers in mine. She turned away, and I couldn't see her face. I don't know if she cried. I don't know how long we sat there like that, unmoving and unspeaking, eyes elsewhere, hands clasped in her lap. There is a kind of time you can't measure. A kind you don't need to. Wouldn't want to.

And then the little girl was standing in front of us, the merest hint of a grin on her face as she shuffled from one foot to the next.

"Tik-tak," said the girl.

Vera dropped my hand and looked up.

"Tik-tak," the girl intoned, louder this time.

All at once Vera's jaw slackened, her eyes scanning the perimeter as she shot to her feet.

"Tomáš?" she called weakly. "Tomáš?"

I knew I'd seen the girl before when she smiled to reveal a toothless black maw.

The Woeful Saga of Kelley and Was-Kelley (cont'd)

Was-Kelley follows the crimson-clad, rot-mouthed Madimi across the tavern and down the worn stones leading to the cellar. He removes a torch from the cellar in order to see better only to find she has vanished. At the rear of the room, past the casks of wine, is a door with a bolt held in place by a large padlock. Was-Kelley hobbles over, finds the lock undone, and stumbles into a passage not twelve hands high, no wider than a confessional, and utterly without light. After a quarter of an hour of hobbling his legs fail, and he commences to crawling. He holds the torch aloft in his right hand, giving him only one arm and half a leg to propel him forward. The tunnel twists and turns, rises and suddenly falls. Another quarter of an hour passes, and the torch is extinguished for lack of air. Was-Kelley can hear the scuttling of rats moving over the floor. He can smell their damp fur as they brush against his face. As the rodents grow more brazen, he registers their claws digging into his arms, feels their teeth piercing the flesh of his face as inch by inch he pulls himself through an enormity of darkness. And when the passage grows too constricted to allow him even this meager movement, he feels the rats writhing beneath him in mass, bearing him from head to toe upon their hundred backs, conveying him towards a flickering light some ways distant. Closer he sees it is candlelight spilling from a crack beneath an iron door. The passage widens and the rats take their leave. He has reached the end of the passage. He clamors upright and leans upon the damp wall and listens but hears nothing, not the beating of his own heart nor the wheezy bellows of his lungs, for since his resurrection the blood has been motionless in his veins.

Was-Kelley raps three times upon the door and waits.

With a great moaning the door opens, and before him is silhouetted a bent figure black robed and white of beard. As Was-Kelley's eyes narrow against the light he sees a second figure in the room, a young man no more than twenty reclining upon a table, his naked flesh glistening and wet. One arm dangles over the edge of the table, and drops of water roll off his pale fingers.

You took your time, the white-bearded figure says. Only upon hearing the voice does Was-Kelley recognize him to be Jacob Eliezer, the Black Rabbi. The years have not been kind. His flesh has grown papery and spotted, his dark eyes further receded into his skull. His eyes are milky and unfocused.

Welcome to the Fifth Quarter, says the Black Rabbi.

The Black Rabbi helps Was-Kelley to stand. *You are in the Chevra Kadisha adjoining the Jewish cemetery*, he tells him. *Here we cleanse the body before burial according to the laws of Halacha. Here is a sacred place. Here I sit nights as the shomrim, guarding against any who should endeavor to pilfer our fine and healthy corpses. A fit job for a blind man! I trust you have no designs upon them?*

The rabbi laughs and Was-Kelley perceives three shapes laid upon another table at the far side of the room, bodies draped in sheets of white. A trunk in the corner is filled with bolts of fabric and a set of heavy iron shears for cutting. The room smells of soap and tallow and putrefaction. The Black Rabbi moves past Was-Kelly and closes the heavy iron door behind him. From inside the room the door is concealed, its surface overlaid with false brickwork. The mystery of the Black Rabbi's comings and goings from the walled Jewish ghetto years ago when he would secretly meet Edward Kelley to discuss gematria was a mystery no longer.

Forgive the foul stench, says the Black Rabbi, moving with all the speed of a wounded goose to a corner where sits the large trunk heaped with fabric. *You never grow accustomed to it, but some nights are worse than others. These fellows must be especially ripe.* After rummaging through the trunk's contents, the rabbi emerges with a parcel draped in a familiar swath of black.

Was-Kelley unwraps the parcel given him by the Black Rabbi and finds the Complication remains as it was the day he delivered it to his melancholy Emperor, unscathed, preserved in all its gilded glory, complete save the winding key. Was-Kelley gazes upon it for several moments then drapes the watch about his own neck and tucks the instrument safely beneath his mud-encrusted cloak. It warms his cold flesh as if alive.

Procuring the piece was no easy task, says the Black Rabbi, his thick white eyebrows drawn together like clouds pushed by opposing winds. He produces from his robe a scrap of paper with listed figures and dates, but before he can present the bill to the resurrected suicide, Was-Kelley has withdrawn his means of payment.

With a single thrust to the Rabbi's throat he buries the gypsy dagger to its hilt. The Rabbi stumbles back and stammers in a garbled tongue as blood issues forth in a fountain of sputtering arcs. As his beard goes from white to crimson, the rabbi tries to steady himself on the table's edge but upsets its balance and dislodges the body thereupon. The corpse topples to the floor and the rabbi is not long in joining it. Supine, their splayed bodies offer a study in contrasts. Still one young, naked, and clean. Old one clothed, besmirched in gore, and twitching as the life pulses out of him.

Was-Kelley slumps heavy against the wall, his back sliding down until he is sitting with wooden leg and broken one both outstretched. He labors in undoing a series of buckles and straps at his knee and disengages the false limb. Taking the appendage in his hands, he runs his fingers over its length until they register

a slight ridge invisible to the naked eye. Was-Kelley digs at the
seam with his fingernails until he has pried loose a hollowed compartment measuring the width of two fingers. The winding key,
solid gold and inscribed with esoteric symbols, the same three-
inch length of precious metal Rudolf had two years previously
dispatched the entirety of his royal police in an effort to claim,
tumbles out of its hiding place and clinks dully upon the floor.
Was-Kelley inserts it into the watch's winding slot. The mechanism
does not yield. The second rule governing the Rudolf Complication dictates that more is required.

Was-Kelly removes the dagger from the old man's neck and
doggedly hacks at the right wrist of the Black Rabbi until the joint
is a flayed and spongy mass. The dagger having proven sufficient
for murder but too blunt for surgery, Was-Kelley employs the heavy
iron shears the Jew had used to cut cloth for dressing the dead.
The old man's bones snap between the blades and his detached
hand drops to the ground where it lands palm up, fingers slightly
extended as if in supplication.

Manipulating the Rabbi's disembodied hand Was-Kelley
finds to be an awkward undertaking. Chick with viscous blood,
the uncooperative and calloused fingers slide between his own,
become at once limp and inflexible, refusing take hold of the
winding key. But after much grappling, Was-Kelley is able to
purpose the dead man's hand for turning the key, which at last
turns with ease, and Was-Kelley turns it until it can turn no further, and then he tosses the lifeless appendage aside and listens.
The watch begins ticking. Was-Kelley's heart beats back to life.

And in that moment is shown him one final revelation, a jumbled vision of his fate now written, the long thread of his future
balled into a knot. Manifestations of Was-Kelley flash by, rich and
poor, powerful and impotent, fat and thin, handsome and ugly,
all engaged in lurid scenes of murder and degradation spanning

centuries untold. Madimi shows him murders ruthlessly efficient, murders whimsical and intricate, each ending with his fingers interwoven with those of dead men and dead women and dead children by the hundreds, some of Madimi's choosing, some of his own. Over the years he will fall into patterns unknown even to himself, and therein will be writ his destruction. He will lose the Complication in a single moment of carelessness but will go on killing past the point of its utility because old habits are the hardest to break. And then Madimi will turn her full strength upon him, abandoning his cause to aid those fated to destroy him. It may happen in five years, it may happen in ten. Time itself she would use as an instrument of torture.

Was-Kelley is lastly given a glimpse of his own end, an image so vague and fleeting he will guess upon its substance until the very moment of its arrival. He closes his eyes and releases his new-drawn breath, and the room is filled with a double ticking as the twin mechanisms of tiny gears and levers spring to life. After so many false starts his end is now beginning, his beginning is now over.

CHAPTER 14

We scoured Stromovka for half an hour, frantically calling Tomášek's name as we charged through clusters of forest, over open spaces of patchwork grass, through a picnic area, and around the pond near the center of the park. Vera would stop pedestrians on the footpath to ask if they'd seen him while I stood mute and useless beside her, watching their startled reactions, scanning the distance for any sign of Tomášek or the little girl. The same girl who'd forced upon me *Prague Unbound* the night I arrived in the city.

The girl had disappeared as soon as she'd delivered her message, run off somewhere as I tried to go after Vera, to calm her down. There was no calming her down. Her pace increased with each stride and sweat darkened her purple scarf.

"Please tell me right now what the fuck is going on," she said, suddenly grabbing my arm as we neared her car. "What have you gotten me into? Stop playing games and just tell me who you are and what is happening!"

"What have *I* gotten *you* into?"

"You are an insane person. Either you are insane or I'm going crazy." She unlocked her car with the remote on her keychain. "Maybe both. Get in."

Last time someone was determined on taking me for a ride I ended up being catapulted through the windshield, but pointing that out now would probably just make me sound insane. I got in the passenger side and she slid into the driver's seat and slammed the door. We wound our way out of the little side streets and were soon ripping through the expressway, Vera weaving through traffic like a racecar driver who'd spent the last forty-eight hours smoking crystal meth. Racecar, another palindrome. It wasn't until we were back in the neighborhood near her apartment that she spoke.

"Where did you get that book?" she asked.

"The guidebook?"

"Guidebook!" She cursed under her breath, slapped her palms against the steering wheel. "That book, when I opened it, the book was . . . forget it."

"What?"

"I'm *not* catching your insanity," she declared between clenched teeth.

"Where is the book?"

"In the pond," she said. "The book, your crazy Right Hand of God folder—I won't have these things in my life. They're a sickness. Just tell me right now what is happening and where I can find my son."

Probably wasn't the best time to point out if she hadn't thrown the book in the pond, maybe it could've provided some guidance, some clue about what to do next. Because I certainly had no idea, and her only strategy seemed to be repeatedly questioning my sanity. Right then I'd have taken crazy thoughts, but in truth I had no thoughts at all. The mental silence was enough to make me want to rip my own brain out of my skull and scream at it.

"Where is my son?" she asked. "Tell me."

Kick it, punch it. Try to beat some life into it.

"Do you know where he is, yes or no? Are you even listening to me?"

I nodded. Stomp on it. Drop-kick it.

"Don't nod! Speak! Tell me something goddamnit."

"Don't nod is a palindrome," I muttered.

"What? What does this mean?"

"You said to speak, so I'm speaking. I have no idea where he is, Vera. I'm sorry."

"The police," she sighed. "I'm calling the police."

And now I had to be the one to argue against getting them involved. The man who'd followed her, the one she'd seen at the Black Rabbit, he wasn't a policeman like she'd thought. He was an ex-cop turned black sheriff who was now working for Klingáč. He had friends inside the force. Someone might tip him off; he'd give word to Klingáč. We couldn't risk it. These were the people who'd killed Paul, after all, and I'd witnessed other examples of their violence firsthand.

"Enough!" she cried. "Just stop!"

Moments later, she slammed the car to a halt on the sidewalk in front of her Smíchov apartment building, vaulted out, and disappeared around the corner. Why were we stopping? I sat in a car parked halfway on the sidewalk and blocking the entrance into Erotic World and waited. I tried gauging how much time had passed by the beating of my own heart but lost track of the pulses. Then I took out the map, the one the journalist had given me.

Tik-tak. Same words the creepy little girl had spoken.

Why would Klingáč make some sort of game of it? He was either going to kill Tomáš or he wasn't, but it was useless pretending he was operating on any kind of rational level, that he'd left a puzzle to be solved.

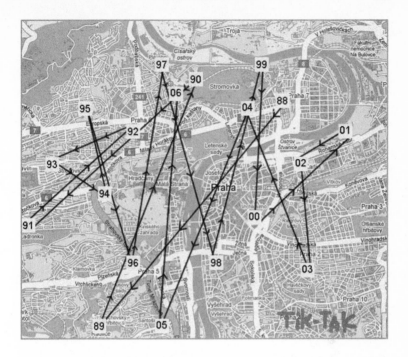

Tick-tock.

Still no sign of Vera. I started getting claustrophobic in the car, so I got out and strolled up the embankment, toward the river. I was only twenty, thirty yards away from the car and would be able to see when Vera came back out. I took a deep breath, rubbed my face with my palms. In the distance beyond, I could just make out the Charles Bridge and its blackened saints. I recalled the newspaper story, the one about the bridge's birthday. How the bridge had been founded some date chosen where the odd primary numbers ran palindromically.

1/3/5/7/9/7/5/3/1.

I ran down the hill just as Vera emerged from her apartment building with a shoebox under her arm, and suddenly it all clicked into place. What was it Martinko Klingáč wanted in exchange for Tomáš' life? Of course. The same thing he'd wanted five years ago. A watch. A large watch worn around the neck, an old watch roughly the size of a tea saucer, small enough to fit inside a shoebox. A watch that went both clockwise and counterclockwise, that ran backwards and forwards. Like a palindrome.

Like *no pets step on.*

Like *racecar.*

Like *don't nod.*

Like Soros.

With that I understood the detective was no black sheriff for Martinko Klingáč. He *was* Martinko Klingáč. My presence at the Black Rabbit had led him straight to Vera. He might have gotten to her anyway, but I'd hastened it along, solidified her connection to Paul. The Right Hand of God serial killer stuff had all been just a smoke screen. I don't know why Soros had fed the ex-pat journalist the same line of crap, unless maybe he thought my brother had some connection to him. Maybe he was just fucking with the *Stone Folio* writer because that's what sociopaths like to do. But when he found out that Hannah was onto him—thanks again to me, to the phone call I'd answered in Soros's car—Soros had killed him. While I was busy passing out and coming to and passing out again in Charles Square, he'd left the scene of the accident just like I had, made his way across town, and ripped Hannah's head off. He'd left the Right Hand of God folder behind because it was meaningless now. There was no suspicious detective determined not to let the case die. No odd cop looking to get even for a derailed career.

Only Martinko Klingáč himself.

Vera pulled open the door, got in the car, and handed me the box. It was heavier than I would have thought, but not nearly heavy enough to counterbalance everything weighted against it. Vera had trouble looking me in the eye. She had trouble putting the key in the ignition and had trouble speaking.

"Well, don't you want to see it?" she asked.

I didn't even have to shake my head. She could feel the disgust crawling over me, emanating out in waves. Anything you could fit in a box was not worth my brother's life. I'm sure the journalist's family would've felt the same way. Same for the people close to the old hippie curator in Malá Strana now struggling to emerge from a coma.

And now Vera had decided it wasn't worth her kid's life, either. A morally upstanding conclusion, but one reached too late to do my brother much good. And would she have come to this conclusion if she wasn't already dying?

I thought about her story, her fairytale seven days of rain. How she'd run sloshing up the hill in the downpour and tried to call my brother from a payphone. How someone had answered, how she'd known it was the unknown third man. Maybe my brother had still been alive at that point. Maybe there had still been a chance to save his life if she would have stayed on the line, told Mr. Rumpelstiltskin she had the Rudolf Complication, offered it up in exchange for letting Paul Holloway live.

She nodded toward the map. "What's that?"

"It's from our friend Klingáč."

"Does it show where he's keeping Tomáš?"

I didn't want to care. Let her reap what she'd sown. But then there was the damn kid. He looked like Paul. Kinda even looked like me. We shared a name. As much as I wanted to let the sins of the father and mother be visited upon the son, the rest of my life would be even more fucked up then it was already bound to be if I had to live knowing I'd let a four-year-old child die when I could've done something to stop it.

If I could do something to stop it.

Tik-tak.

I needed a plan.

A man, a plan, a canal. Panama.

At that last idiotic palindrome my brain slammed to a full and sudden stop. The mental whiplash must have loosed a syllable or two from my lips because when I looked at Vera, she was staring at me with her eyes wide and quizzical.

"An odd cop looking to get even," I muttered.

"What cop?"

I didn't answer. But I'd figured it out.

I knew where to find Tomášek.

I knew where to find Martinko Klingáč.

■

CHAPTER 15

Vera ran her tongue over her lips as her eyes darted from mine to the map and back again. She asked me if I was sure that was the place.

I told Vera I was certain.

I was not within shouting distance of certain.

She put the car in gear and gunned the engine. I put the shoebox housing the Rudolf Complication on the floor. Didn't like the weight of it in my hands, didn't want anything to do with it. Vera kept her eyes glued to the road and her mouth clamped shut. She didn't ask how I suddenly knew where Klingáč would be waiting, which was just as well because explaining how palindromes, the Rudolf Complication, the Right Hand of God, *tik-tak,* and the odd cop getting even all came together in some half-baked geographical guesswork would have taken hours we didn't have, and by the time I was finished, any belief she had in me would have vanished and she'd be back to questioning my mental health.

As we headed southwest I looked at the map again to assure myself the pattern I was seeing was real, not some arrangement I had wished upon it, the way people see Jesus's face in a potato

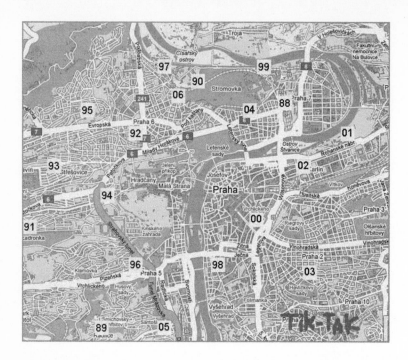

chip. I'd erased all of the crisscrossing connective lines Soros had drawn, leaving only the dates in place.

At first glance there seemed to be no clear progression from one site to the next. My brother was found in 2002 in Karlín, but in 2003 the alleged Right Hand of God dump site jumped all the way to Vinohrady. In 2004, it was the edge of Stromovka park. The next year, some place called Santoška.

But if I skipped every other year, broke it into odds and evens, a pattern emerged. Following only the even numbered years, the sites traced a predictable, roughly circular route counterclockwise around the city.

The odd numbers did the same, moving clockwise.

Forward and backward at the same time. Like *no pets step on*. Like Soros. Like the Rudolf Complication. Were the initials and dates then just an abstraction, puzzle pieces with no underlying

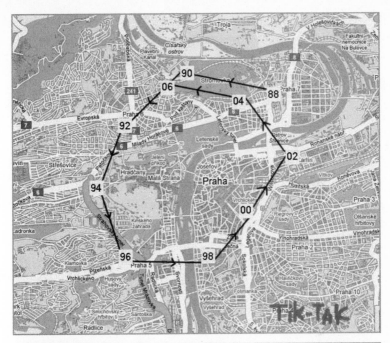

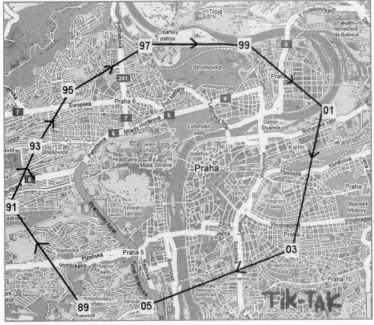

reality? My brother hadn't been an abstraction, and creating this map solely to give me something to decipher didn't make any sense. Did it mean there really was a Right Hand of God killer on the loose? That Soros/Klingáč had in effect been trying to tell first Bob Hannah and then me how to find him?

In crappy thrillers there's often a scene where a psychologist type gives a speech about how every serial killer subconsciously yearns to be caught and punished, which conveniently explains why the killer spent the whole movie leaving not-quite-ingenious-enough clues for some attractive but troubled detective to string together. I didn't believe Martinko Klingáč secretly wanted to get caught, but I discovered that continuing the pattern of odd years would point to a certain spot at the edge of the map, one I'd guided Vera to with more certainty than I felt.

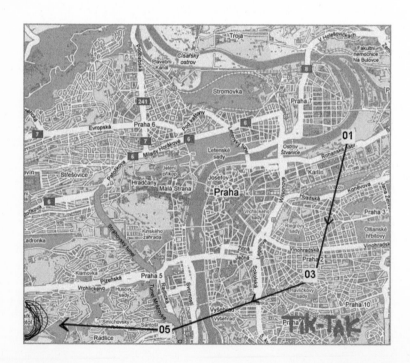

That was as accurate as I could get, and the area would still encompass several blocks. After that we'd just have to trust our luck. Neither of us having had much luck in the luck department lately, maybe we were due.

Vera glided to a halt by the side of the road.

"There," she said. The space across the street was overgrown with trees, a park or forest preserve though there was no signage to indicate as much. Vera told me to give her the box. I felt the watch shift inside as I handed it to her, heard the smooth whisper of fabric on cardboard from whatever protective cloth the watch was wrapped in.

Vera bolted from the car without bothering to close the door and raced down a weedy path into the trees. I followed. The sky had grown heavy with clouds. Rain on the way, rain always coming or going. Leaves rustled in the wind, the sound like a rumor spreading. Vera paid no attention to the chattering tree-tops, slogging upward, head angled in grim determination. She didn't look like someone in a dangerous, unfamiliar place. She didn't even look particularly worried. I couldn't shake the feeling that I was being set up. That I was little more than a meat puppet playing out some drama scripted long ago.

"Where are we going?" I asked.

"Cibulka," she said. "Cibulka Manor." The path sloped upward, and she was breathing so hard she had trouble talking. Sweat blotched her headscarf, the flesh of her face was colorless and waxy and suddenly she looked as ill as she must've felt. "It's an old estate house," she said between breaths. "From, I don't know, fourteenth century, fifteenth century. Abandoned a long time ago. Problems of who was the rightful owner . . ." She sputtered out in a coughing fit and pointed ahead.

Some fifteen feet away a thicket of vines, grass, and knee-high weeds crawled over an archway of discolored stone. Twin wrought iron gates were held together by a heavy rusted chain and padlock the size of small dog's head. Vera shook the gate, the chain rattled. When the sound died out it was so quiet I could all but hear the movement of her eyeballs as she scanned the wall, gauging its height, looking for a way in. She moved off the path, and the smell of wet leaves and damp soil clogged my nostrils as I trudged behind her along the wall's perimeter, ten yards, twenty yards, through the sucking mud and slithering overgrowth. Thirty yards in the wall went from chipped-brick edifice to unshaped layered stones, saplings growing from the gaps and struggling toward the light.

Forty or fifty yards, we came to a hole like the entrance to some animal's cave. Vera was through it before I even had a chance to warn her that we could be walking into a trap. But then she knew it was a trap. What else could it be in place like this? The only question was whether she was the bait or the quarry.

Several dilapidated structures awaited us on the other side. Even in ruins the buildings were stately enough you could almost picture a nice summer pastoral with ladies cavorting about with parasols and flouncy dresses, lords in long-tailed coats and powdered wigs, cooks and coachmen and stable boys bustling about. Now the stone walls were stained and crumbling, the windows smashed out, the roofs a patchwork of chipped tiles and rotting wood. Plywood boards were nailed up over the doorways, except for those ripped away by squatters or bored teenagers. Searching all the buildings would take more time than we had. I nodded toward what appeared to be the main house, and after a moment's hesitation Vera nodded back.

We found a large, busted-out window in the back and climbed inside. Uneven shafts of light pierced the room from holes in the roof above, strewn trash was piled nearly two feet high in places, and the walls were layered in unreadable graffiti. Vera cursed and

I spun to the sound. She was pressing a hand to her forehead. Her headscarf had been ripped off and was hanging stuck from a shard of splintered glass still clinging to the window frame. When she removed her hand it came away bloodied. She winced and nudged me forward with the same hand.

At the far side of the room a short stairwell littered with chunks of dislodged stone descended into darkness. Darkness seeming less an absence of light than a palpable presence all its own, spilling formless in all directions, filling up the space. Vera took out her cell phone, flipped it opened. Feeble blue light penetrated a few feet, enough to keep us from smashing headlong into a wall, tripping over rubble, or falling into a hole if we moved slowly enough. If we moved carefully enough.

And still I brushed against Soros before I saw him.

Feeling his flesh, I jerked back and Vera shrieked. Soros said nothing, didn't even blink or change expression. Nothing of him was visible except his face and the gray stocking cap on his head. His eyes were lusterless, his mouth turned in a frown. Vera moved the light lower.

There was nothing else of Soros to see.

And suddenly I understood why. The rest of him was in Bob Hannah's apartment.

Dressed, like me, in a suit not his own.

Because Hannah was a palindrome, too.

Vera moved the light quickly away, but the afterimage of Soros's head remained in ghostly outlines I couldn't blink away. Then a circle of white light exploded at the other end of the room. A flashlight beam froze us in place, its holder invisible in the gloom. Vera stood just behind me, shielding her eyes. A branching rivulet of blood ran from her scalp and down her cheek, catching the light like quicksilver. Filling the room was a sickly sweet odor so palpable it nearly made me choke.

"You have it?" Hannah's voice called out. He was speaking English but his accent had lost its reassuring news anchor timbre, its regionless Americana. His voice sounded deeper, vaguely Anglican and tense. Martinko Klingáč, Bob Hannah, I knew he was neither of these people, not really. Whatever name he chose he would always be the Right Hand of God.

Vera gently rattled the shoebox.

"Good. Bring it to me."

"Where is Tomáš?"

The flashlight beam swung some fifteen feet to our left. Tomášek huddled against the wall, stripped to his underwear and blindfolded, knees pulled to his chest. His wrists were bound with a zip tie and there was an honest to goodness manacle around his ankle connected to a heavy chain bolted to the wall. Vera started shaking so hard I could feel the vibrations in the floor. She wanted to tell Tomáš that it was okay, that everything was going to be alright. She didn't trust her voice to make anything sound alright. She addressed Hannah instead.

"Let him go."

"The Complication first. Bring it to me. No, better still, let that man bring it to me. Let him do what should have been done five years ago."

Vera looked at me, her eyes a silent apology.

Then she handed me the box.

Despite refusing to look at it in the car, I'd been curious about what a $5 million watch would look like up close. And it struck me Paul must once have been curious, too. After the rain began falling, after he'd taken the flood as his sign, after he'd paddled unseen down the Čertovka canal, hoisted himself into the gallery, successfully located the target. Before he wrapped it in plastic or stuffed it in a waterproof sack there must have been a moment where he took time to gaze upon it. Allowed himself a measure of wonderment that some object built hundreds of years ago was about to become the instrument of his deliverance. Maybe he thought about returning to Chicago a millionaire with a beautiful Czech bride in tow, the prodigal son proving all the naysayers like his big brother wrong. There must have been a moment where he felt pretty damn good about himself, about the future now stretched out before him.

But I would never see what Paul saw, never lay eyes on the object that prompted those feelings I imagined him experiencing five years ago. Vera stepped past me, emerging from my shadow, and leveled a gun in the direction of the flashlight across the room.

"Your hair." Hannah's voice angry and frayed. "You have no— this is a trick!"

The shot was deafening. My ears rang as it echoed off the walls enclosing us. Tomáš screamed and the man cried out, waves of sound overlapping, filling up the room. His flashlight bounced and rolled across the floor. I reached for Vera but she was already gone, had flipped closed her cell phone and was moving, invisible, until she picked up the flashlight and closed in, training its beam on Hannah. His pinprick eyes were focused and unblinking, his face onion yellow and stiff, a mask of itself. One of his legs was sticking out as he sat half-crouched against the wall, clutching his chest, blood running over his fingers.

"Don't kill me," he intoned. "You don't have to kill me."

"Do you have the key?"

"You're being used. You don't know."

"The key! Do you have the key to unlock my son?"

"I have it," he moaned. "I have it."

He reached toward his leg, the one stretched out before him. Vera kept the light and the gun trained on Hannah as he slowly rolled up his pants, past his black shoes, past his socks, to reveal instead of skin a length of tapered wood, black and worn smooth with age. His hands trembled and fluttered over its surface as they rose to find a series of metallic fasteners at the knee. Then his hands stopped. Hannah looked up, eyes narrowed against the flashlight beam focused on him. At length his features slackened. His shoulders slumped and he closed his eyes. He drew a deep breath and slowly released it. That rancid meat smell filled my nostrils and my hand went to my mouth to hold back a gag.

"I'm not giving you the key," he said.

"Give it to me now!"

His eyes opened. "No. I think instead I'm going to kill you."

"Don't you fucking move!" Vera's voice ragged.

"I'm going to kill you," Hannah sighed. "You, him. The boy. That's me. What I do."

"Your hands. Put up your hands!"

"Hands!" He laughed, slowly shaking his head. "Hands?"

Hannah grinned and kept grinning, gray teeth flashing as the circle of light fixed on his face strayed and quivered, Vera trembling so violently she couldn't keep the flashlight still. Then all at once Hannah stopped grinning. His teeth snapped together and his face pinched tight, veins bulging at his temples as he surged forward, going for his wooden leg. Vera yelled for him to stop, but there was no stopping him. He yanked off the false leg. As his hands fumbled for something within I knew what would happen next, was already lurching toward her as if I could somehow reverse time, take it all back, make it all stop.

But time kept moving, and time moves in only one direction.

She fired three rounds, one after the next.

Three flashes of white, the room exploding in sound. Gunshots reverberating, echoing, and finally receding until all that was left was the smell of cordite and rot. And moments later the sound of rain arriving, rain coming down all at once, rain like a child's tantrum too full of its own fury to last.

"Look in the box," she said. "Take a good long look."

I picked up the flashlight from the floor. Then I did as she instructed.

Inside the box was nothing but a mirror.

CHAPTER 16

First thing I'd done when I got back to Chicago was purchase a new pair of shoes. Bought them right in O'Hare, along with a pair of shorts and a golf shirt. I changed into them inside a bathroom in Terminal 5, leaving behind a T-shirt, sweater, and corduroy pants that belonged to Vera's father. My dad's suit had been so thoroughly destroyed Vera didn't think it was a good idea to wear it to the American consulate in Prague in order to get an emergency replacement passport. According to the sob story she'd hastily concocted, I wasn't supposed to look like I'd been living in the Hlavní nádraží train depot after all, just like I'd been jumped outside it. The park near the city's main railway station was known as "Sherwood Forest" for the merry bands of homeless people, junkies, and muggers who inhabited it. Not the most dangerous place in Prague, but one of the dicier ones a tourist could conceivably stumble onto. Listening to Vera concoct the narrative, adding and subtracting details, measuring its plausibility until perfectly calibrated, I realized I was out of my league. Lying came as naturally to her as graft did to my hometown politicians. She was an expert deceiver, and I was going to have to accept that I'd never be certain how much of the truth she was telling. About Paul, about Martinko Klingáč, about her role in stealing the Rudolf Compli-cation. About her certainty the man in the Cibulka Manor cellar was going for a gun when she shot him (he'd wanted her to think that—but there was no gun in the hollowed out compartment of his prosthetic leg, only the key to unlock Tomáš). About her rare cancer she didn't know the English name for. I could tell she was relieved to drop me off at the consulate, to be rid of me. After what we'd been through together, I couldn't blame her.

The extra two days I'd spent waiting at the Hotel Dalibor for the consulate to clear me to leave without a passport or ID were the worst of all. I couldn't contact Vera; my cell phone was busted. I was afraid of what might be on TV or in the newspaper and was sure any moment there would be a knock on the door and I'd peer out to see police fisheyed in the peephole. Not a historically uncommon experience in Prague, a city I've since developed a misshapen fondness for, despite everything that happened.

In the weeks that followed, my plunge into the Čertovka canal was the memory that came to me most often, visiting me in the long, empty afternoons in the weeks after my return. In dreams I'd dive into the canal and find myself immersed in complete dark-ness. In these dreams I'd propel myself toward a bottom I could never reach, and over and over the pressure would build in my lungs, panic would set in, and I'd race back to the surface. Gal-leria Čertovka curator Gustav played no part in these dreams. I was looking for something in that water though, groping blindly, sure it was within reach if I just held my breath just a little longer. I never could.

And the dreams made me think of my brother Paul out on that canal, made me wonder what it must have been like the night he stole the Rudolf Complication, and where the thing finally ended up. If Klingac didn't have it and neither did Vera—and I was sure she didn't, sure she wouldn't risk her child's life just to keep it—then Paul was the only member of the conspiracy left. Had he hidden it somewhere? As I thought about it a scenario entered my mind with such sudden clarity it felt like the answer had been there waiting all along.

Paul paddling a canoe through the submerged streets of Malá Strana, maneuvering onto the Čertovka canal. Breaking the third-story window of the building housing the gallery, hoisting himself inside. Finding the Rudolf Complication right where Vera said it would be. Slipping it inside a plastic bag, lowering himself out the window, back into his canoe.

And then, just as his feet hit the canoe, the boat moving beneath him, shifting and rocking unbalanced upon the water. Paul widening his stance to stop the boat swaying, his hands shooting out to restore his equilibrium. Paul losing his concentration, loosening his grip for just a split second. The bag sailing from his hand. The Rudolf Complication hitting the water and sinking almost without a sound, gone before he even realizes he's no longer holding it. Maybe he even flashes back to that fish he'd dropped on our trip to Wisconsin all those years ago, the summer mom left.

An instant later, boat no longer in danger of toppling, he realizes what has happened. He doesn't need to think about the implications. Maybe he dives after it, groping through the inky blackness just as I'd done while trying to find the curator. Just as I still did in my dreams. Or maybe he just slumps down and sits in the canoe and as it undulates upon the water. He tries to keep the panic at bay. He chews his fist and wonders what to do next.

And instead of deciding to hide out, or trying to flee the city, alone or with Vera, he decides he's just going to have to meet up with Martinko Klingáč that night as planned. Rendezvous some-where on the riverbank. He decides there is nothing to do but man up, face the music. But of course Klingáč doesn't believe his story—who would? Maybe Klingáč had planned to kill him all along once he delivered the piece. This just makes it easier.

Except now Klingáč can't kill him straightaway. Not until he finds out who helped Paul steal the piece, fed him information about the gallery, worked the supposed double-cross. But Paul isn't talking. Maybe Klingáč has accomplices, goons who tie Paul up, toss him in the trunk of a car, are forced by all the washed-out roads to take a winding route to a safe house in Karlín. Once there, in an otherwise evacuated house on Křižíkova, still tied up, Paul is beaten. He is tortured. But still he won't talk except to repeat that he screwed up, that he accidentally dropped the watch in the canal, that it was a mishap no amount of violence would undo. He sticks to his story even as Klingáč breaks Paul's ribs and breaks his nose and threatens to cut off his right hand. And when Klingáč starts to make good on this threat in a scene my imagination shirks from detailing, Klingáč knows it's a lost cause. He leaves the hand intact. Paul is dragged onto the balcony over-looking a courtyard. Floodwaters have turned it into a wide pool some four to six feet deep.

Paul is barely conscious as they heave him over the edge. He splashes down into the water below, the sensation bringing him part way to his senses. For awhile he struggles to stay afloat, thinking there must still be a way out. But his ribs are broken, blood is pulsing out his mouth and the large gash in his wrist. His eyes are swollen shut, his nose broken. He can barely breathe. There is no way out. Paul understands this, accepts it. They didn't get Vera's name. They didn't get anything. Vera is smart, and if she is careful, she'll be safe. He stops struggling and takes one last breath and then slowly expels the air from his lungs, his body stretching limp across the water. Paul washes out of the courtyard, joining the swelling river, and then all that's left is the wavering reflection of the moon.

Grimley & Dunballer Recovery Solutions had no choice but to let me go. First a week, then ten days, then two weeks passed without me bothering to respond to the increasingly concerned messages they'd left on my voicemail. It was inconsiderate, even cowardly of me not to let them know what was going on, but my reason for leaving wasn't something I could easily explain, nothing that would have its own little checkbox on an exit interview form. My dad had left me a little money, enough to live on for a couple years if I was careful. I moved into his house with the idea of staying there until I knew what to do next with my life. It was like graduating college, minus any sense of ambition or optimism.

I spent lots of time looking through that box of old photos I'd found, all the ones my father had kept of him and Paul. And after awhile I started wearing the Tag Heuer watch my dad had left behind, the same kind Steve McQueen used to wear. At night when I couldn't sleep, I sometimes found myself searching Czech news sites. I discovered a short article written in Czech about the Galleria Čertovka that I cut-and-pasted into an online translator to render into English. The resulting text was choppy, but the gist was there had been an assault at an art gallery in Malá Strana in which the gallery owner had been pushed out a third-story window. He'd managed to "shun his attacker" by hiding himself under a wheelbarrow propped at the back of the house. Meaning he'd been cowering unseen just a few feet away while I threw myself into the canal. He'd broken his arm and had received numerous stitches in his head, but had otherwise suffered only a concussion and was discharged from the hospital after one day's observation. "The police have suspected this is not the time," concluded the article, which after much puzzling I took to mean the police had no suspects at present. Detective Soros had either been lying about Gustav being in coma in order to scare me into talking, or it was a simple misinterpretation of the word "concussion." I chose to believe the latter.

There were a fair number of posts related to the detective, though it took lots of clicking through "see related" links to piece it all together. First a decapitated body found in an apartment near Charles Square. Then the body identified as former homicide detective Zdenek Soros, who'd retired from the department in 2002 after suffering a debilitating leg wound in the line of duty. Nothing about him being former StB, nothing about him being a hired thug for some shadowy Eastern European gangster. But then, I reminded myself, all the scary bad stuff I'd heard about Soros had come from a single source—Bob Hannah, the man who killed him. From all other accounts, Zdenek Soros appeared to be exactly who he'd said he was. One story quoted his estranged wife, a woman named Dominika, who said he had battled alcoholism since leaving the police. She begged anyone with information about his murder to come forward. The story ended, as all stories related to Soros did, with a reassurance that police were investigating all possible leads. I didn't need a computerized translator to know that the statement meant they didn't have any.

It was about three months after returning to Chicago that I tried calling Vera on the phone. It must've been her mom who answered, and she sputtered something in Czech before turning over the phone to Vera's father. He was the one who told me Vera had died. It had happened only the week before. I apologized and tried to convey my condolences, but the language barrier made it difficult, and I sensed that Mr. Svoboda didn't particularly want to speak with me. I thought I detected an edge of hostility in his voice, but the man was clearly still in mourning and probably didn't much feel like talking on the phone.

The news hit me harder than I'd imagined it would. I suddenly wanted to get out of the house, just hop in the car and drive. So that's what I did. Just got in my Dad's old car and drove around thinking about Vera. About Paul. Little Tomáš. I'd been meandering aimlessly around the city for about two hours when it started raining, light at first, then heavier. Sometime around midnight I saw the flashing red and blue lights in my rearview mirror and pulled over.

The policeman told me I'd been driving a little erratically but that's not why he stopped me. Apparently one of the brake lights on my dad's car was out. I'd forgotten, I explained, and had been meaning to get it fixed, both of which were true. The cop asked for my license and registration, and as I reached over to pop open the glove box, I noticed a bunch of envelopes that must have fallen from the passenger seat and onto the floor. Stuff my dad had meant to mail and never got around to before the heart attack.

While the policeman did his thing back in the squad car, I sorted through the letters. Bill payments mostly, stuff I'm sure the executor had already taken care of by now, along with a Netflix movie to return and a mail-in rebate form for a drill he'd recently bought. What caught my eye, though, was an envelope addressed to Vera, care of the Black Rabbit Tavern.

When the policeman knocked on my window I nearly jumped.

"You're good to go," he said as I rolled down the window. "Just make sure to get that brake light checked out, you wascally wabbit."

"Huh?"

The policeman smiled and pointed at my forearm. "Your tattoo. Elmer Fudd, right?"

I rolled up the window and drove away. I didn't get far though. I was too curious about the letter. After a couple turns to make sure the policeman was no longer following me, I pulled over and ripped open the envelope, rain pelting the windows and throwing watery shadows over the pages as I read.

Dear Vera,

Thank you for your letter. I regret that I won't be able to take you up on your offer to come to Prague to meet you. It's an offer I've weighed seriously, even going so far as to book a flight there, but after a great deal of deliberation, I just don't think it's a good idea. At least not until I know more—and, more importantly, until you know more. With no address to go on, I'm not sure this letter will even reach you, but if you go to the Black Rabbit every day as you indicated, I figure sending it there is my best shot.

I'm not sure how to go about telling you this, so I will just put it bluntly. The person who made himself known to you as "Paul" is really my son, Lee. He's a good man but he's had some difficulties in his life and has waged a long battle against some pretty severe mental health challenges. The problems started after his mother died—an event he has to this day refused to acknowledge or confront. He stopped taking his meds. Soon thereafter came his first major psychotic break. This happened roughly six years ago.

It was around then that he assumed the identity of Paul. Experts tell me this imaginary brother of his had likely been kicking around his head for some time, but Lee had never actually "become" Paul prior to this occasion. As Paul, his behavior

*became increasingly erratic, threatening, and sometimes violent.
I told him if he continued refusing his meds then I would have
no choice but to see that he entered a full-time care facility.*

*This, I now know, was a mistake. After I issued this
ultimatum, Lee disappeared. For over a year, I had no contact
with him. I knew that he'd flown to the Czech Republic because
he'd stolen my credit card to pay for the flight. Occasionally he
would send postcards as Paul addressed to his brother, Lee. I
have no idea what led him to choose your country.*

*Shortly after the flood, I received a call from the American
consulate. Lee had been found just outside the city on the banks
of the river. He had been discovered shirtless, his body covered
in bruises, his ribs and nose broken, his right arm nearly severed
at the wrist. The consulate told me he'd identified himself as
Lee Holloway but had no memory of what had happened. He
had no memory of the flood. He had no memory of how he got
to the Czech Republic or what he had been doing there for the
last year.*

*Since coming home, Paul has spent a number of years receiving
full-time care at Grimley & Dunballer Recovery Solutions, one
of the Midwest's best mental health facilities. Recent budget cuts
have restricted the number of patients they can house and so he's
been living on his own under the supervision of a health care
worker who checks on him a twice a week. They assure me that
he's made a lot of progress and that—barring some unforeseen
trauma—as long as he keeps taking his meds he's on the path to
a healthy and productive life.*

*I'm sure this news is all quite shocking. And I'm sorry my son
Lee deceived you, though surely you are not alone. He has always
been clever and resourceful, and it wouldn't surprise me if he was
able to procure the kinds of documents needed to give this "Paul"
some sort of official, bureaucratic existence. Lee can't really take*

responsibility for his actions, but as my own failures contributed to bringing this Paul person into your life, I can only offer my heartfelt apologies.

Part of me yearns to know what happened to my son over there during his "lost" year, but please also understand that this was a very dark, very painful period of my life as a father, and not one I think it would be healthy to revisit. You wrote that I'd be interested in knowing "an important part of Paul's life" unknown to me, but I'm afraid all of Paul's "'life" is unknown to me. Paul is a stranger to me, and I'd like it to remain that way. Maybe that's selfish, but we all have to adapt our own strategies for getting on with life. We're none of us really ever out of the woods.

But I hope this letter is in some capacity helpful. Maybe it will bring you a measure of solace to learn the person you were close to didn't drown in the flood five years ago. That he survived, that he's alive and getting a little better every day. I hope the passage of time will bestow these same gifts upon you.

Wishing you all the best,
Lee Holloway, Sr.

Back at home I sat down at my father's desk, rereading the letter from beginning to end, from end to beginning. My father had never been a communicative man, especially when it came to difficult emotional territory, and I knew it must have been a struggle for him to produce a letter like this. I tried to imagine what he could have been thinking while he wrote it, but I was never good at deciphering other people's thought processes. I was never, as my dad had been, what you would call a people person. Vera, Paul, my father—they were all at their core unfathomable, as maybe we all are. Inside of us so often lies a hidden mechanism running counter to the face we show the world. My father was no exception. Five years after being floored by the disappearance of his favored son, the memory was still so painful that he'd chosen to concoct some outlandish scenario involving split personalities rather than face the fact that Paul was gone. I didn't mind that he'd lied about me, devised for me some vague, almost laughable history of mental illness. I understood and forgave him. Like he said, we all have to adapt our own strategies for getting on with life.

But I was glad that Vera never saw the letter. It would have brought her only unnecessary pain and further confusion in those final months of her life when she already had so much to contend with. And I was thankful her parents and Tomáš would never have to wrestle with such sad nonsense amidst their devastation. They deserved better, and I still felt there was a chance, after some time had passed and grief's deep wounds began to heal, to get to know them. Maybe one day I'd return to Prague, to that little mother and her claws. I still had my guidebook after all—*Prague Unbound*—which I'd retrieved from Stromovka Park hours before I left the city, finding it lying dry, unharmed, and waiting for me at the edge of the pond. Yes, I'd go when Tomáš was older, better able to understand the things I had to say. We'd walk those ancient streets and stroll by that slow-moving river, and I would tell him stories about his father. The funny ones, the good ones. There were a lot of those, and even as I sat there listening to the rain, I could feel them taking shape in my mind, waiting for their chance to be told.

ACKNOWLEDGMENTS

■

Many books were consumed and regurgitated in the making of this one, but I must make special mention of Angelo Maria Ripellino's fantastic *Magic Prague*, which I picked up on my honeymoon years ago and haven't truly put down since.

Thanks to my early readers, a hearty and insightful crew that included my parents (Dave and Cynda), my wife (Chee-Soo), along with Jim Nietz, Andy Laing, Natasha Laing, Serapio Baca, and Ashley and Carolyn Grayson. Thanks especially to Margaret Norwood for gently reminding me that sometimes less is more.

I also owe a huge debt of gratitude to filmmaker Arash Ayrom—sorry for making you hike up steep hills and through thorny brambles. Thanks also to Damian Odess-Gillett (the fastest-walking magician in Prague) for not only lending his acting talents, but also for being our location scout and an all-around good sport. I'm also very grateful to the incredible Flanna Sheridan for all her fine work and hospitality—next time, we'll get you good and bloody, I promise. Special thanks also to actors John Branch and Bria Lynn Massie, whose talents made me think I was really standing in an old Czech secret police interrogation room instead of a freezing Portland garage.

Huge kudos go to my extraordinary editor, Dan Smetanka, who saw something in my misshapen manuscript no one else did and vastly improved the novel with six brilliant words. Working with you could not have been a better, more enjoyable experience. I'm also grateful for Charlie Winton, Laura Mazer, Liz Parker, Julia Kent, Kelly Winton, and everyone at Counterpoint and Soft Skull who helped along the way.

And finally, thanks to my agent Jason Allen Ashlock—without your belief, persistence, and vision, this book would never have seen the light of day.